Undiscovered Country

undiscovered country

JENNIFER GOLD

Second Story Press

Library and Archives Canada Cataloguing in Publication

Gold, Jennifer, author
Undiscovered country / by Jennifer Gold.

Issued in print and electronic formats.
ISBN 978-1-77260-031-5 (paperback).
—ISBN 978-1-77260-032-2 (epub)

I. Title.

PS8613.O4317U53 2017   jC813'.6   C2016-907247-9

C2016-907248-7

Editors: Patricia Kennedy and Carolyn Jackson
Design by Melissa Kaita
Cover photos © iStockphoto

Printed and bound in Canada

*Second Story Press gratefully acknowledges the support of the
Ontario Arts Council and the Canada Council for the Arts for our
publishing program. We acknowledge the financial support of the
Government of Canada through the Canada Book Fund.*

Published by
SECOND STORY PRESS
20 Maud Street, Suite 401
Toronto, ON M5V 2M5
www.secondstorypress.ca

For Teddy and Violet

Prologue

In the waiting room of Dr. Shapiro's office is a stack of books and magazines on grief. What it is, how to manage it. How to cope, how to move on. The people on the covers look somber, usually dressed in cardigans: apparently, cardigans are the official clothing of grief. Leafing through one of these tomes, you inevitably encounter what the experts call the "five stages" of grief, a series of phases mourners pass through to come to terms with tragedy. When I picture these steps, I always see a grave-looking medieval knight atop a black horse, successfully completing the challenges in his path. Only instead of slaying the dragon and saving the princess, he's meeting the milestones some well-meaning psychologist set out for him back in the seventies: Denial and anger. Bargaining, depression, and acceptance.

These five steps annoy me. Human experience is not neat

and orderly, ready to be coded into predetermined categories. Real life is messy, and grief is even messier. What if you feel depression right away? Or if you continue to feel anger long after you've accepted the death? Why wouldn't you, really, feel an eternal sort of fury if someone you loved was snatched from you prematurely? But then, Dr. Shapiro long maintained that my response to grief wasn't normal. I had, he intimated by way of ominous diagnosis and multiple prescriptions, crossed the line between grief and madness. I'm glad he's so sure of himself. I guess he has to be, in his profession. I'm not sure of anything. Where does grief stop and madness start?

Ironically, Dr. Shapiro's office was also where I found the crumpled pamphlet for Students Without Boundaries. I guess another patient had left it behind, because there was only the one, abandoned on top of a tattered copy of *The Healing Journey*. Ordinarily, it wasn't something I'd look at twice. But after the funeral, after I watched the earth swallow her and take her from me irrevocably, I picked it up and smoothed out the creases. I read it through, and all I could think was one thing: escape.

That's not what I told people, of course. When people ask you why you're deferring college to venture into poverty-stricken, war-torn South America, you give them what they're looking for. You toe the party line, demurely tossing out comments about "helping people" and "giving back," because that's what they want. People want to hear I was inspired to join Students Without Boundaries because of my poor dead mother and my desire to lessen the suffering of starving orphans. No one wants to hear the truth. The truth is uncomfortable and awkward. It makes demands, it yearns for the respect of a truthful response—or even, perhaps, action. No one wants that responsibility, so they deal in equivocations and half-truths, white lies and niceties. *So sorry for your loss* and *what a noble endeavor* and all that crap.

The truth is, when I signed up to go Calantes, to escape the prison of my own grief, there was a part of me that never believed I'd actually go. I kept waiting for my dad to step in and forbid me to leave, that it would rouse him from the emotional coma he'd been in since Mom died, but he just sort of blinked at me and was like, "That's nice, Cat. Good for you," and went back to pretending to write. I knew for a fact he hadn't written a word in months, because I hacked into his computer one night and there was nothing there, nothing at all, not even a title or "Chapter One" or anything. And since St. Mary's gently put him on some kind of leave when he blanked out and started sobbing in the middle of a lecture on the Modern Novel, I know he's not grading papers or anything, either. When he's not sitting in his study staring into space, he wanders around the house clutching a battered old copy of *The Great Gatsby*. It was my mom's favorite, and Dad used to call her his Daisy, which if you ask me is kind of an insult, because Daisy was a bit of a bitch. But maybe there was something more to it between them. I don't know.

The only person who tried to talk me out of going was Tess, who seemed legitimately alarmed, because my rushing off to Latin America was out of character.

"You cannot go live in a tent in South America." I can picture it clearly. We're in my room, Tess lounging on my yellow bedspread wearing one of my St. Mary's sweatshirts because she's always freezing at my house; my dad has never let our thermostat climb above sixty-eight. He claims humans function better if they're slightly cool, but since he's an English professor and not a biologist, I'm not sure it's really anything other than his personal preference. I'm flopped on the cold hardwood floor on a bean-bag chair. We're studying for the physics final, which seems irrelevant (a) because we've already been accepted to college, (b) we graduate in less than two weeks, and (c) my mom just died, rendering everything else in the universe meaningless.

"You won't even use the bathrooms at the mall," she points out.

"This is different." I toss my textbook aside. "I have to get away. I have to do something. I want to help people."

"You could just volunteer at the Children's Hospital, like a normal person," Tess suggests reasonably.

"No, this is something I really feel I need to do." *And maybe it will wake up my dad.* I don't say the last part out loud. If Tess clues in to what's really going on, she'll do what she's been threatening to do for months and call my Aunt Caroline in California to stage an intervention of some kind. I like Caroline and everything—she's ten years younger than my dad and pretty cool—but I can't deal with her or anyone else swooping in right now. I can take care of myself.

"This is crazy." Tess narrows her eyes. "You couldn't even

go to camp. You remember? You tried to sneak home on the food truck!"

"It's not the same," I insist. "This isn't sitting around the campfire in the dirt singing 'Kumbaya' or whatever. I'll be doing important work."

"Remind me where Carnitas is again?" Tess wrinkles her nose, her freckles bunching into a pattern resembling the Big Dipper. "Is it the one with the natives living at crazy high elevations?"

"It's Calantes, Tess. Carnitas is a Mexican meat dish. And no, that's Bolivia."

"Sorry. I'm trying to think back to fourth grade here. I'm drawing a blank." She tucks her fine strawberry-blonde hair behind her ears, looking pensive.

"Calantes." I grab my iPad from my bedside table and pull up a map of South America. "There. See? It borders Brazil, Colombia, and Venezuela. It's tiny."

"It looks a bit like a sheep's head." Tess leans in for a better look.

"I would have said dog's head, but fine. Anyway, it's in the Amazon rainforest. See the green area?"

She shoots me a look. "Even I could figure that out." She pinches the screen and enlarges the image. It really does look like some sort of animal head, menacing jaws open wide.

"I remember now!" Tess snaps her fingers. "This was Matthew Finnerty and Jessica Wong's country."

I stare at her. "You have the most incredible memory for inane detail." Tess remembers things no one else can—or would bother to. She can tell you what I wore the first day of school every year since second grade.

"Come on, you don't remember stuff like that? You had Peru, which is cool and interesting. I got stuck with French Guyana and I had to work with that weird kid who moved to Florida."

"Sam Rosen."

"See? You do remember!" She grins at me, then her smile fades. "What does Dr. Shapiro think of this?"

"He thinks it's a good idea," I lie. I haven't told Dr. Shapiro, because I'm positive he would end up using it to somehow bolster his ridiculous Bipolar II diagnosis. I didn't know this before I was forced to see a psychiatrist, but apparently there are two kinds of bipolar disorder. There's the one everyone knows about, with the big manic episodes where you go to Neiman Marcus and buy out the entire shoe section and stay up all night trying to solve Fermat's Last Theorem before you crash and crawl into bed for nine months. But then there's a second type, which is kind of like Bipolar Lite, where you just maybe decide to start a novel and bake a cake and read ahead in Advanced Placement biology and then you feel kind of shitty *because your mom died*. I think it's a load of crap, personally, because who wouldn't feel bad if their mother died after a long and miserable illness? And really, if studying extra hard makes you a candidate for psychiatric drugs, there are a lot of overachieving gunners out there who need medication.

I haven't said any of this to Dr. Shapiro, though. I'm not stupid. The more I push back, the longer he's going to want to see me. I don't tell him I stopped taking the Abilify he prescribed, either. It made me feel like a zombie. A vampire zombie, actually, because all I wanted to do all day was sleep with the curtains drawn. When I was on it, I didn't feel like crying when I thought of my mom, and I want to feel that way. I want to miss my mom. You can't just magic away life and all its ups and downs with a pill. Also, the packet insert said it could cause weight gain, and let's face it, how was being fat going to help me?

"Well, I guess if he thinks it's a good idea…" Tess still looks worried. "Does he know about your irritable bowel syndrome?"

"Yes," I say. That part, at least, is true. He does know about it.

"And he thinks that going to live for nearly a year in a tent in the middle of a war zone and digging your own toilets is okay?" She sounds deeply skeptical.

"We didn't really get into the toilets," I admit.

"Cat, you spend half your life worrying about toilets. How could you not get into the bathroom issue?"

"I figure I'll just pack a lot of Imodium."

"So basically, your plan is to try not to poo for nine months?" Tess's expression is growing increasingly alarmed.

"Very funny," I say. "Look, this is something I feel I need to do. I want you to support me. You're my best friend." I pick at the seam of the bean-bag chair. Little bits of Styrofoam spill out onto the floor like fake snow.

"I'm just worried about you." Tess hesitates. "You know your mom would have thought this is crazy."

"Don't do that," I snap, bristling. "She was my mom. She would have wanted me to be happy." I avoid meeting her eyes, though. She isn't entirely wrong.

"She wouldn't have wanted you to defer a year at Stanford to go traipsing around in the mud," Tess persists. "She had all your grass torn up in the backyard. She was hardly the outdoorsy type."

"She took a year off after high school." I stare at the wall across from me and count the daisies on my wallpaper. I've had the same decor since I was a toddler.

"She went to Paris! Why this, Cat? Are you punishing yourself or something?" Tess has resorted to waving her calculator around angrily for emphasis.

I roll my eyes. "Great. Now I have two shrinks? Give it a rest. Anyway, back to vectors. What did you get for problem number three?"

• • •

We must have replayed that conversation weekly over the remainder of our senior year, and all through that summer. Each time, Tess would painstakingly point out all the reasons that going was a Really Bad Idea and, each time, I'd ignore her and change the subject. The strange thing was, the more Tess tried to talk me out of going, the more resolved I became to actually go. It was the same with my dad, and his lack of response. I kept waiting for him to intervene and stop me— even just to comment that running off to the jungle seemed out of character—but he never did, not once. And the less he seemed to care, the more I convinced myself that it was the right thing to do. More than just a way to escape, to leave the misery and the memories behind. I began to buy into what I had been spouting to others. This was my chance to give back. To do some good.

"But what if something happens to you?" Tess tried to talk me out of it, right up until the day I left. "What if you get, like, shot, or something?"

Who cares? I didn't say that out loud, though. No need to set off alarm bells. Instead, I acted dismissive. "I'm not going to get shot. Don't be melodramatic."

When I finally told Dr. Shapiro, he responded exactly as I thought he would.

"Have you been taking the Abilify?" I'm sitting uncomfortably in his stuffy office, which is designed to look like a living room, only it doesn't feel like a living room at all. It feels exactly like what it is: a doctor's office awkwardly pretending to be a family living space. Dr. Shapiro sits across from me, trying to look approachable in his scruffy jeans and T-shirt, his beard wild and scraggly. It's not like it is in the movies, where you lie on the couch and the psychiatrist asks you how you feel about things. There is a couch, but I don't lie down, I just sit on it. It's faux leather, and it sticks to my thighs when I wear a skirt.

"Of course," I lie smoothly.

"I'm thinking we should switch you to something else." He stands up to rummage around his desk, pulling out a prescription pad. "Maybe Seroquel."

Dr. Shapiro's solution to everything is drugs. The talking part is all a ruse, a way for him to get me in here so he can proceed to drug me some more.

"What's wrong with the Abilify?" I ask politely.

"I'm not sure it's working." He gives me a condescending smile, the kind you give to a small child or a grandmother with Alzheimer's. "Caitlin, I think you're having a hypomanic episode."

That word again. Hypomanic. It freaks me out, calling to mind images of shrieking inpatients bound in straitjackets. I'm not claiming I'm normal or anything like that. I'm not completely delusional, but bipolar just seems really crazy. And I think I'm more of a regular kind of crazy.

"I don't agree," I say firmly, staring at him hard. I don't want him to see he's unsettled me. "This is something I've always wanted to do."

"Is it?" He blinks down at his notes and frowns again. "Didn't you once have to come home from camp?" He turns a page. "It says here, 'I asked my parents to come and get me because I hated it. I hated being away, I hated the dirt and the bugs and sharing a bathroom—'"

I feel my cheeks redden and I cut him off. "I was twelve then," I say, trying to look five years older and infinitely more dignified. My bare thighs squelch on the couch, and I blush deeper, because it sounds like I've farted. I move around, squelching some more so that he knows it's just his stupid fake leather sofa and not me breaking wind in public like some kind of social misfit.

"What about your irritable bowel syndrome?" Doc Shapiro pushes his glasses up. He's always doing that. He sweats a lot, so they're always sliding down his nose, like tires skidding on a wet road. He uses his middle finger to do it, so I always feel like he's trying to tell me to f– off, even though I know he'd never actually say that. You can tell he's the type who doesn't swear, who yells 'Oh, sugar,' when he stubs his toe. My dad's parents are like that. My mom used to call them emotionally constipated.

"Why does everyone keep asking about that?" I irritably dig my nails into the sofa. "If I have to go, I'll go, and then I'll take some drugs. It's fine."

"Who's everyone?" He leans in, genuinely intrigued. "Your father?"

I guess there's enough Freud in this pill-pusher to still get him worked up when I talk about my dad. But I won't. Not that there's anything to tell, anyway. My dad is still hanging out exclusively with Gatsby.

"No," I reply shortly. I won't give this jerk the satisfaction of talking about my dad. "Tess. My best friend."

"Oh," he says, disappointed. "Well, it's something to think about." He pauses, looking thoughtful. "Why are you doing this, though? What do you plan to gain from it?"

I frown at him. "I'm going to help people," I say automatically. The refrain is second nature now. "It's a war-torn country. They need our help."

He gazes at me intently, as if he knows the words "war-torn" were lifted straight off the Students Without Boundaries website. "And you want to be the one to help."

"Yes," I say, trying not to sound irritated. *Did I not just say that?*

"You're trying to save them, then." He gives me a penetrating stare. "Because you couldn't save your mother."

I don't know whether to be impressed at this uncharacteristic stab at actual psychoanalysis or exasperated and annoyed. I don't say anything.

"Because, Cat," he goes on gently in that maddeningly slow voice of his, "nothing is going to bring her back. You don't have to do this."

"I'm going," I say resolutely. I meet his gaze until he looks away, scribbling something on his notepad.

"Are you hoping something will happen to you?" he asks, switching tactics. "Because it's normal, after losing a loved one. To think about death. About joining them."

"Joining them? Really?" It's all I can do to keep from rolling my eyes. "Joining them, where? In heaven, with pink fluffy unicorns?"

He sighs. "I don't necessarily mean in an…afterlife. But it's not unusual to have those sorts of thoughts."

I didn't answer. I wasn't thinking about killing myself. If I happened to take a bullet in the jungle, that would suck, but it didn't scare me the way it might have a year ago. I wasn't afraid of death or seeking it, either. I was indifferent to it. If I saw the Grim Reaper coming for me, I'd probably give him the finger and go back to checking my Twitter feed.

"Caitlin?" The doc leaned forward, stroking his beard.

I sighed. "I'm not suicidal, okay? This is just something I feel I need to do."

"Well, I can't stop you," he says reasonably, glancing at his watch. For all his expansive concern, he's quick to put an end to things when my hour is up. "But I would like you to give the Seroquel a shot."

"Fine," I mumble. It doesn't matter, because I won't be taking it. I can stash it with my Abilify; they can keep each other company, do a pas de deux as they swirl down the drain together. "Can I get some more Ambien?"

"You're still not sleeping?" He looks at his watch again, and I almost catch a glimpse of suppressed irritation.

"No," I say flatly.

"Okay." He scribbles something down and hands the slip to me. "That's for a year. Normally I wouldn't prescribe so much at once, but since you're going away..."

"Right. Thanks." I stuff the prescription in my purse. "I guess I'll see you when I get back."

He frowns, tugging at his overgrown beard. "Caitlin, please make sure this is really the best idea for you. Before you go. And if you need anything—"

If I need any mind-altering zombie fat drugs, I'll give you a call, I finish silently. "Right," I say again out loud. "Thanks Doc."

As I pass through the waiting room, I accidentally knock a copy of *Healthy Grieving* to the ground. I hesitate, but don't stop to pick it up.

Chapter 1

Before

"What's wrong?" I know something's up as soon as I see my mother. I've just walked in from school, and she's hovering in the kitchen doorway, clutching a bag of pretzels to her chest the way a toddler holds a stuffed animal.

"Nothing." She smiles brightly. "How was your day?"

"I see the pretzels, Mom." I nod pointedly at the bag and kick my boots into the hall closet. Pretzels are my mother's go-to snack for stress eating. "What's going on?" I brush past her, tossing my backpack at the foot of the stairs before heading to the kitchen.

"I skipped lunch, that's all." My mom trails behind me. "Want some?" She holds out the bag.

I reach in and grab a handful as I settle down at the table, biting into one with a satisfying crunch. "So what's up?"

"I have a lump in my breast." She blurts it out, then covers her mouth in horror.

"What?" I nearly choke on the pretzel before I force it down, coughing. "What do you mean? Are you sure?"

Mom slides into the chair across from me, her head in her hands. "I wasn't going to tell you."

"You weren't going to tell me?" I push the vase in the center of the table out of the way so I can see her. Her long, thick, dark hair tumbles over her arms and her voice is muffled. We have the same hair: thick, dark, and poker straight. When I was little, I would have her braid mine when wet in the hopes I would wake up to a head full of Rapunzel-esque waves. To my dismay, it always came out just as mercilessly straight when I undid the braids, no matter how many times we tried it.

"I didn't want to burden you. You're just a teenager." She is still speaking through her hair, with only her nose poking out. She looks a bit like a Muppet.

"Burden me?" I raise my eyebrows. "Come on, Mom. When has that ever been an issue?"

My mom is not exactly the secretive type. She's shared pretty much everything with me since I mastered peeing in the potty. While my friends' parents shielded their children from the realities of the world in an effort to protect them, my mom was always blunt and matter-of-fact. She didn't believe in nonsense or silly stories, even for kids; she felt it was akin to lying, and she's a terrible liar. When I was four, my friend Ashley had a new baby brother that she claimed was delivered by a stork. My mother clarified that this was not, in fact, the case, and proceeded to explain in gory detail how babies were made and born. It caused quite a stir in the pre-kindergarten class, I can tell you that much. After that I wasn't really invited to Ashley's any more.

"I know, I know. I'm sorry. I just don't know any other way to be." Her head is still in her hands, but she sneaks another pretzel. It's both furtive and adorable, and my stomach starts hurting on cue.

"Look, it's probably just a cyst." I try to sound nonchalant.

"How do you know about cysts?" Her head pops up, gray eyes hopeful. The sudden movement disturbs the vase of daffodils, and a sprinkling of yellow pollen flutters to the glass tabletop.

"I saw it on TV, I think. Dr. Oz, maybe."

Her eyes darken. "I hate Dr. Oz. He's such a self-righteous blowhard. Do you think he even takes his own advice?"

"Yeah, for sure. He spends all his off-screen time on a treadmill with a broccoli smoothie." I carefully pluck a tiny crystal of salt off a pretzel with my front teeth. I love salt; I've eaten it plain, from the shaker. My sodium levels would probably give Dr. Oz a heart attack. Or maybe not, actually, seeing as how he's such a paragon of healthy living and all.

"Will you feel it?" My mom leans across the table and grabs my arm. Her grip is surprisingly strong.

"Feel what?"

"The lump."

"Feel your boobs?!" I pull away, panicked.

"Oh, come on, don't be like that. You nursed until you

were two." My mom is already pulling off her top, a stretchy black turtleneck.

"Ugh!" I make a face. "Please."

"Oh, come on." She's unhooking her bra now, black and lacy. It's nowhere near the sturdy, practical sort of bra you'd picture your mother choosing, and I avert my eyes, not wanting to see or think about my mom in sexy lingerie.

She continues talking as if nothing's happened. "Breast-feeding is natural. You loved it."

"I know, but I don't want to think about doing it as a toddler." I sigh and stand up. There's no way around this, I'm going to have to feel up my own mom. She's never going to take no for an answer.

"It's over here." She gropes her right breast and grabs my hand. "There. Can you feel that?"

I can feel it. It feels like a wad of old, hardened chewing gum stuck under her smooth skin. My heart pounds and I pull my hand away. I stare openly now at her naked breasts. You can't see the lump at all; the breast looks entirely normal. Round and uniform. I notice with a jolt that her left breast is slightly smaller than her right, something we apparently share but have never discussed. I feel another sharp cramp in my left side and wince.

"You think it's bad, don't you?" Her voice is quiet.

"I don't. I don't!" I protest as she redresses. "I felt it, but it's probably just a cyst, like I said before."

"What if it's cancer?" My mom blurts it out.

"Mom!" I recoil. "Don't say that!" I clutch the edge of the

table, my knuckles turning white. A pretzel falls to the floor and snaps into pieces.

"You were thinking it," she says. "I'm just saying it out loud."

"Don't even think it, then." My voice is firm. "It's a cyst. Are you going to the doctor?"

"Yeah, tomorrow."

"What does Dad say?" I bend down to collect the pieces of the broken pretzel. I consider just eating them, but think better of it and toss them behind me, into the sink.

"I wish you wouldn't do that." She frowns at me. "It clogs the drain. Is it so hard to throw your garbage in the actual trash can?"

"Hey, I just felt your boobs for you!" I feign indignation.

"Point taken." My mom walks over to the fridge and swings it open to release a cool whoosh of air, rummaging inside for a Diet Coke. "Dad says it's probably a cyst, too."

"See?" I say. Against my better judgment, I take a Coke too, leaning against the kitchen counter as I flip open the top. Caffeine aggravates my IBS, but I want to share this moment with her. Diet Coke is another of my mother's vices, one we both used to share.

"It's hardly reassuring. Last I checked, your father was an English professor." My mom takes a swig of her own can and exhales deeply with satisfaction before noticing mine.

"Should you be drinking that?" She frowns. "I thought it made you sick."

"I'm fine," I lie. I sip my drink and stare out the window

to the backyard. The leaves are already mostly gone, while those that are left die slowly, fading from fiery shades of red and gold to brown. It's windy out today, and my old tire swing moves back and forth in a slow, rhythmic fashion, as if propelled by a ghost.

My mom follows my gaze. "Remember how you loved that swing?" She sounds wistful. "You'd swing for hours at a time."

"Yeah," I say. "I'm sixteen now, though. A little old for swinging."

"Sixteen…" Her voice trails off. She's not the type for nostalgic weeping over photo albums, but her eyes look glassy.

"What's for supper?" I hastily change the subject.

"Well, about supper." My mom turns to me, biting her lip. "After I found…it, I didn't feel much like cooking."

"Totally fair," I agree, trying not to laugh. This happens at least twice a week, for any of a wide variety of reasons. My mother hates to cook, which is a shame, because she's actually quite good at it.

"Japanese?" She suggests. She opens a drawer and riffles through it, looking for a menu, her dark hair sliding like a curtain over her face.

"Perfect," I agree, then pull her in for a hug. "It'll be fine," I say firmly, even as my own stomach seizes, promising to exact its revenge for the Diet Coke.

She hugs me back tightly, and I close my eyes and pray that I'm right.

Chapter 2

After

The first thing I see when I get off the plane in Calantes is a goat. I've seen goats before, obviously, but this is the first one I've seen outside a petting zoo, let alone at an airport. It would feel very Third World, only the guy standing next to the goat is swearing loudly in Spanish on an iPhone, holding something like a Starbucks frappuccino. Every so often he kicks the poor goat for no reason. The goat takes it, bleating quietly to itself and shuffling its hooves. It doesn't try to make a run for it, even though it's not on a leash. My eyes travel to the door, which is flanked by about a dozen soldiers with machine guns. One notices me staring and smiles lasciviously.

"Caitlin Marks?" Someone taps me on the shoulder, and I jump about six feet in the air.

"Sorry!" The guy holds up his hands as I whirl around,

ready to defend myself. "I didn't mean to startle you. I'm from Students Without Boundaries."

"Right," I say, relaxing. "I thought you'd be holding up a sign."

"We don't like to do that," he says. He lowers his voice. "You don't want to give people any unnecessary information."

They taught us that at orientation. Something to do with stealing and ransoming your luggage, I think. "Right," I say again quickly. "I remember now."

"I'm Emerson Anklewicz." He puts out his hand, and I shake it as I follow him past the goat to the baggage claim. The floors are cracked terra-cotta tile, and I can feel the grooves beneath my feet as I walk. There's a large fan overhead; the airport is not air conditioned.

"It will take a few minutes for the bags to be unloaded," says Emerson. I guess he does this all the time. "How was your flight?"

I shrug. "Fine, I guess. Long." I don't mention that I watched *The Notebook* twice. There are some things you just don't share with a guy.

"You connected in Mexico City?"

"No, in São Paolo." I don't remember much about São Paolo. I spent my layover slumped bonelessly in a chair, asleep enough to have dreamed that I missed an English final, but sufficiently awake that I could have fought someone who tried to pry my carryon out of my arms.

"Nice." Emerson nods, and I nod too, though I don't actually know why we're nodding at each other. I notice he's dressed pretty much head to toe in navy clothing emblazoned with SWB in white. I wonder if that's required, or whether he chooses to go around wearing swag. He's not bad-looking—his close-cropped, curly brown hair is pretty cute—but he's channeling some kind of weird nineties vibe, wearing his SWB hat backwards.

"There's my bag." I point to the large red hiking backpack jostling its companions on the carousel, relieved that it showed up. I hadn't wanted to check it, but it had stalwartly resisted all my efforts to cram it into the overhead bin. Finally, I had yielded it to a smirking flight attendant, red-faced.

Emerson leans forward and neatly grabs it for me. "Thanks," I say, reaching out for it.

"You sure?" He eyes me skeptically, taking in my diminutive height and small frame.

"Yes," I say quickly, before I can change my mind. I hoist it onto my shoulders and make an effort not to wince. "I need to be able to carry it myself, right?"

"It can't hurt." Emerson leads me towards the exit. "We don't do a lot of traveling by foot, but I guess you never know." He pauses. "Do you have your passport and papers ready?"

"Yeah." I dig through my purse and find both. A packet of Imodium—I have at least twelve just in my handbag—peeks out of the top of the passport, having somehow managed to wedge itself inside. Discreetly, I shove it back into the bag.

"*Bienvenudo a Calantes.*" It's the soldier who was staring at me before. I hand him my papers without meeting his eyes.

"Catalina Marks, from the USA," he drawls in thickly

accented English, latinizing my name. I don't correct him, just nod my head. My heart pounds and my stomach starts to churn.

"You come to help *los rebeldes*," he says darkly. *Los rebeldes*. Rebels.

"Just helping to treat the sick. Children and the elderly." This was the reply I was taught to provide in orientation. It felt very different giving it in person, in real life. I feel a bead of sweat trickle from my hair right down to the small of my lower back. Still avoiding eye contact, I focus my glance on a large map on the wall, which is brand new, unlike most of the decaying airport.

The guard snorts and rattles off something I can't quite catch in rapid-fire Spanish. I stand perfectly still and don't say anything. He leans in towards me, leering, so close I can feel his breath on my ear. He smells like cigarettes and stale bread. "You don't speak Spanish?"

"I do!" I look up, panicked. "*Pero solo...solo hablo un poquito de Español.*" I only speak a little bit of Spanish. I had been required to do the Spanish crash course as part of orientation. Not for the first time, I curse my decision to take French in high school. Tess would have said it was a sign I should have gone to Paris.

Sergeant Sleaze says nothing. He reaches into his pocket and pulls out a cigarette. Fumbling for a lighter, he thrusts my papers back at me before lighting up and exhaling loudly. I try not to gag as he blows a toxic whorl of smoke right into my face. I notice Emerson is already through the door, looking worried.

I wonder if I messed up the Spanish and accidentally insulted his mother or something.

"No you worry, Princessa." He steps aside, giving me that stomach-curdling grin again. "I let you go."

"Gracias," I stammer. He presses up against me as I try to get by, and I feel the butt of his machine gun against my stomach. I shudder and practically fling myself at Emerson.

"Did he give you a hard time?" Emerson gives me a sympathetic look. He digs into his pocket and pulls out a roll of Mentos, offering me one. The foil wrapper is crumpled, and there are bits of lint stuck to it, but I take one anyway, because it's something to do.

"Thanks." I bite into the mint, enjoying the satisfying crunch before it gives way to the soft interior. "He was just kind of a jerk."

"They're all like that." He shakes his head. "This place is really screwed up. You'll see soon enough."

I look around me. The ground is dusty, with tufts of grass and weeds growing here and there, as if someone forgot to water their lawn for three or four years. It's littered with cigarette butts and other trash: rotting food, torn items of clothing, empty bottles. A few feet away, I notice a baby doll on its back. Its head is cracked open and you can see the mechanism inside that opens and closes the eyes. There is something horrifying about it, and I feel my insides churn as I look away. There's a chain-link fence around the airport and it's topped with barbed wire. More soldiers with machine guns and cigarettes patrol the perimeter.

"Over here." Emerson motions toward a red vehicle that looks like a cross between a Jeep and a pickup truck and unlocks the doors. I toss my things in the back, but Emerson shakes his head. "You can't leave it there," he says, picking up my backpack. "It will get stolen."

"While we're moving?"

"You have no idea." His expression is grim. He shoves my pack under my seat for me, and helps me inside. "Like I said, this place is screwed up."

Emerson starts the car and clicks the lock switch at least five times. I wonder if he's paranoid, or if it's really that bad outside. As if reading my mind, Emerson catches my eye. "This is your first time in a Third World country." It's a flat statement, not a question. My lack of experience must be glaringly obvious.

"Yeah." I slump forward in my seat, my hair falling like a curtain around my face so he can't see my reddened cheeks. "It's not yours?"

"No, it is." He's blushing too. "I didn't mean it like that. Some of the others are just, like, veterans at this sort of thing. They've volunteered in Africa, or whatever."

"Not me." *I can't even believe I'm here,* I add silently. Out the window, I notice a small group of children waving to us from the side of the road. They don't look old enough to be in preschool, let alone wandering the road by themselves. Emerson notices them and toots the horn. They clap, delighted. Their faces are filthy and their clothes are ripped and smeared with dusty dirt. The oldest one—she's maybe five—picks up the youngest and props her on her hip, just like a mother with a baby. I stare, transfixed. I have never held a baby.

"The beginning is tough." Emerson is talking, and I try to concentrate on his voice. "It's a lot to get used to psychologically, all the poverty and violence. But it's not too bad for us. The barracks are decent, and the food isn't that awful. Anyway, you start to feel lucky about having food at all."

"How long have you been here?" I steal another look at Emerson. He's very tanned, probably from spending a lot of time outdoors here. He also has a smattering of freckles across his cheekbones and nose. He's not exactly good looking, not in a Hollywood sort of way, but there is something pleasant about his face. His eyes are warm, and when he smiles it feels genuine.

"Almost a year," he says. "I go home soon. Back to college. I took a year off to come here."

"Where are you studying?" I ask politely. Outside, I notice a trio of dead birds smeared on the road and cringe.

"UCLA. Architecture." He gives me a shy smile. "I've been helping to design the orphanage."

"Wow." I reach for another Mentos. Emerson's dropped the pack in the cup holder, and my mouth is dry and sticky, as if I swallowed a tablespoon of tapioca pudding. Flying will do that to you; it's the recycled air. My dad taught me that. Before he lost his mind, my dad was an airplane enthusiast. I think of his collection of model 747s and feel a crushing sensation in my chest, as if my insides are crumpling like an empty soda can.

"How about you?" He makes a sharp left, and I grab on to the door handle to steady myself. "You also taking a year off?"

"Yeah, but I haven't started." The sun is blinding, and I lower my sunglasses. "I've deferred. Stanford. Undeclared major."

"Wow, right out of high school?"

"Something wrong with that?" I cross my arms across my chest, feeling defensive.

"No, it's great," he says sincerely. "It shows a lot of commitment. A lot of people here are just résumé-building. You know, for grad school or whatever."

"Seriously?" It seems like a long way to come to résumé build, and I wonder if that's the standard now. My parents made me volunteer Saturdays at a food bank, citing not only the joys of altruism but the benefits of listing the work on my university application. Now I wonder if they were being naïve. Maybe handing out canned goods was good enough to get you into law school or whatever back in the eighties, but it sounds like it might not cut it now.

"Oh yeah. Though to be fair, it's still hard work, no matter why you're here."

The road narrows as we drive down a steep hill. It isn't paved, just covered in gravel. In the distance, I catch a glimpse of the thick, green, tree canopy of the Amazon rainforest. Emerson follows my gaze.

"That's the jungle," he confirms, reading my thoughts. "It's hard to believe this was all jungle once, really."

I think of the airport, the barren ground, the dusty roads. It's hard to imagine any of it having been the source of thriving life. I picture my battered copy of *Lonely Planet: Calantes*, and the photos of tall grasses and ancient trees, colorful birds, and oversized flowers.

"You know the history?" Emerson looks at me quickly, before turning his eyes back to the road, which is winding its way down the rest of the hill. My stomach is empty, and I feel slightly queasy. I take a deep breath, hoping my bowels won't choose this particularly inopportune moment to showcase their irritability.

"Yes." I nod, exhaling. It had been touched on briefly in orientation, of course, but I'd also done a lot of my own reading on Calantes's long and sad history. It was a thriving hub during the Amazon rubber boom of the nineteenth century, and the capital city of San Pedro was second only to Manaus, Brazil, in its wealth and importance as an international destination for rubber. But when the rubber-tree seeds were smuggled out of the Amazon, no country suffered as much as Calantes. San Pedro had slowly crumbled over the years, its European-style buildings either destroyed or decaying, its once-paved streets cracked and unrepaired. A revolving door of corrupt leaders had plunged the tiny country into a lingering depression over the last half-century, most of them succumbing to greed and involvement in what had become Calantes's main source of income since the rubber collapse: drug trafficking.

"These guys now—General Alvarez and his crew—they're beyond corrupt." Emerson shakes his head in disgust. "There was a democratically elected government here for ten years, and things were finally looking better. And now this."

I frown at his reference to the previous government.

"Wasn't President Carias convicted of collaborating with drug cartels and stealing from taxpayers to build a saltwater pool for his mansion?" I shift in my seat, feeling a rumbling in my stomach that I pray is just hunger and not the prelude to a full-blown attack. I feel thankful the windows are rolled down.

Emerson reddens. "He wasn't perfect," he admits. He doesn't look at me, his eyes firmly fixed on the uneven terrain before him. "But the army is even worse. It's a huge step backwards for Calantes."

I don't say anything. He would know better; he's been here, on the ground. Besides, I had seen the news reports, and the pictures. One particularly famous shot that had gone viral was of one of Alvarez's soldiers lighting a cigarette off a woman's burning hair. My stomach turns as I recall it, the victim's anguish contrasted with the manic laughter of the soldier. The car takes another twist, and I feel the Mentos rising in my throat, coupled with another grumbling sensation.

Thankfully, moments later Emerson slows to a stop. We've arrived. The base is a hodgepodge of burlap tents, abandoned trailers, and old wooden barracks. They look ridiculously rickety, and I can't help picturing the big bad wolf huffing and puffing and blowing them down. Kids my own age mill about in jeans and T-shirts. I notice a girl with two long red braids carrying a guitar and have the urge to roll my eyes. I can almost picture Tess raising her eyebrows at me. See, she would say. It's exactly like camp. Guitars and "Kumbaya."

Emerson follows my gaze. "That's Sari," he says, nodding

at the girl with the guitar. "She does music therapy with the little ones."

Of course she does. Feeling like the biggest asshole on the planet, I follow Emerson into a rusty trailer that's been painted with the distinctive blue-and-white SWB logo. "Office" is scrawled on the door as an afterthought, in what looks like black marker. The door is propped open with a broken chair. "This is the main office," says Emerson, unnecessarily. "Come on, I'll introduce you to Tricia."

The office isn't much more than a desk, a couple of dented filing cabinets, and a fan, which oscillates slowly, gently rustling the papers on the desk each time it breezes by. I step in front of it, enjoying the sensation of moving air on my face.

The girl at the desk smiles pleasantly. Her hair is a wild mass of brown curls valiantly trying to escape the ponytail they've been scraped into, and when the fan blows by, the loose tendrils fly upwards, forming a ruff around her face. "Nice, isn't it? You're welcome to come and stand here in front of my fan anytime," she says, putting out her hand. "I'm Trish. I run the office."

"Cat," I say, shaking her hand firmly. "Cat Marks."

"Cat," she repeats. "I like that."

"There were four Caitlins in my first-grade class," I explain. "Cate and Caity were already taken as nicknames."

"Ah," she says knowingly. "My oldest sister is a Jessica. I totally understand."

"I like Cat," says Emerson, unexpectedly. I look at him, and he blushes and kind of shrugs. "I know a lot of Katies, but I've never met a Cat."

31

I notice a dish of colorful lollipops on the corner of Trish's desk and eye them hopefully. Hard candy helps soothe my stomach. Trish sees me looking and grins, handing me the bowl. Gratefully, I select a red one and noisily tear off the plastic wrapping.

"So, Caitlin Marks." Trish swaps the candy dish for a blue file folder and spreads it open on the desk. "Here is your name tag and handbook."

"Name tag?" I pop the lollipop into my mouth.

"It's for orientation," she clarifies.

I push the sucker to one side with my tongue. "I had an orientation back in Ohio," I say, frowning.

"This is more like an icebreaker," Emerson interjects helpfully. "You know, like games. To get to know the others in your group."

Icebreaker. Glorious. I imagine Tess rolling on the floor, helpless with laughter. We both hate those intolerably cutesy, forced games. I try not to cringe as I pick up the name tag with two fingers, as if it's contaminated with hepatitis.

"You're in Barracks B," continues Trish. "Bed four."

"Bed four," I repeat. I sound like a toddler, my mouth full of candy.

"And Emerson here is your buddy. We have a buddy system here," she adds, catching my look of confusion. "We pair the newbies with experienced volunteers to help them get adjusted. It's like a mentorship program."

"Right," I say. I look over at Emerson, who smiles at me. I wonder if he thinks I'm going to sleep with him. Then I wonder where people have sex, because we all live in barracks and having sex in a communal living arrangement is sort of gross. Not that I would really know, because I've never had sex. I may be the only person on the planet who graduated from high school a virgin, but to be fair, I did have a lot on my mind.

"And the tuck shop and pay phones are in Barracks H." Guiltily, I realize Trish has been talking while I've been thinking about sex, and I've missed all of it. Now I won't know where the bathrooms are, or how to get Internet. I hope it's all in my handbook.

"Don't worry, all of this is in the handbook," says Trish, as if reading my mind. "It's a lot to take in right away, especially after seeing all the poverty on the drive in."

"Yes," I say quickly, feeling ashamed. She thinks I've gone maudlin over the underprivileged children, rather than thinking about hypothetical sex.

"And thank you," Trish adds. Her dark eyes are warm and sincere; they make her sweet face almost pretty. "We really need the help out here. We get the fewest number of volunteers. We don't have the cachet of Africa or the Gaza Strip."

I wonder if it's the first time "cachet" and "Gaza" have been used in the same sentence. I figure this is not a good time to mention I chose Calantes because Gaza seemed terrifying and Burkina Faso required more shots.

"I'll take you over to B Barracks now," says Emerson helpfully. "Thanks, Trish."

"Thanks!" I add. She waves with a smile as we step out of the trailer. Little clouds of dust puff up at my feet with each step, as if the ground is smoking. I crunch down on the lollipop, biting the sweet remains. I feel better, for now.

"Trish is great," he says. "She used to be a volunteer. Back in 2009."

"And now she's working for SWB?"

"Yeah. She's the site manager. She came back after she got her MBA in non-profit organization management."

I didn't realize masters' degrees were that specific. Clearly I have a lot to learn.

"This is B," he says, gesturing to one of the broken-down barracks I'd noticed from the car. It has a giant, sloppy "B" spray-painted in orange on the door, but I don't mention this, because right now Emerson is pretty much my only friend, and I don't want him to think I'm a sarcastic bitch, even if it happens to be true.

There's no one else inside when we open the door into the stale heat. "The others should be here soon," says Emerson, looking at his watch. "I know Anthony went to pick up two newbies for three, and Erin is going later to get the last."

"It's four to a room?" I look around. There are four metal twin beds carefully placed, one in each corner. Each one has a bedside table, a trunk, and a bookcase tucked beside it. Mosquito nets hang over each bed like woven chandeliers. I've never seen a mosquito net in person before. They look a bit like canopies, giving the room a weird kind of squalid grandeur.

"Yeah." Emerson points to a corner. "That one's four. You put your clothes and anything perishable in the trunk, everything else in the bookcase. Oh, and keep your toiletries in your trunk, too."

"Why?" I ask, curious.

"Because otherwise they melt," he says simply.

"How would they melt?" I frown, picturing my shampoo. As far as I know, it's already liquid. *What happens to shampoo when it melts? Can it melt? How would I even know?*

He looks at me quizzically. "It's hot here?"

"No, but how does it melt them?"

He thinks I'm crazy now, I can tell. "The soap. It gets hot, and it melts."

"Ohh." *Soap. Of course.* "I—I use body wash." Realizing I've just divulged Too Much Information, I stop talking and look away, mortified. Emerson looks amused, and I hope at this point he actually does want to sleep with me, because otherwise he's just going to think I'm deeply weird.

"I'll leave you here to unpack and rest a bit," he says, chewing on the inside of his lip. At least both of us are uncomfortable. "Does that work?"

"Yes," I say gratefully, gazing longingly at my new bed. I'm happy to have somewhere to lie down after what felt like an endless trip, even if the mattress looks like it was previously occupied by a sumo wrestler and the blanket is scratchy-looking blue polyester.

"Great, I'll see you later," says Emerson. He flips around his baseball cap, fiddling with the brim. "I'll come back and take you on a camp tour."

"Sure." My voice is muffled by the musty pillow. I'm

already flopped face-first down on the bed. Emerson says something else, but my eyes are half-closed and the words don't register. I don't bother to turn down the bed before falling asleep.

Chapter 3

Before

I know from the look on my mother's face it's bad news long before she opens her mouth.

"No," I say. I feel the blood leave my head and plunge to my feet. I sway, dizzy, and grab on to a kitchen chair to steady myself. "Don't say it."

"He doesn't know yet." Her voice is quiet. She's holding a glass of wine in one hand, taking gulps as opposed to sips. "But he thinks it's bad, based on the mammogram."

"They can't tell it's cancer from a mammogram," I jump in. I know this, because I have spent the past week googling breast cancer like it's my job. I now know that a lump can only be declared cancerous once it's been biopsied, which involves sticking a giant needle deep into your boob to extract a sample of tissue. There was a video of the procedure on YouTube, but

I couldn't bring myself to watch it. Just thinking about it nearly sent me running to the bathroom.

"He said it was spiculated, though." She reaches for the bottle of Chardonnay on the counter and tops up her glass. "Apparently, that is bad."

"Oh." My heart plummets. Spiculated is bad. It means that the lump has spikes protruding from it when it shows up on an X-ray, and those spikes tend to mean malignant cancer. I picture a spiky mass, bright green, with crazy eyes and a scowling mouth, like a character in a video game you squash for two hundred points.

My mom is watching my expression, her eyes growing wide. "It is bad, then. I was right." Her voice is high and thin with panic. "What did you read?"

While I have been devoting my time to becoming the world's first high-school junior to earn a specialty in breast oncology, my mother has been studiously avoiding the Internet. "Don't tell me, Cat," she'd say, when I tried to explain anything to her. "I don't want to know."

I don't blame her for acting this way. While I deal with fear by learning everything I can, I recognize that hiding in bed with an iPad and pretzels as an equally reasonable strategy for coping with stress.

"They can't tell anything until the biopsy," I say firmly, but I don't make eye contact. Instead, I focus on a point just above her head, on the kitchen cabinets. I notice a tiny spider there, trying to move around undetected. Ordinarily this would bother me, but it would seem I've moved on from being afraid of spiders.

"I'm going to have to do chemo." She's tearing up now. My heartbeat stutters, then picks up; I hate seeing my parents cry. It feels unnatural. Parents are supposed to be brave and stoic and stable, and right now my mom is weeping, with a glass of wine held loosely in one hand. "I'm going to lose all my hair." She sets her glass down on the table and wipes her eyes with the back of her hand, leaving a trail of smudged mascara. "Is that shallow? It is, isn't it? I have cancer and all I can think of is my hair." She gives a painful little hiccup, a cross between a laugh and a sob. "What if I have a giant birthmark on my head?"

"Maybe you should lay off the wine," I say gently, putting my hand on her arm. She's wearing the sweater I bought her for Christmas last year. It's baby-soft and purple, made of real cashmere.

"You're right," she says. "That fucker Oz says it can raise your risk of breast cancer." She throws back her head and gives a crazy kind of cackle.

"Okay, enough." I grab her glass and dump the remaining contents into the sink, and tuck the bottle back in the fridge. I refill her glass with water and hand it back to her. "Drink," I say.

My mom gulps it down, obedient as a child, and goes over to place the glass in the dishwasher.

"If I die," she says, her palms flat on the washer, "you're going to have to remember to run the dishwasher at night. Your father will never do it."

"Mom!" I massage my temples against a gathering head-ache. "You can't say stuff like that!"

"I know." She comes over to me and puts both her hands

on my shoulders. She looks at me searchingly, her eyes full of pain. "I'm so sorry, Cat."

"It's okay," I reply, because what else can I say. I wrap my arms around her, inhaling deeply. I take in her scent—vanilla deodorant and Pears shampoo. I don't know how long we stand there like that.

• • •

My mom gets her biopsy results the same day I get my midterm back in Chem. I knew it would be bad news, because I aced the Chem test. Karma is like that. The Universe giveth, the Universe taketh away, or something along those lines. But anyway, as soon as I see that ninety-six, I feel my stomach bottom out. I stare at the poster of the periodic table of the elements tacked to the wall, wishing I could reverse the two numbers.

"What's wrong?" Tess mouths. She's watching me from across the aisle, a quizzical expression on her face. "Bad?"

I shake my head, and flash her my paper. She furrows her eyebrows in confusion, and I gesture at my breasts in explanation. Tess just looks increasingly baffled. Jonah Campbell, who sits next to her, winks at me suggestively.

"Ms. Marks?" Mr. Josefson, the chemistry teacher, regards me with an odd expression. "Is everything...all right?"

I feel my cheeks flame as I cease poking at my chest with a number-two pencil. "Yes, Mr. Josefson." I slouch down in my seat. "Sorry."

Jonah gives a snort of laughter, but I ignore him. Instead,

I stare at the series of neat red checkmarks on my near-perfect midterm, overcome with trepidation. Why couldn't I have blown it?

I don't call or text my mom to find out. In my heart, I know that, if it was good news, she would have sent me her own text, full of her trademark caps and exclamation marks and series of completely random emoji. Instead, it's been radio silence all day.

It's dark when I enter the house. All the lights are off on the main floor, which is unusual. Ordinarily, my dad has to nag us into shutting off the lights, because "do you know how many papers I have to grade to pay for the electrical bill," and so on. But today, it's dark, and dark is never good. I've seen enough movies to know which way this is going.

I walk into the living room, where I find my father on the couch. The TV isn't on, and he hasn't got any books or a newspaper or anything, he's just sitting there, in the dark, staring at the wall. He's clutching a family-sized bag of plain Lay's and there's a bag of red licorice half-empty on the table. I don't remember either of these things being in our pantry, and I wonder, briefly, if my dad actually made a stop at the grocery store to load up on stress food after the hospital.

"Dad?" I venture cautiously. I hover in the doorway, watching as he takes another heaping handful of chips.

"Cat," he says with a start. "Shouldn't you be in school?"

"It's four," I say quietly. I brace myself, waiting for the words I know are coming. I half hope he won't say anything, because until he says it out loud, it isn't real.

"Is it? Already?" He looks confused for a moment, then shakes his head. "Sorry." He struggles to look at me, and I can see his eyes are filling with tears behind his round frameless glasses. His thinning gray hair, usually combed neatly to one side, is sticking up in various directions. It looks sort of fluffy, like a ruffled baby chicken.

"It's okay," I say brusquely. "You don't have to say it." I fold my arms around myself for protection.

"Oh, sweetheart." He's crying now, and I feel the panic rise in my throat. "Don't worry. Everything is going to be okay. The doctors were very positive."

He keeps talking, but I don't hear him. The doctors were very positive. It's funny how a statement about positivity really isn't very positive at all.

"Where's Mom?" I interrupt. He's blathering on about support groups, which irritates me. My mother isn't the support-group type. She'd probably rather have an extra biopsy than bare her soul to a roomful of strangers.

"She's sleeping," he said. "They gave her something to help her sleep. She was upset."

I take the stairs two at a time, and poke my head into my parents' bedroom. My mom is curled up on top of the duvet, still in her clothes.

On the dresser, I see a small bottle. Xanax, it says. Alprazolam. Quietly, I open the bottle and shake one into my palm.

Chapter 4

After

"Was that a rat?"

I'm still half-asleep when I hear the girl's voice, loud and bordering on shrill, followed by the thud of her luggage being dumped on the ground. I groan loudly and sit up, squinting blearily at the new arrival.

"Hi," I say. "I'm Cat Marks."

She's very petite, with long, straight jet-black hair and almond-shaped eyes. Her skinny jeans are tucked into a pair of little black boots with impossibly high heels, and she's wearing several tank tops in different colors layered over one another. Her purse is Louis Vuitton, and there's something about her that suggests it's real, not purchased furtively on a side street in Chinatown, or whatever.

"Margo Chang-Cohen," she says abruptly. She looks

around, an expression of disdain on her face. "Wow. This place is even more disgusting than I thought it would be. That's special."

I yawn and release my hair from its ponytail, fastening the yellow tie around my wrist. "Did you say you saw a rat?"

"I think so." Margo peers around suspiciously. "I saw something move over there." She points toward the back left-hand corner of the room, and we both stare, waiting. Nothing happens.

"Whatever." She shrugs. "Nothing we can do anyway. It'll be like home."

"You have rats at home?" I eye the designer bag doubtfully.

"Not *in* my home, obviously. But I live in downtown Toronto, so yeah. Rats. You see them on the subway tracks and stuff." She sits down gingerly on bed number three. "Assuming there are rats in South America."

"Aren't there rats everywhere?" I frown. My eyes dart around the little barracks, on alert now for furry little creatures. All I see are dust bunnies and dirt, and what looks like a crushed can of Diet Coke in one of the front corners.

"No. There are no rats in Alberta. But I can't say for certain about anywhere else." She opens her purse and begins rummaging through it.

"Why no rats in Alberta?" My curiosity is piqued.

"No clue." She pulls out a Butterfinger. "I read it once, in a magazine. Want some?"

"Sure." She snaps off a half and hands it to me. Bright orange crumbs rain to the ground, adding to our potential vermin situation, but I'm too tired to do anything about it. We chew in silence, while I continue to survey the room for signs of non-human life. Except for a couple of disturbing insects, it seems okay, but I still can't help worrying about rats, especially when the night rolls around. I saw a story on the news once of a baby who had been attacked by rats in her crib. They tried to gnaw off her face. It was in London, though, where rats and people have a long history of mutual enmity. I'm not sure how it is here in the jungle.

"Hello?" A new voice, this one male, pipes up from the doorway. A tall guy about my age hovers, looking uncertain. "This is Barracks B, right?"

"Well, there was a great big letter B on the outside wall," says Margo. I can't tell if she's intentionally being sarcastic, or if she's one of those people who manage to sound that way even when they're being nice.

"I thought the barracks were…segregated," says the boy.

"Segregated?" Margo raises an eyebrow and swallows the last of her chocolate. "You mean like the American south? I don't think so. I'm pretty sure that's illegal now."

"No. No!" He turns an unfortunate shade of scarlet, clearly flustered. "Like, guys and girls. Separated."

"So, you're not a racist, then," Margo smirks.

"No! I'm Latino! How could I be?"

"Relax, I'm just playing." She waves him over. "I'm Margo, and this is Cat."

I smile feebly. "Hi."

"Taylor Mendez," he says. "Nice to meet you guys."

Taylor is tall and olive-skinned, with wavy, almost black hair worn to his shoulders and a pair of expensive-looking aviator sunglasses perched on his head. He's wearing skinny jeans with PUMA sneakers and one of those T-shirts that is meant to look retro, but is actually brand new and mass-produced in China or Bangladesh or some other place where they force toddlers to work sewing machines for five cents an hour. It has an eighties-looking box of Rice Krispies printed on the front.

"Well, that's it then." Margo nods.

"That's what?"

"You have a girl's name. That's how you ended up here."

"Taylor is not a girl's name!" He looks affronted.

"Taylor Swift? Taylor Momsen? Taylor Schilling? Come on."

"What about Taylor Lautner?" he challenges.

Margo waves her hand dismissively. "He doesn't count. The *Twilight* movies were crap. He won't be in anything else of note, mark my words."

"Didn't Trish notice you were a guy?" I interrupt. "Maybe the dorms are coed."

"Is that the office manager? She wasn't there." Taylor waves the paper in his hand. "This was on the counter for me. It says Bed Two."

"Well, you're welcome to stay." Margo nods at bed number two. "I don't have any issues with a coed dorm. I lived in one my freshman year."

"You're in college?" I ask eagerly.

"Yeah, of course." She eyes me suspiciously. "Why? How old are you?"

"I just graduated. High school," I add quickly. "I'm taking a gap year before college. I deferred."

"I should have done that," says Taylor. He drops his bag on the ground, and sinks down on one of the opposite beds. "I just finished freshman year."

"That's a weird time to do a year abroad," says Margo, frowning at him.

"Let's just say I needed to get away," he answers. He's not giving us anything else—his tone of voice makes it clear that conversation is over, for now. Margo shrugs and turns back to me, kicking off her spike-heeled boots. She takes a bottle of violet nail polish from her purse and shakes it briskly with one hand, peeling off her socks with the other.

"So why are you guys here?" she asks, carefully painting her big toe, chin resting on her knee. "And not the bullshit helping-people reason. The truth."

The truth. My breath catches, as if I'd been hit in the stomach by one of Margo's stilettos.

Taylor gives her a slantwise look as he opens his bag and retrieves a granola bar. "You start," he says, tearing off the crinkly wrapper.

"Sure." Margo finishes her left foot, and wiggles her toes as if this will hasten the drying process. She replaces the brush with a delicate touch and looks at us evenly. "My cousin got into law school."

I wait for further explanation, but apparently none is forthcoming. Margo starts on her right foot, swearing under her breath as she accidentally smears purple polish around her cuticle.

"So?" Taylor asks. "What does that have to do with anything?"

"So, my dad is a competitive prick," says Margo, her tone matter-of-fact. "He basically told me, if I don't get into medical school, he'll never be able to face his brother—that's my Uncle Steve—ever again. And I don't have the extracurriculars to get into med school. And my Spanish is pretty good, so here I am." She makes a face. "It's just a year, right?"

Taylor looks mildly repulsed. "No offense, but that's, like, the worst reason I've ever heard for volunteering." He swallows the last of his granola bar. "Do you even want to go to med school?"

"Not really," Margo says. Finished with her toes, she swings her feet around so they're dangling off the edge of the bed. She's so short that her soles don't even brush the ground. "I'd probably be better off alone in a lab somewhere, but my parents are both doctors, and they'd never get over the shame of a daughter with a PhD."

"That's insane," says Taylor. "Why do you have to do what they say? You're an adult."

Margo narrows her eyes at him. "You have no idea what they're like. Lucky you, that you're so…unencumbered by your family."

Taylor turns yet another deep shade of scarlet. It's like red is his skin's natural spectrum. He looks away silently.

"So why are you here, Cat?" Margo turns to me. "Got into a crap college? Bad breakup? Parents' divorce?"

For a minute, I don't say anything. I stare at my hands, weaving them in and out of each other. Finally, I look up, and take a deep breath.

"My mom died," I say. "Breast cancer."

"Shit," says Margo. All the sarcasm has leached out. "I'm really sorry."

"Yeah, it's been…terrible." After months of pretending, I feel surprisingly liberated by my confession. "Everyone asks, 'Are you okay?' and I say 'Yeah, I'm dealing,' but really, I'm not. Not at all, actually. I'm a fucking mess."

"Of course you are," says Taylor. His eyes are full of sympathy. "Your mom died."

"Were you close?" Margo asks quietly.

I feel tears prick at my eyes, and my nose tingles the way it does before I start to cry. "She was my best friend."

They're both quiet. I take a deep breath. "When I first signed up, I didn't think I'd actually go. I thought my father would step in and…I don't know…save me from myself, I guess. But he's been on his own planet since the diagnosis, not that I can really blame him. I kind of lost it when she died."

"Lost it how?" Margo looks interested. She pokes at her toes and makes a face as a bit of polish smears her finger.

"I got really depressed." I shudder, remembering the black hole that swallowed me the moment my mother's heart stopped beating. "Before that, when she was in treatment, I was okay. My dad was useless, so I handled everything, and I went to school, and I was doing everything, and then when she died, I just…crashed."

"Did they make you see someone?" asks Margo. She has a knowing expression on her face.

I flush, and don't answer. *Way to go, Cat. Now they're going to think you're crazy.*

"It's okay," she adds. "I've been in therapy since I was fifteen."

"Sixteen for me," says Taylor.

I look at them, taken aback. I've never met anyone else my age who needed to see a psychiatrist. "Yeah," I say. "Dr. Shapiro."

"Did they let you get away with depression?" asks Margo. She draws her knees into her chest, hugging them.

"What do you mean?"

"Did you get diagnosed with depression," she clarifies, "or did they turn it into a bigger issue? Like, for me, when I felt depressed, they said I had a borderline personality disorder. Same thing happened to most of my friends."

"Most of your friends have seen a shrink?" Now I'm totally flabbergasted.

She shrugs. "I went to a hypercompetitive private school," she says. "It's a cultural thing. So—let me guess. Generalized Anxiety Disorder?"

"Bipolar II," I mutter, not looking directly at her. "He said my...my behavior before she died was hypomanic."

Margo makes a noise that sounds like a cross between spitting and laughing. "Bullshit!" she crows. "They're so full of shit. I should have guessed. Bipolar II is the diagnosis *du jour*.

All the rage right now in the head-shrinking community. Let me guess—Seroquel?"

"Abilify," I answer, still amazed that she's such an expert in all things psychological. "But he was talking about switching. Not that I take any of it. I flush it all down the toilet."

Taylor speaks up. "I've been on Abilify. They should call it Inabilify. I was a zombie on that drug. I couldn't get out of bed for three months."

"Me too!" I exclaim. "It's the worst!"

"Clearly you've never been on a tricyclic," says Margo bitterly. "The old-school antidepressants? You can't imagine."

I have no idea what she's talking about, but Taylor looks aghast. "Dude, why not an SSRI?"

Margo shakes her head. "They made me suicidal. I tried to kill myself on Paxil."

She drops it so casually, she could have been talking about lactose intolerance. It takes me a moment to react. "You…you tried to kill yourself?"

"Yeah. It's a lesser-known side effect of the SSRIs in teenagers. Selective serotonin reuptake inhibitors," she adds helpfully, seeing the bewildered look on my face. "You know, like Prozac or Effexor."

These I've heard of, so I nod dumbly. My dad's on Effexor. It hasn't done much, in my opinion. I wince; thinking about my dad is like being punched suddenly in the gut. *Does he miss me?* I wonder. *Does he even notice I'm gone?*

"I take Pristiq now," says Taylor. "It's like Effexor, but it doesn't make you fat. I gained ten pounds on Effexor. I had to work out three hours a day for six months to take it off." He shudders, his hands clutching at his now-flat abdomen.

Margo looks at Taylor with sudden interest, studying him. "Are you gay?" she asks, suddenly. "I wouldn't have guessed."

I stare at Margo in horror, feeling my stomach seize in an uncomfortable and familiar way. *You can't just ask someone if they're gay, can you? Like asking them if they're vegetarian, or have they been to Disneyland? It's personal. I wonder if this line of questioning is normal in Canada. They legalized gay marriage ages ago, so perhaps it's basic conversation up there.*

Taylor stares at her, open-mouthed. "You can't just ask someone if they're gay!"

"But I just did. And you are." Margo rolls her eyes.

Taylor exhales. "Yeah," he admits. "I am."

"Shall we assume that's why you're here?" Margo leans back on her pillow, and makes a face. "Ugh, this thing is like a rock. I knew I should have brought one from home."

Taylor scowls. "Actually, if you must know," he says, jerkily unzipping his hoodie to reveal a UCLA T-shirt, "I'm here because I blew my freshman year and let my family down."

I let my family down. I wonder if he's the first person in his family to go to university. Or if he lost a scholarship, or something. I feel a pang of jealousy at his having people to let down; I doubt my father would notice if I joined Al-Qaeda. The pains in my stomach intensify briefly, but I try to ignore them.

"Oh, so you do care what your family thinks," says Margo, raising her eyebrows. "Talk about the pot calling the kettle black."

"It's a bit different," snaps Taylor. "My father is Arthur Mendez."

The name sounds vaguely familiar. Instinctively, I reach for my iPhone, before remembering it's not good for much other than a camera and calculator out here in the wilderness. I feel a twinge of homesickness for Google, if it's possible to feel homesick for a search engine.

"Arthur Mendez, really?" Margo looks reluctantly impressed. "Like the Su Casa Arthur Mendez?"

"Yeah," says Taylor, shoulders slumped. "That one."

Now I remember, too. Arthur Mendez is a millionaire who opened the Su Casa chain of motels. For years, he was the star of his own commercials, which always ended with a close-up of him saying *Mi casa e su casa!* with a wide, blinding grin. Clearly I was wrong about the scholarship thing. Taylor wasn't a financial-aid candidate, that's for damn sure.

"But why should it matter?" I break in. I'm not usually the forthright type, but I can't help myself. "Isn't your dad, like, famous for being self-made?"

"Exactly," says Taylor, his face darkening. He riffles through his bag and pulls out a pack of cigarettes. They're Virginia Slims, and I see Margo smirk at his choice of brand. "He never had the chance to go to university, so he expected me to go and become, like, a lawyer and MBA. He's always going on and on about how he feels inferior because he doesn't have an education, so he wanted to make sure I had what he didn't have, and blah, blah, blah." He fishes out a fancy silver lighter that looks as if it might double as some kind of James

Bond spy device and flicks it open. "Now I've blown that, so not only am I a huge disappointment for being gay—which I'm sure he cries about when I'm not around—but now I've blown the school thing too."

"That's all very tragic, but do not even consider lighting that cigarette in here." Margo points at his hand, looking disgusted. "I have asthma."

Taylor gives an exaggerated sigh and tosses the pack of smokes back in his bag. "Of course you do."

Margo glares at him. "What's that supposed to mean?"

"Nothing." Taylor pulls the sunglasses perched on his head down over his eyes. "Forget it."

"You know, you can cut the whole 'poor me' act," says Margo irritably. "At the end of the day, you're still a hotel heir, even if Daddy is upset. The rest of us don't have a trust fund. And Cat's mom is dead."

"Thanks," I say mildly, pulling my hair back and braiding it. "I love being reminded like that."

She at least has the decency to blush. "Sorry," she says. "But seriously. Whining millionaires piss me off."

"Do you encounter many?" I ask, interested. I loop a hair tie around the end of my braid. I feel cooler and less encumbered with my hair pulled back, and my stomach settles slightly.

"I went to private school," she says dryly. "I've met my share."

"I'm a failure and I'm gay," Taylor snaps back. "You wouldn't understand. You've probably never even gotten a B."

"Of course I've gotten a B." Margo rolls her eyes again.

"What was it in? Gym?"

Margo turns away and mutters something about it not mattering. I try to hide my grin, while Taylor smirks triumphantly.

"So what made you come here, of all places?" I break the awkward silence, looking over at him.

He shrugs, fiddling with his lighter. "Students Without Boundaries was recruiting outside my Stats final. I knew I'd failed, so I went right ahead and signed up. Calantes was the only placement with openings left, probably because no one's heard of it."

"How could you be so sure you'd failed?" It seemed like a drastic move to make before even getting your score.

"I handed it in blank," he says, his tone matter-of-fact.

Oh.

"I need a smoke," he says abruptly. He grabs his bag and makes a quick exit, without looking at either of us. I can feel Margo's eyes on me, but I don't return the stare. I haven't quite decided if we're friends yet. My stomach cramps again, and this time I know there's no ignoring it.

"I'm going out to make a phone call," I mumble, sliding off my bed. I rush to the bathroom, nearly giddy with relief as I lock myself in a stall. I sink down on to the toilet, and as my bowels give out, I wonder what the hell I was thinking in coming here. I picture Tess shaking her head, her freckles growing increasingly prominent as she begged me not to do this. I think of Dr. Shapiro, and wonder if he has ever had diarrhea in a stiflingly hot public bathroom. I fumble in my pocket for an Imodium, ecstatic at the minty sensation as it dissolves on my tongue. While I wait for the episode to pass, I watch a huge, shiny, brown beetle with a strange orange pattern on its shell scurry around the drain under the stall door. It is just out of the reach of my feet, though I don't know if I could bring myself to step on it, even if it were an option. I imagine the sickening crunch it would make, and shudder.

When it's finally over, I head to Barracks H without speaking to anyone, including the guy manning the tuck shop at the front. I plunk myself down at one of the phones and take a deep breath. I don't have to look at the buttons; my fingers know the number by heart. I wait impatiently as the phone rings its usual four times before I hear her.

"You've reached Paula Marks. Sorry I missed your call! You can leave a message, but I'll probably forget to call you back. Try me by email at PaulaM at Netwave dot com."

Hot tears stream down my face as I replace the receiver. I've been paying my mom's old cellphone bill for months without telling anyone. Sometimes I call it two or three times a day.

I pause, then dial the number again.

Chapter 5

Before

"How do you think I'd look as a blonde?" My mom carefully positions a wavy, platinum wig on her head and turns to face me. "Too much?"

"You look like an eighties pop star," I say, recoiling. "Take it off."

"Ugh." She tosses it on the counter. "I hate this."

"I know." I can't look at her. "Me, too."

We're at a hair salon that specializes in hair loss. The windows are tinted, and women enter and exit through the back, so as not to be spotted going in and out. The stylists' stations are all private, as are the wig-fitting rooms. I never dreamed that places like this existed. I wish I still didn't know.

"I'm sure Serena'll be able to help us." I flounder for the right thing to say, though these days it's getting harder and harder. "She's probably done this hundreds of times."

Serena is the salon owner. She's the one who warmly ushered us in, and then promptly left us in this terrifying room while she finished up with another client. It's filled with mannequin heads that smile with empty eyes, and the walls are decorated with Before and After photos that make me feel faint. Bald women with missing eyebrows and lashes stare at me wherever I look, their eyes on me from every corner of the room. No matter how hard I try, I still can't picture my mother that way. But it's coming, there's no way around it. She starts chemo next week.

"Sorry about that." Serena is back, a subdued smile on her face. I am duly impressed; she has perfected the Cancer Smile. Friendly, but not too enthusiastic. Sympathetic, but not pitying. Not many people have mastered it this expertly. "Do you see anything you think you might like?"

Reflexively, my mother reaches up and touches her own hair. Thick and dark and sleek like mink, it's the almost the exact opposite of the frizzy blonde disaster she tried on moments ago. She stares at herself in the mirror and doesn't answer.

"We're looking for something that looks like her natural hair," I begin, when it's clear my mother isn't going to speak up. "Just maybe shorter."

"Good choice," agrees Serena, nodding. She scrutinizes my mom, who's still gazing at her reflection, her eyes dull. "Perhaps a nice chestnut bob? Something with bangs? Bangs are very trendy this year."

"That sounds great," I say quickly.

Serena unlocks a cupboard and pulls out a few wigs, spreading them out on the counter. "So you have some options," she says, fanning out the locks with deft fingers. "The first is synthetic."

My mom finally snaps out of her reverie and turns to look at Serena. "I don't want synthetic," she says quietly. "I want it to look like real hair. I know it's expensive, but I want it to feel like real hair."

"Good choice," says Serena smoothly, whisking the synthetic away and tucking it back in a basket. "And a human hair wig will be a considerably cooler option."

"Right," says my mom. She picks up one of the wigs in front of Serena and places it on her head. "Like it's not a billion degrees wearing a squirrel on your head."

"Mom." There's a familiar, stabbing pain in my lower abdomen, and I imagine a squirrel scurrying around my small intestine. "Let's just listen, okay?"

Serena smiles nervously. I wonder if she's not used to cancer patients who make a lot of bitter jokes, but then I wonder how she could be anything but used to it.

"That one you're wearing is Indian hair," she says, pointing. "It's lovely and very reasonable."

"It looks great," I say, watching Serena adjust it on my mom's head. "It looks just like your hair."

It does, too; there's no way you would know it wasn't her own, even if you were looking closely. I wonder how many people I saw every day were wearing wigs, but I just didn't notice them.

"Is your hair naturally straight?" Serena removes the wig and inspects my mother's hair, eyebrows knitted in concentration as she stares at the roots.

"Yes. Why?" My mother touches her hair again, and this time doesn't let go. I wonder if she even realizes she's clutching a fistful of hair just under her left ear.

"Indian hair is a bit different than straight European hair," Serena explains, picking up a third wig. "This is European. It won't frizz too much in the humidity, for example. But the Indian one will. It might be very different than what you're used to. If you open the oven, for example, it can frizz the hair right up."

"Oven?" My mom stares at her blankly. "I have cancer. I don't plan on cooking."

Serena titters nervously. "Of course," she says. "I just wanted to make sure you're aware."

My mother glances over at me, her expression dubious. "What do you think, Cat?" She grabs the two wigs, one in each hand, as if she's weighing them. "They look so similar."

"They look the same now, but the Indian one will frizz," I point out. "Are you going to be able to handle that?"

"Frizzy hair *and* cancer?" My mom covers her face in mock horror. "I don't know which is worse."

I sigh and look at Serena. "Will it be harder to blow-dry?" I ask. I'm the one who will likely end up caring for it. If my mom is sick, she won't want to, and I don't imagine my dad would be much use.

"It might be," says Serena. "It depends what you're used to.

If you're used to washing and blow-drying straight European hair, then yeah, it might be tougher. But I don't want to pressure you one way or another."

She places the third wig on my mother's head, adjusting it delicately. Of the three, it looks the most like her. I watch her face closely. It relaxes ever so slightly as she sees how color, texture, and sheen all match her own.

"I guess we'll take this one," she says. She doesn't say anything for a few seconds, then looks up at Serena. "So how does this all go down? The hair falling out, I mean."

Serena re-engages the Cancer Face and sits down next to my mom. "Do you know which kind of chemo you're getting?"

"Taxotere and Cytoxan," my mom says. Her voice trembles slightly. "I start next week."

"It will start to fall out around two weeks after," says Serena gently. "At that point, we recommend coming back. We can cut it for you, make it easier to deal with."

My mother nods, and takes a deep breath. "Does it come out in clumps?" she whispers.

Serena shakes her head. "It depends on the person," she says. "It's different for everyone. But many times, yes."

We pay for the wig. It comes with an eerie, faceless plastic head, and Serena carefully places it in a large paper shopping bag. Swinging it over my shoulder, I catch a glimpse inside and shudder. It looks like my mom's head has been chopped off and dropped in. Nauseous, I look away and lead my mother out of the store.

...

She starts chemo on Thursday. I want to go with her, but both my parents say no, it's not necessary, that I have to go to school and take my English midterm. So, while my mother is at the hospital having "poison dripped into her veins" (her choice of words, not mine), I actually have to sit and write an essay on *The Catcher in the Rye*.

Holden repeatedly wonders where the ducks at the pond in Central Park go in the winter. What do the ducks represent? How do they factor into the larger themes of the novel?

I stare at the paper and begin writing. I actually read the book back in eighth grade—my dad has a huge library I've been working my way through since I learned to read, and *Catcher* was a favorite of my mom's—and had been excited to see it on my eleventh-grade English syllabus. Now, though, I just scribble down whatever comes into my mind. Anything to just finish and get it over with.

When it's done, I don't even bother checking it before handing it in.

"Are you sure, Cat?" Mrs. Jacobs, my English teacher, raises her eyebrows when I'm the first to walk my exam booklet over to her desk. I'm usually a perfectionist, painstakingly fixing commas and correcting spelling right until the bell rings.

"Yes," I say brusquely. "I need to get home. My mom started chemo today."

"Oh, dear." Her wrinkled cheeks redden, clashing with

the thick layer of candy-pink blush she's caked on. Her eyes no longer meet mine. "I'm sorry. You should get going."

"Thanks, Mrs. J." I give her a grateful look and drop my paper in front of her. She gives me a wan smile—she hasn't had the opportunity to master the right Cancer Face. Hers is still painfully awkward.

Tess is waiting for me at my locker. "How'd it go?" she offers me some gum. "I just had geometry. Brutal."

"Whatever." I take a piece and pop it in my mouth, enjoying the burst of mint. "My mom should be home soon. Let's book it."

Tess walks me home. Her house is first, but she insists I shouldn't be alone. She's nervous, I can tell; she keeps twisting strands of curly blonde hair around her index finger and fiddling with her hat.

"Have you heard from them?" she asks. "Did it go okay, at least?"

"Nothing," I say. "My dad can't text. He still has a phone with buttons." I shake my head.

"And nothing from your mom, I guess." Her eyes are full of concern.

"No." I tighten my scarf around my neck. Even for November, it's cold, and the air has that smell about it that winter is coming: a scent of burning leaves, frozen earth, and damp wool. "She would have texted if she could. But she has an IV in her arm and stuff, I think. You know, to get the chemo."

"Right, of course." Tess looks markedly faint. Doctors and blood and needles terrify her. She's been putting on her best brave face these past months, letting me confide in her after googling myself into a state of fear-induced hysteria. Only once did she ask me to stop, when I talked about the shots in the stomach my mom might need to boost her immune system during chemo.

"Please," she'd said, turning the color of my grandma's pea soup. "I'm doing my best here, but needles in the stomach are more than I can take."

Which, of course, was fair. A couple of months ago, it might have made me squeamish too. Now, though, it is as if I am made of stone when it comes to medical information. My mom refused to read the pamphlet on chemo side effects, and my dad said he would read it later, which he never did: the competent, capable man who was once my father has since been replaced with a frightened, depressed doppelganger, who has put on at least five pounds in junk food and wanders around the house in the dark. So, I read it. All of it. Nausea, vomiting, diarrhea, taste and smell disturbances. Mouth sores, aches and pains, runny nose. Hair and nail loss. Memory loss and mental fog. Someone had to know what was coming, and, as luck would have it, that someone was me.

Tess hugs me at my front door. "Give your mom my best," she says, tears in her gray eyes. Tess has known my family since first grade. She's slept at our house and eaten in our kitchen and once went with my mom and me to New York to see *Spring Awakening*. We all stayed in the same hotel room in Times Square and shared giant cupcakes as a midnight snack. This hasn't been easy on her, either.

"Cat." My dad is at the door when I walk in, his face visibly relaxing with relief. "I'm so glad you're back." I can see the crumbs on his pants, and I know he's been into the chips again.

"What happened? Is she okay?" I feel my heart speed up. I'd read online that some people have severe allergic reactions to chemo. Had that happened to Mom?

"She's fine," he says hastily. "She's sleeping. She had a…a bit of a panic attack toward the end, so they gave her something to sleep."

"Was it awful?" My voice comes out as a whisper. I unlace my boots and take off my mittens, white with little pastel bows, a gift from my mom last winter. I'd been sure I'd blown my history midterm, and she'd wanted to cheer me up. *BC*, I think grimly. *Before cancer.* Back when a lousy midterm grade was a tragedy, the worst thing that could happen. *Had I appreciated my life back then? Does anyone appreciate what they have before tragedy suddenly strikes?* I doubted it.

"It wasn't great," my dad says, sighing, his face haggard with exhaustion. His sparse hair has gone even grayer since The Diagnosis, and his usual odd style of dressing has become even stranger. Right now, he's wearing a plaid flannel shirt with a patterned tie and pinstripe pants. He looks like a parody of the absentminded professor that he is. "There were no major reactions, nothing like that, but she was so scared." His voice breaks. "I didn't know how to help. Nothing I said made any difference."

"I think Mom is beyond words," I say gently. "Even yours."

She's awake when I go in. She looks so small in the bed;

she's lost a lot of weight since her surgery. There's no medical reason behind it, I don't think. She's just not eating. She pushes food around on her plate, making little piles and tucking bites into napkins like a picky preschooler.

"Hi, Cat." Her knees are drawn up to her chest, arms wrapped around them. "How was English?"

I make a dismissive gesture and crawl into the bed next to her. "Was it scary?" I put my hand on her shoulder.

"Oh, Cat." Her voice breaks. "It was terrifying. I saw the IV bag and I just totally lost it. I'm sure the nurses thought I was nuts. Dad was completely freaked out."

I take her hand and squeeze it. She squeezes back, and we sit there like that, for ages, neither of us saying a thing.

Chapter 6

After

"Welcome, everyone, to orientation." Sari, who I spotted earlier with the guitar, waves enthusiastically at the group. We're seated in a circle outside in the field behind the living quarters. The sun is setting, but it's still hotter than the hottest day of summer back home. I've been told it never really cools down during the dry season. I'd read about the heat, of course, but my only frame of reference then was the cloying humidity of a July vacation in Florida. This was more like existing inside a wood-burning oven. Taylor and Margo are there, as are five other kids I haven't met yet. I spot the guitar propped up against a nearby stump and try not to cringe. I'd be willing to bet my tuck money she's going to try to get us to sing by the end of this kindergarten-style meeting.

"I know you've had orientations back home, so this is more

like an icebreaker—so you can all get to know each other!" She smiles and brushes her wavy red hair off her face. Her eyes are wide and earnest, and she has a sprinkling of freckles on each cheek like a Raggedy Ann doll. She looks like she should have her own children's television show, where she makes up her own earnestly quirky verses to "Wheels on the Bus."

"We'll start by introducing ourselves. Please give us your first name, and an adjective that describes you, using the first letter of your name. For example, I'm Smiley Sari!"

"Jesus Christ," mutters Taylor, looking appalled. He tries to stand up, but Sari wags her finger at him. "Oh, no you don't!" she exclaims in a sing-song voice. "Everyone has to participate. Come on, it will be fun! Taylor, you start."

Taylor sits back down, his cheeks scarlet. "I'm Taylor," he mutters. "And I'm..." he pauses, looking ill.

"Terrific!" pipes up Sari. Margo snorts with laughter, and Taylor puts his head in his hands.

Margo is up next. "I'm Metropolitan Margo," she says, her voice expressionless.

"I'm not sure that 'metropolitan' is the sort of adjective we're looking for," Sari interjects, her smile never slipping from her lips. "It doesn't really describe a *person*. How about marvelous?"

"How about murderous?" says Margo to me under her breath. To Sari, she smiles benignly. "Why can't metropolitan describe a person? If I had said Texas Margo, you would have pictured me with cowboy boots and a rifle."

"Texas doesn't start with M," says a boy from across the

circle. He's wearing a pair of purple hipster glasses, the thick plastic kind from the sixties or whatever. I look up to see if he's joking, but he seems totally serious. Taylor coughs into his sleeve trying to hide his laughter.

Margo gives the boy an incredulous look. "Did you really just say that?"

He looks affronted. "Well, it's true. The adjective has to start with the first letter of your name."

I bite the insides of my cheek to keep from laughing.

Margo shakes her head despondently. "I knew this was a mistake."

"There you go!" Taylor looks up, tears in his eyes from laughter. "Mistaken Margo."

"Maybe we should move along." Even Smiley Sari has lost her smile, and there is an edge to her voice. "Who's next?"

"Me, I guess." I pick at the grass between my legs and avoid looking at the others. "I'm Cat. Um…" My voice trails off. I can't think of a single word that starts with C other than 'cookie,' like the Sesame Street song.

"Cool Cat?" offers Sari. I feel a surge of irritation.

"No," I snap. "What is the point of this if you're just going to speak for us?"

Taylor hisses through his teeth. "Ouch," he says, delighted. "*Burn*." Margo looks taken aback and grudgingly impressed.

Instantly, I regret my words. Outbursts like that one are how I ended up on Dr. Shapiro's couch. I told the gym teacher she could go to hell when she chided me for not being able to climb a rope. That was around the time they first saw the spots on my mom's brain, so I didn't get in trouble or anything. Everyone just exchanged knowing looks and mouthed "cancer" at each other, and bristly old Mrs. Wolf actually put her arm around me before packing me off to the principal's office.

Sari, for her part, has the grace to look abashed. "You're totally right," she says humbly. "I was defeating the purpose of this exercise. I stand corrected."

I don't say anything. I can't look at her, because I'm embarrassed over losing it, and now she's being the Bigger Person and all.

"I'm Chaotic Cat," I say finally. "I have a lot going on." I fold my arms protectively across my chest, noticing the black streaks of dirt on the backs of my hands. I try to brush them off, but it only aggravates the problem, smearing mud across my palms. *What have I gotten myself into?*

"Great!" Sari scans the group nervously, eager to move on. "Who's next?"

"I am." A petite blonde with beautiful, long curly hair raises her hand. She has a strong Southern accent; it comes out as "Ah am Merciful Melody."

"That's lovely!" Sari beams at her, grateful, probably, to have someone who is not actively sneering at the icebreaker activities.

"Yes," says Melody. "Just like Our Lord, Jesus Christ."

For a second, everyone falls silent. I scrutinize my sandaled feet, again not wanting to meet anyone's eye. The awkwardness is practically tangible.

Margo is the first to speak. "This isn't a Christian program, is it? Because I'm getting on the next plane out if I somehow missed that in the brochure."

Sari is about to reply when Melody pipes up. "It doesn't have to be a Christian program." She stares at Margo, gleaming eyes earnest. "The work of Our Lord Jesus Christ is everywhere. If you look deep inside your heart, you'll find Him there."

"I don't think I will," says Margo. "I'm half-Jewish and half-atheist."

Bespectacled boy frowns from across the circle. "I'm not sure you can be both."

Margo scowls. "It was meant to be flippant. Do you have Asperger's or something?"

A guy in a Baltimore Orioles baseball cap snorts. The girl next to him, clad in cut-offs and a vintage Aerosmith concert T-shirt, is actually shaking with the effort of trying not to laugh.

Melody frowns, her hands on her hips. "Is it okay to insult people, then? To make fun of Christians, and people who can't breathe?"

It's too much for Aerosmith girl. She lets out a raucous guffaw, then stuffs her fist into her mouth, turning away from the circle.

"Asperger's," says Margo, looking at Melody, her expression disbelieving. "Not asthma."

"Whatever," Melody replies, unfazed. "I forgive you."

Taylor makes retching motions and Melody frowns at him. "I forgive you, too."

"I'm gay," he says. "Still merciful?"

Melody doesn't flinch. "Hate the sin, love the sinner," she says primly.

"You know what?" Sari stands abruptly and goes over to retrieve her guitar. "Why don't we skip the name game and have a bonfire? Maybe make some s'mores?"

Orioles guy—his name is Gavin—leaps up to help Sari start a fire, nearly tripping over himself with eagerness. Turns out he's a survival hobbyist of some kind, like that guy on TV who wanders the forest for days on end with no supplies, whispering manly comments to the camera about eating insects and grubs to stay alive. Gavin seems nice enough, but watching him furiously rub sticks together to spark a flame is deeply annoying when Taylor is waving around his lighter.

Everyone is in better spirits when the s'mores are passed around. I bite into the gooey mess of chocolate, marshmallow, and graham cracker and immediately feel restored. I haven't had s'mores in ages. My mom and I used to make them over our gas stove with chopsticks. She was a pro at toasting marshmallows so that they were meltingly soft on the inside and crispy on the outside. I tried it by myself, once, and my marshmallow caught fire. I took it as a sign and haven't attempted it again since.

"You okay?" Margo is next to me, delicately nibbling at a roasted marshmallow on a stick. "I think maybe we got off to a bad start. I'm not really that big of a bitch."

I lick some melted chocolate off my fingers and nod, trying to smile. "Me neither," I say. "Just jet-lagged and bipolar."

We both laugh. Taylor sidles up to us, carefully balancing three perfectly assembled s'mores, which he passes out. "Ladies," he says, nodding. "We have a problem."

"Oh?" Margo gives him a wary look. "I was just apologizing to Cat here. I think we all got off to a bad start."

"Forget it." Taylor waves a sticky hand dismissively. "We have bigger fish to fry now."

"We do?" I hold the s'more in my hand without eating it. I'm starting to feel queasy.

"Guess who our fourth roommate is." He looks grim.

"Not Asperger's boy?" Margo looks aghast.

"No, his name is Scott, so no gender mix-ups there. Guess again."

"Oh, no," I groan, realizing who Taylor is referring to. "Scarlett O'Hara?"

"Yup." Taylor polishes off his s'more and turns to gesture at Melody, who is sitting next to Sari singing an enthusiastic rendition of "Michael Row the Boat Ashore," putting pointed emphasis on the "hallelujah" part. Everyone else is milling around, discreetly avoiding her. Even Sari's eyes are cast downward, concentrating hard on her guitar.

"Maybe she's not that bad," I say doubtfully. "We shouldn't stereotype. You wouldn't want her to stereotype you, right?"

"True," says Margo. "You wouldn't want her to assume you like musicals, or whatever."

Taylor grins. "I do like musicals."

Margo shrugs. "Forget it, then. Just no one bring up evolution."

I start to laugh, and Margo and Taylor join in. I don't notice Emerson sneak up from behind and tap me on the shoulder.

"Hey," he says. "Glad you seem to be settling in."

"Hi," I say. "Have you met Margo and Taylor? They're my roommates."

Emerson looks at Taylor, surprised. "The dorms aren't supposed to be coed."

"He has a girl's name and he's gay," says Margo bluntly. "So it's all good. We're cool with it."

Taylor grits his teeth. "It is not a girl's name."

"Yeah, there's that guy from those vampire movies," Emerson offers.

Taylor claps Emerson on the back. "Dude, you're my new best friend."

"Bet you can't remember his last name, though," Margo challenges. "Can you?"

Emerson frowns, thinking. "Is it Campbell?"

"Not even close," she says smugly.

Taylor is about to retort, but stops when we notice a fifth person has joined us.

"Hi y'all." Melody wiggles her fingers and turns to me and Margo. "I think we're roommates."

"Yup." Taylor grins at her. "Your bed is next to mine."

She steps back, a horrified expression on her face. "But you're a boy!"

"Maybe I'm just transgendered," he says, leering at her. "You need to be less judgmental. Jesus wouldn't want you to judge."

"Are you really a girl?" she looks faint. "I thought you said you were…gay." She whispers the last word, as if she can't bring herself to vocalize such blasphemy.

Margo snorts. "There are gay girls, Melanie. And anyway, he's shitting you. He's a guy with a penis and the whole bit."

Melody flushes pink. "It's Melody, and I would appreciate if you would refrain from using foul language."

"What did I say?" Margo looks genuinely puzzled.

"You said the 's' word and the 'p' word," she says primly.

"The *p word?*" Emerson laughs. "Penis is an anatomical term."

"Yes, well, last I checked this wasn't an anatomy class." Melody looks indignant.

"Look at the fire!" I interject hastily, pointing. I'm not in the mood for another argument. "It's really going now."

Everyone turns to look at the campfire, which, thanks to the efforts of Gavin the Ultimate Survivor Guy, is now blazing with the perfection of a gas fireplace against the night sky. I stare into the flames, mesmerized at their motion and brightness. Inhaling the tangy smell of woodsmoke, I breathe deeply and step closer so as to feel the warmth of the blaze against my bare arms and legs. I'm not cold, but the intense heat makes me feel alive.

"Any requests?" Sari points to her guitar. "I'm happy to oblige."

Melody raises her hand, but before she can suggest "Jesus Loves Me" or whatever, Emerson pipes up. "Play 'The Rainbow Connection,' Sari."

"Rainbow Connection?" Margo looks skeptical. "Like Kermit the Frog?"

Emerson puts a finger to his lips, and Sari begins to play,

strumming lightly in preparation. She really does have a beautiful voice: it's somehow both husky and sweet at the same time, and she hits high notes like a pro. She motions for us all to join in, and I hum along, remembering parts of the song from that one summer I went to camp. I listen to the lyrics and find myself surprisingly moved. It may be sung by a talking frog, but as Sari sings about ethereal voices and what's on the other side, I picture my mother, waving to me from the other side of a rainbow, her hair long again and whipping about her laughing face and delicate shoulders.

Chapter 7

Before

I'd done a lot of reading on hair loss once we knew which chemo my mom would be getting; I wanted to be prepared. I didn't want to walk into her room one morning and find her there, weeping over a pile of chestnut hair, a blanket pulled around her bare head. Just thinking about it made me feel as if someone had kicked me in the gut with a pair of steel-toed Doc Martens.

"The follicles will open between days fourteen and seventeen after chemotherapy is started," read most articles. Forums where breast-cancer patients and survivors posted their questions and advice said the same thing. Many said their hair loss was sudden, that they woke one day to find a small animal-like pile on their pillow.

It didn't happen that way for my mother. It wasn't one,

dramatic loss, but rather a slow, agonizing process. It fell out bit by bit, hair by hair, like thousands of bitter tears or abandoned dreams. One day at dinner, I noticed strands of hair all over the back of her dining chair, like a finely woven pattern of lace. The next day, I saw it in the shower, a little clump near the drain. On the fourth day, I find her over the sink, my father's clippers in her hand.

"I just want it gone," she says, her face pale. Her hands shook as she took another swipe at what was left of her hair. She'd laid a plastic bag over the sink, and the hair fell into it with a soft, crunching sound.

"I'll help," I say, steeling myself. Tears prick at my eyes, but I blink them back. I can't let them fall, not now. "Let me do it."

Bravely, I take the clippers in hand and shave off the last of my mother's beautiful brown locks. In fewer than ten swift movements, she is bald, a faint dusting of stubble all that remains.

"I look like a monster," she whispers, staring at the mirror. "I look like that painting. *The Scream*. Edvard Munch."

"No. No!" I shake my head furiously, forcing myself to look at her. "You look cool. Like…like Natalie Portman in *V for Vendetta*."

"Cat, cut the shit. I look like the villain in a Hans Christian Andersen fairy tale." She turns away from the sink, looking exhausted. Dark circles rim her eyes, and her cheeks are increasingly hollowed. "Where's my Xanax?" She reaches into the medicine cabinet, rummaging around.

"Should you be taking so many of those?" I try to sound

casual, but I'm scared. She's been popping them like they're Life Savers.

"It helps with the nausea," she replies defiantly. She clutches at the bottle, holding it just out of my reach, as if I might try to take it from her. "The doctor said it's okay. I have cancer." She laughs, an unhinged sort of laugh, and places a pill on her tongue.

"Do you want some water?" I reach for the tap, ready to turn it on.

"No." She looks ill, as if I've suggested she lick the inside of the toilet bowl. "It tastes disgusting."

"Water, too?" I feel another stab of worry. The last couple of days, she's barely eaten a thing. Everything tastes horrible, she says.

"It tastes like someone took a pair of socks, wore them out in the rain, then put them in a garbage bag with a rotten banana and tied it up and forgot it in a cupboard for a week and then took it out again." She gags as she swallows the pill dry.

"That's…specific," I say lamely. "Is there anything you think you could eat? Or drink? Soda? Milk? Orange juice?" My mom covers her ears, her face tight with nausea. Sweat beads the hollow above her upper lip. "Please," she says. "Don't."

"I'm sorry." Unsure what to do, I stuff my hands in my pockets, feeling wretched.

"It's okay." Her expression softens. "Why don't you come sit with me, and we'll watch 'Make It Over.'"

"Sure," I say automatically. The last two weeks, I've spent every moment I'm not at school on my parents' bed, tucked against my mother, watching home-renovation shows. We'd never watched them before; I didn't even realize my mother was so into home decor. Now, we were both practically bona fide interior designers and contractors. My mom had even begun keeping notes; she planned to renovate the bathroom when this was all over. She said that, otherwise, she'd probably keep throwing up every time she had to pee, from learned association.

I help her back into bed and climb in next to her, trying not to stare at her head. I'd never admit it to her, but it scares me, and I hate that. I want to be a bigger person than that, to be able to look past it, to not let it bother me, but I can't. I look at it and I want to scream and cry and rail against fate and the forces that brought things to this point, where my mom, the one who everyone always complimented for being so pretty and youthful, sits shriveled against a pillow like a bald old man.

Hastily, before the tears rise again, I grab the remote and flip to the Home and Garden channel. I can see my mother visibly relax next to me, her body going boneless, and feel grateful to the network drones who thought it was a good idea to run home reno shows twenty-four-seven, something I'd previously thought was bizarre.

Downstairs, I can hear my dad. He's barely left his study in weeks. He sits there in the dark, with his bags of potato chips and red licorice. His computer is on, but I don't think he's doing much. He's noticeably heavier around the middle, but I don't say anything about this. It occurs to me he's not right, that he shouldn't be this way, but I don't have anything left for him. I push away the memory that suddenly pops into my head. I'm six, the last of my friends to learn to ride a bike. Dad comes home with a new helmet, a purple one that glows in the dark.

"Why did you buy that?" I demanded. "I can't ride. I'll never be able to ride."

"You couldn't ride before because you didn't have this." He plunked the helmet on my head. "This is a magic helmet. You'll see."

"Magic?" I touched the strap, eyeing him doubtfully.

"Tomorrow," he said. "I promise."

We spent the entire next day practicing, with Dad running behind me, hand on the back of the seat. His smile never once wavered, nor did his enthusiasm. By the end of the day, I was riding on my own.

"It *was* magic," I said, running my hand worshipfully over the purple plastic.

Dad pulled me close to him and ruffled my hair. "It wasn't magic, Cat," he whispered. "It was you."

Now, my stomach turns with guilt. Should I go down there? See if he's okay? Make him something proper to eat?

Beside me, my mother takes my hand. Her fingers are cold, despite the layers of blankets. *He can take care of himself,* I tell myself firmly. *You can't take care of everyone.*

I turn my attention to the TV, where a couple is knocking out all the walls of their main floor. They're actively involved in the process, smashing at drywall and plaster with oversized hammers. I imagine myself hacking at our living-room wall, bashing it until it falls down. Even in my head, it feels satisfying. I nestle into my mom and pull the blankets over us both.

•••

"I'm glad you came out tonight." Tess puts her hand on my arm. "It's important you take a break once in a while."

"I go to school." I zip my coat higher and fumble through my pockets for my gloves. As if on cue, little snowflakes begin to drift to the ground like tiny frozen paratroopers.

"Cat, going to school is not a break. Going to school is the opposite of a break." Tess shakes her head, and peers at me, worried. "It's like you're starved for fun, Cat."

Fun. The word makes my insides twist like spaghetti curling around a fork. Why should I be having fun while my mother lies in bed, unable to eat? It seems wrong on every possible level. Still, Mom insisted I go to Marianne's party tonight.

"You have to go," she'd declared. She was picking cautiously at a croissant, which she had thought she might be able to eat. "I'm feeling not too bad today. It's a good day."

"No way," I'd replied automatically. I hadn't gone out on a Saturday night since The Diagnosis. "I'm staying right here. Maybe we'll watch a movie? *Bridget Jones*? *Love Actually*?"

"Cat, you're going to end up with no friends. I don't want that. You don't want that. Please. Go."

She looked up at me, her eyes brimming with sadness and guilt. They seemed so huge these days, from the weight loss; it made her look vulnerable and kitten-like. She reached to adjust her tiny cotton hat—chemo caps, the nurse had called them, to prevent heat loss through the skull—and clasped her hands together.

"It doesn't help me to have you ruin your social life and become a recluse," she'd said firmly. "Now go get dressed. And put some makeup on, for heaven's sake. You look almost as bad as I do."

Tess was thrilled when I texted her.

YAY! U r going out!
Yeah. Come by 730?
Def. C U soon!!

I took my mom's advice and dabbed at my lashes, then smudged on some sooty eyeliner. For the first time in months, I looked fully awake. Tess notices the change immediately.

"You look better already," she declares, sizing me up at the end of my driveway. "More alive."

"It's just mascara," I say, gesturing toward my face.

"Really?" She frowns, squinting at me in the snow to get a better look. "I don't believe you."

"Okay, you're right. Also eyeliner."

"Funny." She sticks her tongue out at me.

"It's true. I had to stop wearing eye makeup when my mom was diagnosed."

"How come? Is it carcinogenic?"

"Probably," I say, making a face. These days, it feels like everything causes cancer. Like my body is crawling with all kinds of unseen malignancies ready to strip away my health and my hair at any moment. "But I stopped wearing it because it makes a mess. You know, when you cry." My voice wobbles.

"Oh God." Tess abruptly goes ashen. "I'm sorry, Cat. I didn't think of that."

"Not your fault." I shrug.

"Still, that's…awful."

"Forget it," I say quickly, afraid she might start crying herself. Even if I'm literally incapable of fun, I don't want to ruin Tess's night. Marianne Ambrose's annual Christmas party is the Social Event of the Year in our town, for what that's worth. Andy Kemper's Fourth of July picnic is a close runner-up, but seeing as that won't be for months, I want Tess to enjoy herself.

By the time we reach Marianne's, my feet feel like two Popsicles. I'm still dreading the party, but at least the warmth of her house is welcome.

"Tess! Cat!" Marianne waves from the stairs and winds her way through a sea of classmates towards us. As usual, she looks perfect: impeccably coiffed hair a shade of red that could never be copied and bottled, huge green eyes done in vintage cat's-eye makeup, and a dress that definitely wasn't purchased at the local mall. "So glad you guys could come."

She reaches us and puts a hand on my shoulder, balancing a red plastic cup of something that looks suspiciously like beer in the other. "Cat," she says somberly, trying on her best Cancer Face. It needs work, but I'm not inclined to give her pointers. "It's so *good* to see you here."

"Thanks, Marianne." I smile wanly, bending to unlace my boots.

"How's your mom?" She uses the hushed tone I've come to

call the Cancer Voice. It may or may not be used in conjunction with the Cancer Face. Items sold separately.

"As good as can be expected, I guess," I reply cautiously. I've learned that people don't actually want an honest answer to this question. It makes people uncomfortable to hear that someone is seriously sick, spending most of their time with their head hung over a toilet. People don't want the truth; they want a glossed-over, Hollywood version of it. Pretty, rom-com cancer, if you will.

Marianne nods sympathetically and leads us down the hall. The house is beautiful—it's an ancient Victorian, but recently renovated, with a gleaming, brand-new kitchen that looks like something from one of my mom's shows. Even the oven looks fancy, less like a cooking appliance and more like a shining, stainless-steel spaceship. "There's snacks and drinks in here," she says. Then she lowers her voice conspiratorially. "Kevin's older sister got us some beer. It's under the table there, in the Coke carton."

"Great," I say automatically. She squeezes my shoulder again and goes back to the foyer to greet more guests.

"Beer?" Tess bends down and pulls out two. I hesitate, then take one. Why not, I think to myself, shrugging. Life is short.

I pop open the tab and pour some into a plastic cup. The first sip makes me shudder. It's even more disgusting than I remember, bitter and yeasty in my mouth.

Tess drinks some of hers and grimaces. "This is deeply gross," she says, putting it down on the counter. "I'm getting a Diet Coke. Want one?"

I shake my head. "I'm good." I swallow another mouthful of beer and try not to gag. I wonder how long it takes to get used to it, much less enjoy it.

"If you're sure." Tess shrugs and heads over to the refrigerator.

I grab a sprinkle-covered shortbread from the table, leaning back against it as I take a bite. I haven't had any yet this season. My mom usually bakes up batches and batches of shortbreads and gingerbread men around the holidays, but this year, obviously, there have been no cookies.

"Hey." A guy I recognize from school—a senior—reaches around me to grab a shortbread. "It's Kate, right?"

"Cat," I correct him. "Cat Marks."

"Rory." He winks at me, and swallows a cookie nearly whole before reaching for a handful of Doritos. "I've seen you around."

I don't know what to say, so I gulp down some beer. It doesn't help the situation any.

"You a hockey fan?" He reaches under the table for a beer of his own and swigs about half the can in one go, his throat muscles rippling like a snake's.

"Um…I guess?" I don't know how to answer. I've actually never seen a game in my life. "I'm on the team," he clarifies. "Left wing. You should come some time."

"Uh, sure." I swallow the last of the beer and instantly regret it as a wave of dizziness overtakes me. I haven't eaten anything today but a yogurt, and that was nearly ten hours ago. My head feels unpleasantly detached from my body, as if it's bobbing among apples in a barrel full of water. I think of my mom's faceless wig-holder and my stomach clenches.

"Let me get you another one," says Rory, motioning toward my empty cup.

"No, no, that's okay," I say hastily. I look around for Tess, but she's fallen into a conversation with some of her drama friends, and I don't want to bother her.

"Want to go sit down somewhere?" Rory smiles at me. He cracks open another beer with a hiss, and I wonder how many he's had.

"Okay." I glance quickly at him as he snatches another handful of chips. He's pretty cute—I know a lot of girls would be thrilled at the attention. His blond hair curls loosely, falling just below his ears, and he's got one of those thousand-watt smiles that lulls you into believing you're happy, too, just from watching his mouth go so wide. Not sure what else to do, I follow Rory into a small den. There's another couple—seniors—in there. I recognize one of them from my fourth-period calculus class. They're bent over the coffee table doing something intricate with their hands.

"Buddy," says one—Graham, I think his name is. He nods at me. "Kate, right?"

"Cat," Rory corrects quickly. He motions for me to sit down.

"Want one?" The other one, whose name I don't know, offers me something in his outstretched hand. I bend forward, taking a closer look at it. It's a joint. So that's what they're doing. I peer at the table, almost intrigued, as Graham carefully rolls little white papers and lights the ends.

"No, thanks," I say quickly. I'm feeling sick and lurching from the beer; the last thing I need is to throw pot into the mix.

Rory takes one and inhales deeply, lips thinning as he holds the smoke in his lungs. Graham punches him in the arm. "Dude, you can't smoke that in here. Marianne said no smoking. Her parents'll smell it."

"Are her parents home?" Rory looks surprised.

"Tomorrow," Graham clarifies. He rises, scooping up his little pile of contraband. "You coming outside?"

"No, thanks." Rory passes the joint back to Graham. "I'll catch up with you guys after."

Once they're gone, Rory and I sit in strained silence for a few minutes. It's uncomfortable, and I actually find myself wishing I still had my beer, so that I had something to do.

"So." He scoots closer to me on the loveseat. "Tell me about yourself."

Oh God. I stare at him blankly. My head is spinning, and "myself" suddenly feels like a test I haven't studied for. "Not much to tell," I manage feebly. My stomach churns, and I close my eyes, suddenly nauseous. I should never have drunk that beer so quickly.

"So modest." He winks at me again. I'm vaguely impressed by his control of fine motor functions after both beer and weed. "I know you're taking a whole bunch of AP classes. Big college plans?"

"I guess." I blink, struggling to focus. "Maybe somewhere out west. California."

"Cool," he says approvingly. "I've always wanted to go to LA."

Another awkward silence descends on us. I suppose I should ask him about his hockey or something, but I can't even remember what position he said he played, and it would look rude to ask him again so soon.

"You have really pretty hair," murmurs Rory, inching even closer. He puts an arm around me, and leans in.

I close my eyes and let him kiss me. Hooking up with older guys at parties isn't really something I do, but between the beer and the cancer, I'm feeling a little reckless.

He slides both arms around me, pinning me down on the couch. "You're so hot," he mumbles, kissing my neck. I wince, trying to breathe under his bulk. It feels like he's crushing my lungs, and I gasp for air. Unfortunately, he takes this as a sign of encouragement and presses himself tighter against me.

His hands are at my waist, and creeping up my shirt. I stiffen and try to push him away, but he doesn't notice. Increasingly panicked, I try to speak, but his mouth is on mine again, and he clearly isn't getting the message.

Now he's pawing at my bra, unsuccessfully trying to unfasten it. "No," I say, pushing his hands away. "No!"

"Oh, come on," he gasps. "Don't be like that." He gropes at me again. I picture his hands touching my breasts and my mind instantly goes to my mother, breast scarred and hair stolen. "NO!" I shout, thrashing. "Get off me!"

"Jesus Christ," he says, leaping off me and backing away,

back of his hand swiping over his mouth. "You didn't have to fucking kick me! What the hell is wrong with you?"

"I said *no!*" I'm shrieking now, my arms wrapped protectively around myself, shrinking from him. "I told you to stop!"

"I was going to!" People are peering around the door now, drawn by the commotion. "You didn't have to kick me in the goddamned balls!"

My head is pounding. "Just get away from me," I force out, my voice shaking. "Don't touch me."

"Don't worry." He scowls, and makes a little whirling motion by his head, like I'm insane. "I don't want to come anywhere near you."

"Cat?" Tess has appeared by my side, her arm wound around me protectively. She glares at Rory and gently leads me out of the room.

"I don't feel well," I mumble, leaning my head against her shoulder. I feel dirty and somehow pathetic, and some small part of me—the old Cat, who cared about social norms—is mortified that I caused a scene. "I want to go home."

"Shhhh," she says, rubbing my back. "Don't worry about that asshole, Cat. We'll get you home right now."

Someone brings us our things. A crowd has gathered to watch, and I can hear the words "cancer" and "mom" being whispered around the house.

We get outside and I stumble down the front steps, almost tripping on a broken cobblestone. Tess steadies me, and firmly takes my arm.

"I'm going to be sick," I say suddenly. I break away from

Tess and rush for the bushes, my hand over my mouth. I don't care who sees, as I vomit all over myself and Marianne's mother's frozen rose bushes, the ice-covered thorns scratching at my face. I throw up until there is nothing left, until exhaustion hits and I am left lying on the ground, curled into a ball.

Chapter 8

After

"Put some elbow grease into it, Marks!" A girl named Alicia stands over me, hands on hips, barking orders like a gym teacher. Actually, she even looks like a gym teacher: short hair, muscular, eyebrows in major need of a wax. All that's missing is the whistle around her neck.

"I'm trying," I gasp, heaving another shovelful of dirt. My T-shirt is soaked with sweat. I'm not wearing a bra, but the only guy here right now is Taylor, and he's about as interested in my boobs as I am in digging this well.

Of the four of us, I seem to be having the most trouble with this particular charitable exercise. For her diminutive size, Margo is freakishly strong, probably from the ballet classes she was forced to take until she rebelled at fourteen and microwaved her toe shoes. Taylor spends hours toiling at the gym, apparently, so his physical prowess in unsurprising. And Melody—well, she's Melody. It's possible she's in agony over there with her hoe, but you'd never know it. She was singing "Onward, Christian Soldiers" until Taylor told her he'd kill her in her sleep if she didn't shut up.

I feel something in my back twist in a way that I can tell immediately is Not Good, Very Bad, lack of medical training aside. Groaning, I drop my shovel and clutch at my side in agony.

Alicia sighs. "What is it now, Caitlin? The people of this village need drinking water!"

I don't see you doing anything, I think to myself as I reach for my bottle of water. I long for the six-week mark, when we get our final placement. I won't be applying for anything involving physical labor.

"I hurt my back," I manage. "I need a second."

She sighs, shaking her head. "I don't know why girls like you even bother."

Taylor sucks in his breath, and even Melody stops her humming. Margo, who is wearing earbuds presumably cranked to a high level to block out Melody, doesn't react.

"What exactly is that supposed to mean?" My tone has dipped into sub-zero. *Girls like me?*

Alicia shrugs, not looking particularly sorry. "Suburban princess types. Never encountered a day of adversity in your life other than a bad-hair day. Here so you can get into Yale law school or whatever." She spits on the ground. "Coming here should be for people who really want to help and work hard."

"Who the hell do you think you are?" My voice trembles. "You know nothing about me. Nothing."

"You put on makeup to dig a well," she retorts, disgusted. "That speaks volumes."

Margo, by now, has noticed something's up and turns down her iPod, glancing between the two of us.

"You want to talk about adversity?" I'm shouting now. "My mom had metastatic breast cancer. I was there when we got the news it had spread to her brain. I was also there when she died. Oh, and I made the funeral arrangements because my dad spends most of his time now wandering around in the dark with a bag of chips." I stare at my hands and realize I'm holding the shovel again and the others are all backing unsteadily away.

"I'm sorry," says Alicia, her face ashen. "I'm sorry, okay? Can you put the shovel down?"

I toss the shovel back to the ground and give it a furious kick. My toe promptly begins to throb, but I ignore it. "I wear makeup because I feel better about myself when I look nice," I add, glaring at Alicia. "And since about ninety percent of the time I feel like downing a bottle of pills, I'd say some lipstick isn't such a big fucking deal, would you?"

"I get it. I'm sorry," she repeats, watching me warily, her eyes flicking back and forth between me and the shovel.

"That was awesome," says Margo, swinging her shovel over her shoulder. She narrows her eyes at Alicia. "I'm wearing mascara, too, bitch. You want to take me next?"

Alicia is about to say something else when I cut her off.

"Oh, and another thing. I'm from a small town, not the suburbs. So, if you're going to try to stereotype me, at least get it right."

"If we're on the topic of stereotyping, I'd like to point out that Asians and Jews are not known for their strengths in manual labor." Margo fans herself with her hands. "My dad has to call a guy to change a light bulb. I could use a nap."

"We aren't close to finishing," pipes up Melody. "The villagers need the water."

"Anyone else sick of Sister Mary Sunshine over here?" asks Margo loudly. "Because I've just about had it."

"I vote break," chimes in Taylor. "We've been at this for three hours."

"We'll take a break," concedes Alicia. "I think everyone could benefit from a half hour off and some protein. Meet back here at fourteen hundred."

I make an effort not to snort at her use of military time. We're a student volunteer organization, not the freaking army.

"I'm going to get a granola bar," says Margo. "You guys coming?"

"Yeah," I say. "Losing it always makes me hungry." I turn to follow Margo, who's headed in the direction of the tuck shop.

"That was awesome," says Taylor. "I really thought you were going to hit her with the shovel."

"Strangling her with that whistle would have been easier and less messy." Margo makes a face. "Every time she blows that thing I want to punch her in her chapped mouth."

Melody opens her mouth to say something, but Taylor

cuts her off. "Don't bother, Scarlett. We don't want to hear it. We know we're going to hell and we're cool with it." Sometimes I wonder why she bothers hanging out with us, since she seems to enjoy us about as much as we enjoy her. Though I guess she isn't exactly spoiled for choice around here. Even Gavin the Ultimate Survival Guy isn't keen on Jesus—or, at least, on Melody's take on Him.

"Four granola bars," says Margo to Sari, who is working the tuck counter. She looks over her shoulder at the rest of us. "Anyone want anything else?"

"I'll have a bag of pretzels," says Taylor. "And a pack of gum."

"I'll take a Diet Coke, please," says Melody.

Sari passes out the goods. I take a bite out of my granola bar and make a face. I hate granola—the dry, grainy texture makes me gag; it tastes like getting popcorn kernels stuck in your throat, except on purpose—but I learned quickly that, when you're working hard, a KitKat doesn't quite cut it.

"You know," comments Margo, watching Melody crack open her Coke with a hiss, "I wouldn't have guessed you for a Diet Coke junkie." Melody, who drinks about a half-dozen cans of the stuff a day, swallows a mouthful.

"Why?" she asks warily.

Margo shrugs. "It doesn't seem very Christian."

Taylor shoves a handful of pretzels in his mouth and nods enthusiastically. "Totally," he says, crunching loudly. "Like, Jesus wouldn't drink Diet Coke."

"There was no Diet Coke in Biblical times," points out

Melody, her voice frosty. "There is nothing un-Christian about Diet Coke."

"I don't know about that," says Taylor. "Jesus wouldn't have a vice like that."

Melody bristles. "It's not a vice."

"It's a vice when you have six a day," says Margo, sounding bored. "Trust me. I'm an expert on vices."

"Really," Taylor continues, his voice deadpan. "You need to ask yourself. What would Jesus drink?"

Melody glares at him and stalks off.

"Maybe we're too hard on her," I say. I watch her as she walks away, stopping to take a swig of soda. My mom liked Diet Coke. It was her vice, too. I wonder how many she would have had to drink a day to cope with Calantes. I feel the usual pang, the hollowed-out feeling of loss that winds me when I think of my mother. The advantage of being here, of spending hours digging in the mud, is that the pangs come less often. There's simply no time to feel anything but exhaustion and hunger.

Margo cocks her head at me, surprised. "You can't mean that," she says. "She told me she would pray for my heathen soul."

"She has nightmares," I say quietly. "She cries." Night after night, when the hum of the insects and my memories conspire to keep me awake, I listen to Melody pleading with someone in the dark. It's always the same dream. "No," she shouts, thrashing. "Don't touch her! Leave us alone!"

"It's probably the mefloquine," says Margo dismissively,

referring to the malaria pills we all take. "It's a common side effect. Nightmares, I mean."

"I guess," I say, though I'm not sure. Drugs or no drugs, the ghost of Melody's tormentor feels real enough to her—and to me.

"Glad I'm a sound sleeper," says Taylor. He offers us some pretzels. "She annoys me enough during the day."

"Me, too." Margo grabs a handful of pretzels and eats them slowly, first delicately scraping the salt off with her perfect teeth; she likes the salt as much as I do. I take a pretzel to rid myself of the lingering taste of granola, but manage only two bites before I'm reminded again of my mother. Mom eating pretzels in the kitchen, leaning up against the breakfast bar; in her bed, even though the crumbs made my dad crazy; in the movie theater, smuggled in her purse, because she preferred them to popcorn. I drop the pretzel to the ground, discreetly crushing it beneath my sneaker. The bugs are upon it in seconds, a swarm of them. I can't decide if it's revolting or fascinating.

"Our break's almost over," announces Taylor, polishing off the last of his granola bar. "Field Marshal Alicia will be waiting for us." He takes off his cap and fans his face, exposing his recently shorn head. He buzzed it about a week ago, unable to cope with the heat. It's growing back quickly, though at this point he's sprouting a headful of porcupine quills.

"Ugh," says Margo. She grabs Taylor's hat and fans herself. "I think for my placement I'm going to apply to teach kids' art classes."

"I thought you hated kids." Taylor looks surprised.

"I just want a job where you sit down. That all right with you?"

I wonder idly what I will apply for. Working with kids? Bossing people around with a whistle? Cooking? None of them sound all that appealing, though all are better options than digging wells.

Melody is already back at the well site, digging away, even though Alicia has yet to return. Her empty Coke can rests under a nearby tree. Taylor stares at it pointedly, while Melody studiously avoids his gaze.

"I'm not doing a thing until the dictator gets back," declares Taylor. He sits down on some gnarled old tree roots, hands dangling between his legs. "Let Scarlett work herself to death."

Melody doesn't take the bait, though her shovel hits the ground with slightly more force.

"What time is it?" Margo sounds irritated. She doesn't have a watch—she always relied on her phone, which is useless out here. She never knows what time it is, which drives the rest of us crazy.

"Can't you just write your parents for a freaking watch?" Taylor snaps.

"Can't you just stop being a total jerk?" Margo retorts. "I asked for the time, not, like, a bank loan."

I'm about to interject when I hear the deafening rattle of gunfire somewhere close by and drop to the ground. It's funny; I've never heard gunfire before—not in real life, anyway—and yet there was no mistaking what the sound was. Not for a moment did I even consider the possibility it was anything else. They prepped us for this in orientation, but the academic description of a raid and gunfire is not quite like experiencing it firsthand.

"Get down!" I shout, following the protocol we've been taught. "Someone is shooting!"

The others drop to the ground and freeze like pets rolling over and playing dead. In the not-too-far distance, we hear shrieking and more shots. I hide behind my shovel, my teeth rattling as if I've been shoved unclothed into a freezer. I guess this is what "frozen with fear" means.

"What the—" begins Taylor, but the rest of us cut him off.

"SSSSH!" we all hiss in unison.

More shouting, more gunfire. I curl into a small ball, still clutching my shovel like it's some kind life preserver. *A shovel isn't a match for a rifle*, the little voice at the back of my head reminds me. I feel a familiar pain spread across my abdomen and clench my jaw as my intestines cramp violently.

"What are you doing?" Margo whispers, her eyes wide as I slither across the dirt towards the trees.

"Stomach," I grunt, doing a pathetic and increasingly urgent military crawl, my shovel dragging behind me.

"Oh, shit," says Taylor.

Literally, I think grimly. The others are familiar with my IBS, but this is the first time they'll have to witness it. I find a decent-sized tree and yank down my SWB standard-issue shorts, sighing with relief. I wonder if this is how I will die, my pants down, in a South American country no one has heard of. Trying not to make too much noise, I reach for some toilet paper. I stuff my pockets with the sandpaper-like tissue they stock in the bathrooms here before we leave each morning. From my shirt pocket, I retrieve some hand sanitizer. Overwhelmed with self-pity, I grab my shovel and belly-crawl my way back, a slow process. They watch me, wide-eyed, as I drag myself back on my forearms. The gunfire has quieted, for now.

"Please," I say quietly, closing my eyes. "I don't want to hear anything about it. Okay?"

"I'm impressed, frankly," says Taylor, propping himself up slightly. "I would have just crapped my pants, I think."

"Stop talking!" Margo's harsh whisper cuts him off. Beside her, Melody prays under her breath, her shoulders rocking back and forth slightly. Briefly, I think of joining her, but I turn away. I gave up on God when He gave up on Mom.

Red-faced, Taylor falls silent. We lie there, waiting. I don't know how much time passes—five minutes, maybe? Ten?—before a pair of Spanish-speaking voices draw closer. Much closer.

"Is anyone there?"

I freeze again as I realize the lightly accented voice is addressing us. It's as if someone has taken an egg and cracked it against the back of my skull, letting the cold yolk trickle down my back. Slowly, I turn around, my arms raised above my head the way I've seen people do on television.

Two guys about my own age hover over us. One looks grim but tough; he is tall and dressed only in faded khakis and a green shirt with the sleeves torn off, a rifle slung casually over his shoulder like a messenger bag. The other looks as if he might have to go take his own turn at the tree. He has the look of an IT nerd, the kind they send to fix the computers when they're down at school. He pushes his glasses back up with his index finger as they repeatedly slide down his nose, and stares at us warily.

"You may get up," he says, addressing us hesitantly. "Don't be afraid."

Margo makes a sound that conveys what presumably we are all thinking: that we are very afraid, and that simple reassurances are unlikely to sway us. Shakily, I rise, helping a white-faced Taylor to his feet. We are both covered in thick layers of mud. I scratch without thinking at a mosquito bite on my arm, and watch the black slime take residence under my fingernails. Margo stands next to us, her arms folded protectively across her chest. She has a stripe of mud down the side of her face that looks almost like war paint, making her seem fierce despite her diminutive size. Instinctively, we all put our hands in the air. I guess I'm not the only one who's seen a lot of *Law and Order*.

"There's no need for that," says the tall boy. He looks almost offended. "It wasn't us who was firing."

Margo eyes the pair shrewdly, her hands gracefully descending to her sides like a pair of wings.

"Who are you?"

"Good question," he answers, smiling at her. She doesn't smile back, but it doesn't faze him. We wait, expectant.

"I'm from the village," he continues. "We're doing a perimeter check. We just had a raid. That was the gunfire."

I try to remember if I've seen him before, but whenever I've been down to the village, I've stuck to my task, whether it's digging or cooking or painting walls. Some of the volunteers have integrated more with the locals—Margo sometimes engages people in conversation—but I've hung back, figuring we can't have anything in common. Their living conditions both sadden and repel me, and I find relating difficult. It doesn't just feel as though we are from different countries, but different planets.

"I've seen you," says Margo slowly, frowning. "You're the one they call the *Politico*."

"My name is Rafael," he answers, avoiding replying directly. "The raiders have been dealt with."

"Are they dead?" I blurt out. I don't know why I ask. I'm not sure I care.

"No," says Rafael shortly. "We exchanged gunfire and they left. It happens every few weeks."

Exchanged. I feel an odd, hysterical urge to laugh. As if gunfire is like Pokemon cards on the playground.

"Is anyone dead?" Taylor now, his voice cracking slightly. He wipes the sweat from his forehead and leaves behind a trail of mud. The knees to his jeans are torn, and his left leg is cut from his sudden drop to the ground.

"No." Rafael shakes his head. "Everyone is fine." He looks over at his friend, and the two of them revert to quiet Spanish. Again, it seems as if they are speaking at double-speed, and I wonder if people here actually speak faster, or whether it's just that everything sounds faster when you can't understand it. I wonder what they are saying.

The second boy speaks up, his voice much more heavily accented than Rafael's.

"What is wrong with your friend?"

For the first time, I realize Melody has not risen or made a sound. I look over. She is still crouched on the ground, rocking gently back and forth.

"Melody?" I kneel slightly, trying to get a better look at her face. "Are you okay?"

She lifts her head slightly, and I notice she is still clutching her shovel. Her teeth are bared, giving her the look of a feral animal, and her eyes dart back and forth like pinballs in an arcade game.

"Melody," I repeat. "It's all right. You can put the shovel down."

"No!" she shouts. Her voice shakes, and she raises the shovel so that it is shielding her face. "Don't touch us! Leave us alone!"

I think of her thrashing in the dark, of her screams. I wonder if she has been attacked before. I try to make eye contact with her, but she won't look at me. Her eyes are wild, and I realize the lines separating reality from nightmare have blurred for her. She doesn't know where she is.

"Please," Rafael intervenes. "Put it down."

I reach out and place a hand on her trembling shoulder. Melody howls like a cat who has had its tail trampled on and raises the shovel, as if to strike.

Stunned, I stare, transfixed, at the shovel coming down toward me. I feel someone push me out of the way before I stumble to the ground.

"Sorry," says Rafael breathlessly. He's fallen too, and has landed half on top of me. "She was going to hit you."

I try to thank him, but nothing comes out. I study his large, dark eyes and the faceful of stubble that can't hide a faded scar running down his left jawline. I wonder briefly how he got it. His hair is cut short and haphazardly, as if he did it himself without a mirror and in a rush. Our eyes lock, and I look away, unsettled, as I disengage from our tangle of limbs.

The IT Geek has Melody in an armlock, and with Taylor's and Margo's help has wrestled away the shovel. Melody thrashes and sobs in his arms, her eyes still wild and blank.

"She needs help," I say. Rafael is immediately back on his feet, but I'm on the ground in the dust, hugging my knees against my chest. I have a vague memory of a childhood swimming instructor teaching that this is a life-preserving position, that it's the go-to position if you're stuck in icy water. I wonder if it applies to war-torn, steamy-hot rainforests as well.

"Eduardo can carry her back to your base," says Rafael, referring to IT Geek, who is apparently much stronger than he looks. He is still holding Melody firmly about the shoulders, rocking her slightly and whispering to her softly in soothing Spanish. Her eyes are closed and she seems to have relaxed somewhat.

"I will walk you all back," says Rafael. He bends and offers me his hand, and I take it. It's rough with callouses and warm, almost hot. He pulls me quickly back to standing position and lets go, but I can still feel the dry heat of his palm against mine.

"Why?" says Taylor, looking wary. "Are the gunmen still around?"

"No," says Rafael, but his hand is on his rifle again, as if instinct has called it there. "But this is a dangerous place."

Margo is nodding now. "Dead American kids are bad press," she says. "Especially for a country no one's even heard of."

Rafael flushes at that, but says nothing. He taps at his other side, which I realize has a holster and a handgun. I recoil, shrinking back toward Taylor.

Rafael is watching me. "Don't be afraid," he says again, softly now. "I won't hurt you."

I nod, but I can't help but stare at the gun. I tear my eyes away to watch a bird swoop by overhead. Its voice is clear and mournful, like a call to prayer. It disappears into the tree canopy, and I envy it its freedom.

"Follow me," says Rafael, and we do.

Chapter 9

Before

"You have to take the spring SATs," says Tess, aghast. We're at Starbucks, our biology homework fanned out on the table in front of us. I shrug, tearing open a packet of raw sugar and sprinkling it delicately across the foamy top of my cappuccino.

"I don't know if I can concentrate right now," I say honestly. I take my stir stick and scoop up a mouthful of foam, savoring the sweetness of the melting sugar, a trick I picked up from my mom. She pops unbidden into my head, an image of her gagging down a glass of water. Suddenly, the sugar doesn't taste as good. I become aware of its texture, hard and gritty, like little bits of broken teeth. I push the drink away and turn back to Tess. "I have a lot on my plate."

"But, Cat," Tess swirls her straw around her iced coffee, her freckled nose wrinkled with worry, "what about Stanford?"

"I'm not dropping out of high school," I say flatly. "I'm talking about taking the SATs in the fall. Like most people," I add.

"I know, I just…" Her voice trails off. She shakes her head, her strawberry curls nearly catching her straw. "We always talked about early admission."

"I'll just have to take my chances," I retort. I take a deep breath. I don't want to fight with Tess. None of this is her fault. "Look, I just can't do it right now." My voice shakes, and I feel my shoulders slump. I stare down at my overpriced drink, watch the foam slowly dissolve. I want to take the spring SATs, of course I do. It's always been our plan, mine and Tess's. Early admission for me at Stanford, and for her at UCLA. We've talked about it since middle school, dreaming our overachieving college dreams together.

"I'm sorry," she mumbles, picking up her biology text so she doesn't have to look at me. "I understand."

"I still want Stanford," I assure her, stirring another packet of sugar into my cup just for something to do. "We're still on track. I just can't manage the studying right now. All that mouse is to cheese as cat is to mouse crap."

Tess forces a laugh. "If that's the best you can come up with, you're definitely better off waiting."

"See?" I take a sip of cappuccino, grimacing. Now it's cloyingly sweet. "I'm not ready."

"Technically, you can take it in October and still get early admission," says Tess, brightening. "It might not be an issue at all."

"There you go." Absently, I shred a napkin. Mom's genetic-testing results were due back today. Dad had canceled his office hours to stay home with her and wait; neither would let me take another day off school.

"I won't have you wreck your grade-point average because of me," she said, her voice hoarse. "I'll be fine."

"But—"

"No, Cat." She shook her head. "School."

I didn't push it. The last thing I wanted was to upset her, to sap her of her strength unnecessarily. She looked so tiny in the king-sized bed, blankets drawn up to her chin. Her gray eyes, always so large and lively, looked smaller and exhausted without lashes, and the little pink cotton cap she wore indoors to cover her head made her seem young and vulnerable, like a newborn.

"You haven't heard a word I've said," says Tess now. She's looking at me, expectant, as if she's been waiting for a response. Guiltily, I meet her gaze.

"Sorry," I admit. "My mind is elsewhere. Standard procedure these days." I blink and rub my temples, pressing my thumbs into them.

"Page sixty-three," Tess says helpfully, pointing at a section in her textbook.

"Base pairing in DNA."

"Right." I find the right page and stare at the words. They march around the page like ants, evading me, and I find my mind wandering again.

Tess sighs and shuts her textbook. "Maybe we should just

forget bio," she says. She takes a long swig of her drink. "We're not getting much done."

"I'm sorry," I say again. I shake my head, try to focus. "Turns out I'm a lousy study partner."

"Not lousy," Tess says quietly. "Just distracted."

I exhale loudly, pushing back in my chair. "The genetic-testing results are due today," I admit.

"Oh, geez." Tess looks appalled. "And I asked you to review DNA with me!"

I burst out laughing despite myself. "Tess, that's not why I'm upset."

"But *DNA!*"

"Forget it." I down the last of my drink. "Seriously."

She shoves some papers in her backpack and leans across the table, her gray eyes full of concern. "This is the test that shows whether your mom is genetically predisposed to getting breast cancer, right?"

"Yeah." I pick up another napkin and continue shredding. I watch as the little pieces fall into my empty cup, settling down like feathers in a nest. "It's called the BRCA gene. It causes breast and ovarian cancer. They think there's a good chance she might have it. Her grandmother died of ovarian cancer."

"Shit."

"It's okay," I say quickly, but I'm lying. It's not okay. Because if my mom has the gene, then there's a good chance I have it, too. A fifty-percent chance, to be precise.

Tess's eyes grow wider, and I know she's arrived at this conclusion on her own.

"I'm not going to get tested," I say firmly, before she can ask the question. "I don't want to spend my life waiting for the bomb to drop."

She doesn't say anything. I see the tears gathering in her eyes, and I hastily begin packing up my things. I don't want to cry. Not here.

"Is it okay if we study tomorrow?" I ask quietly. "I'm just not in the right headspace right now."

"Of course." Tess stands up and grabs my hand. She looks like she's about to say something, but then changes her mind. Instead, she squeezes my fingers tightly.

"Are you going back for art club?" she asks finally. We both joined the art club in September, but I've barely made half the meetings. I shake my head.

"I need to get home," I say. "Results were due around three." I check my phone; it's now a quarter past.

"I'll walk you back," she offers.

"No," I say quickly. "You go to art. You love it."

"I don't need—"

"Go." My voice is gentle, but definite.

She leans in for a hug. "Call me later," she says softly. "Promise."

• • •

I know right away it's not good news, because my mother is ugly-crying, big heaving sobs that shake her too-thin frame and turn her face red and splotchy. My dad is patting her arm awkwardly, still dressed in the flannel pants and torn T-shirt he wore to bed last night. With a heavy sigh, I dump my coat and backpack to the ground and stare at both of them, waiting.

Dad clears his throat. "Cat," he begins, his voice gentle, "we don't want you to panic."

My expression doesn't change, even though my heart is fluttering wildly in my chest, like a butterfly trapped in a mason jar. "So it's bad," I say, my tone matter-of-fact. "She carries the gene."

"Yes, but it doesn't mean you do," he says quickly. "It's a fifty-percent chance. So, that's still a fifty-percent chance you don't have it."

"I know how to add and subtract from a hundred, Dad." His face falls, and I feel a stab of guilt. I look away, ashamed, my eyes landing on a portrait of the three of us taken maybe ten years ago. My hair is still in pigtails, and both my parents have a full head of hair.

My mom follows my gaze and sobs harder, her face obscured by a wad of Kleenex.

"Mom?" I go over to her side of the bed and kneel down. "Mom, it's okay. It doesn't affect treatment at all, and it doesn't necessarily mean anything in terms of remission or cure, either. I've been doing some research, and—"

"I don't care about me," she says, sniffing. "I care about *you*. I don't want *you* to get it."

"Forget it." I can't think about that now. Me having breast cancer is unfathomable. I can't even picture myself married, or having kids, or even at college, really, let alone grappling with my own terminal illness. "I don't want to know, regardless."

"But, Cat." She grabs my arm. "You could take precautions."

"Take precautions?" I echo, baffled. Condoms flash across my mind, brightly colored like a selection of lollipops. I've been through sex ed—the word precaution is paired in my subconscious with barrier contraceptives.

"Preventive surgery," she says urgently. "Like Angelina Jolie."

It dawns on me what she is referring to, and I recoil. I will not have my breasts chopped off, no way. They've never really even been used, not unless you count Mike McLeod's unskilled groping at last year's homecoming. They're not even finished growing, or at least I hope they aren't. I picture them lopped off, in one of those metal surgical trays like a pair of sunny-side-up eggs, and feel nauseated. *What do they do with them, once they've been removed? Throw them out with the trash? Burn them? Bury them underground in some kind of creepy boob cemetery?* I shudder.

"I'm not cutting off my boobs," I say flatly. "Forget it."

"Not now," my mom says, "but later, once you've finished breastfeeding, or—"

"Finished breastfeeding?" Incredulous, I hug my arms protectively across my chest. "I haven't even taken the SATs!" I flash back to my earlier conversation with Tess. Maybe I'll take the spring exam, after all. The pace of my life seems to have picked up considerably. I glance involuntarily at the clock, as if it might give some actual sense of the passing of time.

My dad intervenes. "I don't think we need to talk about this now," he says. "I think maybe Mom should get some rest—"

"I don't want to rest." Angrily, Mom kicks the blankets off the bed. "I need to get out of this room."

Dad and I exchange a glance. "Honey—" he begins, but my mom quickly cuts him off.

"Don't 'honey' me," she snaps. "I feel claustrophobic. I need some air." She swings her feet off the bed. She's wearing pink, cupcake-printed pajama pants and a thick pair of yellow thermal socks.

"It's pretty cold out there," I venture. It's February, and there's at least a foot of grimy snow on the ground. The groundhog saw his shadow last week, and we're gearing up for another six weeks or so of winter.

"I don't care." She stumbles slightly as she reaches for a thick wool sweater. "I've finished the chemo. I need to start trying to get my strength back."

The chemo officially ended last week. The nurses apparently celebrated by bringing in sparkling grape juice and cookies, which my mom tried to nibble without gagging. So far, though, nothing much has changed; the doctors say it could be months before her strength returns. Or her sense of taste.

I wince as her little cloth cap slips off when she pulls the sweater over her head. While I know she doesn't have any hair under there—I've witnessed it—whenever she's wearing a cap or a wig, I don't have to acknowledge it. I don't want to see the baldness, the few stray hairs that cling here and there.

"Someone hand me the squirrel," she commands, arm outstretched.

Hesitantly, I retrieve the wig and pass it to her, feeling

guilty at the instant sense of relief when she positions it accurately. To her, it's a dead animal on her head, phony and uncomfortable. To me, though, it's a way to pretend her hair hasn't fallen out and that none of this has happened.

"Come out with me for a few minutes," she says, looking at me. She finds and carefully zips her parka, and fishes her gloves out of the pockets. "Just out here, on the balcony." She gestures to the little deck that's off the master bedroom. My parents have barely ever used it.

"Sure," I say with a shrug. My dad's eyes meet mine, worried, but I shake my head ever so slightly. It will be okay, I communicate to him silently. He nods slightly and passes me my coat, which is still in a heap in the doorway.

"Put a hat on," says Mom sternly as I unlock the patio door. "I may be an invalid, but I'm still your mom."

I grin and pull my earmuffs out of my inside pocket. "You don't have to worry," I assure her. "I hate being cold."

She walks over to the railing, and leans over it onto her elbows, breathing deeply. "I'm sorry," she says. "I kind of lost it in there. I should never have brought it up."

"No," I agree quietly, joining her at the railing.

"It's just so hard, as a mother, to think of your child suffering in any way." Little puffs of white smoke accompany her words; the air is freezing. "But you shouldn't have to grow up so fast. At sixteen you should be thinking about boys getting to second base, not a mastectomy."

"No one calls it second base anymore."

"Well, whatever the current slang is for having a guy touch your boobs, then." She grins slyly.

I glance over at her and she is laughing, her cheeks rosy and healthy-looking from the cold. The wind whips at the wig, blowing the hair around, and it looks natural, like real hair. It's the best she's looked in months.

My feet feel frozen, but I don't say anything. We stand there for a long while, the two of us, not speaking a word. I follow her gaze to the neighbor's yard. They have one of those little ponds for giant goldfish. Kurt, our neighbor, dug it himself, lovingly placing rocks and planting shrubbery around the small pool. In the summer, it has a little waterfall running into it, but now, the water is frozen over. I wonder what happened to the fish. *Can they live under the ice? Does Kurt take them inside until spring?* I picture the fish swimming around in buckets all winter, frantically bashing their heads against the plastic and pining for better times.

"Where do the ducks go?" Mom asks, smiling faintly, as if she's caught my train of thought, and I remember that *Catcher in the Rye* is one of her favorites.

I think back to my English essay. I'd blabbered on about the loss of innocence and scored an A minus, but Mrs. Jacobs had also pointed out that the ducks, and where they go, could also represent larger questions about life, mortality, and the other side.

"Think about it," she'd said to me, when she'd handed back the paper. "Holden's brother has died. Where has he gone? Where do any of us go? Where do the ducks go?"

"They fly south," I say now, quoting my essay. I take my mother's hand. "They fly south, and they're reborn. They come back changed, older."

"Is that what they teach now?" She inhales deeply, enjoying the cold air. "I always thought it had to do with death."

I squeeze her hand harder. "But the ducks don't die," I point out. I'd said this to Mrs. Jacobs as well. "They just go away."

"But maybe that's what death is. You just go someplace else." My mom waves her hand vaguely, gesturing towards the sky.

I don't say anything. I stare at the pond, looking for any flashes of orange beneath the frozen surface, but there are none.

"Don't worry." Mom puts a hand on my shoulder. "Kurt has a huge tank in his basement for the koi in the winter."

But I am not thinking about the koi anymore.

Chapter 10

After

Before I came to Calantes, I couldn't picture what the local villages would look like. There were pictures in the brochures, of course, but they were stills of men assembling buildings or mothers nursing their infants. They captured moments as opposed to conveying a sense of an overall picture, and for some reason, I kept picturing the Al-Qaeda camps they show on TV, shot in Afghanistan. Only those are in the desert, and Calantes is in the heart of the Amazon rainforest, so obviously it made no sense. I also had the awareness that there might have been something vaguely racist about this thought, so I never would have admitted it out loud.

So, there was a bizarre moment when we had first gone into a village and I discovered a complete lack of goats. Whenever I've seen those camps on CNN, there are always goats. I'm not sure why. I'm not even sure if goats are desert animals, though I suspect not, since there was one at the San Pedro Airport. But anyway, no goats, either. What there were, were chickens. And people, too, of course. Lots of people, too many to be living in such a small space. Old people, young people. Babies crawling in the dirt or swaddled tightly in their mothers' arms. But it was the chickens that really caught my eye, at first. I had never seen so many chickens in one place.

"Are those *chickens?*" From behind me, I heard Taylor's voice, incredulous at the sheer number of roaming fowl, wandering aimlessly and pecking at the ground.

"Gives a whole new meaning to 'free range,'" I muttered. Emerson, who had been our guide that day, looked at me, eyebrows raised, but didn't say anything. I wondered if making jokes in a poverty-stricken village was inappropriate. My mom, who had coped with her cancer by tapping into her inner comedienne, had clearly bequeathed to me this unique trait. Instead of appreciating the gravity of such moments, I now turned into a stand-up comic, channeling my mother and her biting wit. It's a bit of a self-defense mechanism: your brain can't cope with the emotional overload of stressful situations and turns to humor to keep you from completely losing it.

Now, I stand amid the chickens, still unnerved at their proximity and sharp beaks. Chickens seem much more threatening in person. I can tell Taylor feels the same way, because he keeps edging closer to me. Mostly when we've been in the village, we've been supervised, shepherded from building to building: from the children's activities to the kitchens to the wells. This is the first time we've just been left to stand there, to observe the reality of life and the day-to-day goings on.

People eye us, but avert their gazes and don't come over, and I wonder what we must look like to them, in our shorts and T-shirts. Some are too busy to even look our way; almost everyone seems occupied with one task or another. A group of boys is counting some kind of fruit I don't recognize, while a trio of girls is doing what appears to be laundry. They're hunched over giant buckets, with long staffs for stirring, and I can't help but think of the opening of *Macbeth*. They look like a coven of witches hovering over their cauldron, only instead of eye of newt they're mixing up filthy T-shirts and stained socks. The smell, unfortunately, is distinctly toe of frog; it's awful, and one of the girls wears a makeshift mask.

"I'm not choosing laundry," whispers Margo, looking revolted. "You'd need an N-95 mask to block that stink."

"Shhh," I hiss, looking around. "They'll hear you."

Being in the village makes me feel incredibly awkward. I start to feel as though everyone is silently judging me as a spoiled American brat. Margo thinks I'm paranoid, but I can't help it. I feel as if I should apologize for every item of clothing I wear, every silly thing I say.

"There's your boyfriend," says Taylor, smirking. He elbows me in the ribs. "He's looking at you."

I give an irritated sigh as I follow his gaze to Rafael. The night after the raid, after we'd been escorted back and were tucked safely inside our mosquito nets, I'd made the mistake of mentioning in passing that I thought Rafael was hot. Taylor hasn't let up since.

Rafael, wearing a faded red T-shirt, is standing against a tree with his arms crossed, nodding at a girl with a long braid that nearly reaches her waist. His expression is serious, and I doubt he's even noticed I'm here. I watch as he says something to the girl, whose hands are gesturing in all directions with a certain urgency. It seems that Rafael has some kind of authority here, but it's not clear if it's in any sort of official capacity.

"He could be married for all we know," I say crossly to Taylor. Taylor whistles loudly, attracting Rafael's attention. Our eyes meet, and he lifts his hand in a small wave.

"He's coming to see you," sings Taylor playfully. I can feel my neck getting hot and red in the back, as if I've been burned by the midday sun. I glare at Taylor, and casually nod at his feet.

"That chicken is eating your shoelace."

It has the desired effect: Taylor jumps back. "Shoo!" he shouts, waving his hands. "Shoo, shoo!"

The chickens ignore him and continue their pecking. Margo doubles over in helpless laughter, and even the laundry girls all pause briefly to chortle and point at Taylor, who is now shaking both his legs and hands at the bobbing birds.

Rafael arrives, looking puzzled. I glance over for the girl with the long braid, but she is nowhere to be seen. "What is he doing?"

Margo grins. "I think it might be the hokey-pokey."

Now I'm laughing, too. Taylor does a sort of half-spin as one of the chickens stabs at his toes with its beak, and Margo continues in a deadpan voice. "Yup, there he goes. Turning himself around."

Rafael is confused, but he smiles and briefly places a hand on my shoulder. It's a casual move—the way you touch someone you don't know very well in a country where touching is a social norm—but it feels heavy there for a moment as he brushes the strap of my tank top.

"How are you?" he asks. His voice is serious. "How is the other girl? Melanie?"

"Melody," I correct him.

It's been just under a week since Rafael and Eduardo escorted us back to the base. Melody has been off-duty ever since, and spent the better part of three days lying on her bed, staring silently at her mosquito net. After that, she was transferred to another barrack, and I've only caught glimpses of her since. I wonder what sort of placement she will choose. If she opts for something here in the village, there won't be any way for her to keep avoiding us.

"Don't worry about Melody." Margo's tone is harsh. "She has Jesus."

"Oh," says Rafael politely. "Is that her boyfriend?"

I start to laugh, before I realize that this is a perfectly reasonable question in a country where Jesus—pronounced the Spanish way, of course, *hey-zoos*—is a popular name. Still, Margo and I laugh like a pair of giggling middle-schoolers, until I realize that the laundry girls are now watching us as they fish clean but permanently stained clothing from their cauldron, laboriously wringing them out. I feel foolish and spoiled and mean, like the archetypal clueless North American teenager. Biting my lip, I sober up.

"She's religious," I say lamely.

"Ohhh." Rafael looks embarrassed, but doesn't pursue it.

"I never asked you your name," he says instead. "It was very rude."

"Well, there was gunfire and a near-miss with the shovel," I say reasonably. I put out my hand. "I'm Cat."

He looks confused again. "Cat?"

"Caitlin," I explain. "It's a nickname."

"Ah!" He brightens. "Catalina."

It sounds pretty the way he says it, and I try to forget that it's my dad's favorite salad dressing. Thinking of my father still feels like being sucker-punched to the gut: when I picture his face, I feel like I can't take in enough air. The emails I've received from him are perfunctory: *How are you, I am fine*, like I'm ten years old and at sleepover camp. When I call, he doesn't answer.

"And you are Taylor, I think," he continues, turning to Margo.

"Nope." She nods at the real Taylor, who has successfully fended off several fowl. "My name is Margo. That's Taylor."

Rafael is caught off guard, but recovers quickly. Margo, watching his expression, gives a satisfied smirk. "You thought I was Taylor because it's a girl's name, right?"

Now it's Rafael's turn to blush, a rosy glow beneath the burnt brown sugar of his skin. "I should not have assumed. I was only thinking of Taylor Swift."

"Did I hear my name?" Taylor looks harried. The chickens have disbanded, but it's not clear who the real victor was.

"He thought I was you," says Margo triumphantly, "because you have a girl's name."

"Maybe he thought you were a boy," retorts Taylor, "because you have no boobs."

Ouch. I wince as they get going, hurling insults back and forth. Rafael looks shocked.

"Do they always do this?" he asks.

"Only when they're in a good mood," I say. I shift back and forth on my feet, both out of nervousness and because my hiking boots are damp inside. There is no way to stay dry in the Amazon, and the water is constantly penetrating my socks. I can feel them, squishing and squelching with every step I take, as if I've filled my boots with saturated sponges. It drives me crazy, and I spend long stretches of the day fantasizing about wringing them out and drying them off. It's a bit like having food caught in your teeth at a restaurant, and you spend half the meal planning your eventual dental-floss attack strategy.

"Is something wrong with your feet?" His eyes travel downward.

"Oh." I feel a rush of embarrassment. "They're just wet. From the jungle."

He looks relieved. "I was worried it was a snake."

"Snake?" I shiver. "Can a snake get in a shoe?"

"Yes." His expression is serious. "It's quite common in the jungle, though in the clearing here it's less of an issue."

I imagine a snake infiltrating my boot and swallowing my

foot whole. In my mind, the snake looks like some sort of sci-fi creature, a Harry Potteresque basilisk with glowing eyes. *Mom hated snakes*, I think, imagining how she would have recoiled at Rafael's explanation. I feel the familiar wave of sadness overtake me, trapping me underwater, stealing my breath. Here in the jungle, it is easier to forget my grief. Sometimes, it feels like something I forgot to pack, something there wasn't room for in my suitcase, and I feel I've won, I've escaped. Then I remember, and it feels as fresh and raw as it did the night she closed her eyes for the last time.

Rafael must think the expression on my face still has to do with the snakes, because he leans in again to touch my shoulder. "Do not worry too much about snakes in your boots, Catalina. They look very sturdy."

I glance down at my hiking boots. I'd bought them on sale, but what I'd paid for them was still probably enough to feed the village for a week. I can't look Rafael in the eye, even though I know he's trying to be kind.

"What's this about snakes?" Taylor pokes his head in, looking worried.

"I was concerned Catalina had a snake in her boot," explains Rafael. He gestures at my feet.

"There's a snake in my boot!" Margo drawls in a Western accent. We all stare at her.

"You know, *Toy Story!*" she looks around expectantly. "Come on. Disney movie? Toys come to life? That's what Woody says if you pull his cord."

"Woody?" Rafael looks confused.

"He's a cowboy toy, with a pull cord." Margo mimes the action. "You haven't seen *Toy Story?*"

"No," says Rafael stiffly. "I have seen the sequel, *Toy Story 2*, but I don't remember about the snake."

At this we all fall quiet, and I marvel at how privileged our North American lives are. While Rafael is explaining the possibility of actual, live snakes burrowing into our footwear, our immediate associations are with pop culture. Smiling cowboys.

"*Bueno,*" says Rafael, breaking the awkward silence. "Have you decided on your placements?"

"We're here to see where you need the most help," I say quickly. "We're sort of…undecided." It's true. None of us has been able to decide since our altercation. I don't know what the others are thinking, but it's left me both afraid and wanting to do more.

Rafael nods. "I can help you, if you would like."

"She would definitely like," says Taylor slyly, and I glare furiously at him.

Rafael turns to Margo. "You could help Sofia's group with preparing food."

Margo bristles. "Because I'm a girl, I should be in the kitchen?"

"Not the kitchen," says Rafael patiently. "With the chickens."

"Huh?" Margo looks behind him at a group of chickens, pecking furiously at the ground. Taylor eyes them suspiciously.

"Slaughter," clarifies Rafael. "Sofia's group needs someone to help slaughter the chickens, and you look like—how do you say it in English?—that you could handle it."

I laugh out loud. I can't help it.

Margo glares at both of us. "What else is there?"

Rafael looks thoughtful. "Elena's group is also looking for help," he says pleasantly, "with the latrines. Plumbing can be a problem in the jungle, and—"

"I'll take the chickens," interrupts Margo hastily. Rafael whistles loudly, and a tiny slip of a girl with braided hair appears at his side.

"This is Sofia," he says to Margo. "She will teach you what you need to know."

"Great," says Margo. She throws me a sympathetic look over her shoulder as she leaves. "Sorry about the caca," she says. "Good luck."

I look at Rafael warily. Our eyes meet, and his expression softens slightly. He reaches over and brushes something off my shoulder. I stiffen at the unexpected touch.

"Mosquito," he says, looking embarrassed. "Sorry."

"No, no," I say, blushing. "Thank you."

"Don't worry," he says. "Elena does not really need help with the latrines. Your friend seemed like she needed a bit of— how would you say it in America?—a kick in the pants?"

I laugh a little. "Margo is tough," I say diplomatically.

"What about me?" interjects Taylor. He's also looking wary. "I don't want anything to do with the chickens."

Rafael looks thoughtful, eyeing Taylor's muscular build. "Chopping wood?"

Taylor makes a face. "Nothing with sharp objects," he says. "I once needed twelve stitches from slicing a bagel."

"Well, we should certainly keep you away from an ax then," says Rafael gravely, but I can see he's trying not to laugh. He pauses. "How are you with computers?"

Taylor brightens. "Okay, I guess. Good. Like some basic HTML and stuff. You have Internet, right?" He looks around hungrily, as if somewhere close by someone has a sleek new MacBook Air and a high-speed WiFi connection that's just out of his reach. Slow connections and crappy computers are a reality of life at the base camp, making sending and receiving email nearly impossible, let alone checking a Facebook account or Twitter feed.

Rafael nods. "You can help Eduardo. He does communications and social media."

Eduardo. That was the other guy with Rafael after the shooting. The one who looked like an IT Geek. I can't help but grin—I was right.

"Where is Eduardo?" Taylor asks, looking around. The laundry girls take out another load for wringing and drying. These are all baby clothes. Tiny sleepers with mended holes and worn fabric, cloths for diapers, with the scrubbed stains still faintly visible. I think of the bulk diapers and cheap sleepers on sale regularly at home and feel another wave of First-World Guilt.

Rafael explains where to find Eduardo and his computer. I hope, for Eduardo's sake, that his Internet connection is fast and that he likes celebrity gossip. I once found Taylor angrily banging on one of the keyboards, trying to load up Perez Hilton.

When he's gone, I wait expectantly for my assignment.

I know I can say no to Rafael, but I also know that I won't. It's still not clear that he has any kind of authority here—not officially, anyway—but he radiates leadership. *Politico*, Margo called him. Political. I wonder what that means, and once again feel the pangs of my privilege-associated shame. *In my world, if you were political, you might run for student council.*

"Anna desperately needs help in the *Enfermería*," Rafael says tentatively. His face searches mine.

In the what? I wrack my brain, trying to decipher what he's saying without having to ask and look stupid.

"Enfermería," he repeats, noting the blank look on my face. "Like…nurses. For sick people?"

"Oh!" Comprehension dawns on me. "The infirmary!"

"Yes!" He nods, relieved at our mutual understanding. "Could you help?"

Again, I think of my mother. "Yes," I say quietly. "Yes, I can."

Chapter 11

Before

"What are you up to?" Mom leans over and peers at the textbook open in front of me. She's wearing a soft, fluffy white bathrobe and a tiny cotton hat in mint green with a little matching flower. The flower, she explained once, reminds her that she's still a woman, even with all her lovely hair hidden in a large plastic freezer bag in her closet. She doesn't know I know it's there, but I do. Every time I help her get dressed, it's there, staring at me, a tangible symbol of what's been lost these past months.

"SAT prep," I explain. I put down my highlighter and yawn. "I can't even begin to explain how boring it is."

"Didn't you just take the SAT, back in the spring?" Mom frowns and tightens the string of her robe. It's huge and billowing on her, like everything nowadays.

"I think I can get a higher score." I pick the highlighter up again and twirl it between my thumb and forefinger. "A lot of people do this now."

"But you did so well." She wanders over to the fridge and opens it up, peers inside. I stiffen; she so rarely eats these days. She's had radiation for a month and her appetite is even worse than it was during chemo.

"Can I make you something?" I ask, trying to sound casual. "I'm happy to do it. Eggs? Pasta? French toast? There are some fresh muffins in the breadbox over there—I made them this morning. Lemon poppy seed."

She makes a face. "You're acting like the parent of an anorexic teenager."

"Well, you barely eat." I fold my arms across my chest. "You need to eat if you're going to get better."

"It's not my fault." The skin around her eyes sags with fatigue; she pinches the bridge of her nose. "It's hard to eat when food tastes disgusting."

Chemotherapy has altered my mother's sense of taste. The doctors say it will return to normal, eventually, but right now everything still tastes revolting to her.

"Imagine a bag of strawberries," she said, when I asked her to explain. "Now, imagine you leave them in a dank, dark cupboard for two weeks. Then imagine taking them, blending them with sour milk and shaving cream, and then adding it to all your food, like some kind of marinade or dipping sauce."

"Wow," I said. "You should have been a horror writer."

"It's just so vile," she'd said, shuddering. "Imagine eating chicken and it tastes like spoiled produce and bad milk."

Now, in the kitchen, she goes over to the muffins and stares at them.

"All natural ingredients," I say. "I used freshly squeezed lemon juice."

"I'm scared to eat one," she admits.

"Just try it," I coax her. "Just a couple of bites."

Reluctantly, she selects a muffin and carefully places it on a plate, as if it might be radioactive. She returns to the table and sits down across from me.

"So you really think you need to take the test again?"

We're back to the SAT now, probably to distract me from the fact that she is fastidiously picking apart the muffin, but not actually eating it.

"I want my score to be as high as possible," I say. "I don't want to have to worry about backup schools."

"But do you have time? Even with all your AP courses, and the play, and…" Her voice trails off. The unspoken words—*me*, or *my cancer*—hang between us.

I pretend not to notice, and shrug. "I'm managing okay," I say, honestly. "My grades are up."

"Dad says you've been going to bed later and later."

"Dad's one to talk."

Traitor, I think, fuming. All the nights I've been up late studying, rehearsing, or aimlessly trolling the Internet, he's been right in the next room, eating himself into a food coma and binge-watching *The Walking Dead* on Netflix. And did I tell on him? No, I did not. I thought there was, like a code, or something for situations like this. *Compadres* in cancer.

"He's just worried about you. We both are. Are you getting enough sleep?" She takes a small morsel of muffin and places it gently on her tongue. I wait for the ensuing gagging response, but there is none. Looking surprised, she chews and swallows the piece and reaches for another, larger one.

"These actually taste okay." She gets up. "I could use a Diet Coke."

Throughout her cancer-related food travails, Mom has maintained that the only thing that tastes "normal" is Diet Coke. This makes me anxious, as what, exactly, is in it? *Is it a food product at all, or just a can of chemicals?* I'm not sure I want to know.

"I'll take a Perrier, if we have it," I say. She tosses a small green plastic bottle, which, of course, I miss. It falls to the ground, rolling back and forth and fizzing with angry-looking frothy bubbles.

"Sorry," she says, and I can see she's trying not to laugh.

I give her a mock glare. "You married Dad knowing he was a spaz. Didn't you worry about passing inferior genes on to your offspring?"

Instantly, our banter dies, and the cheerful mood evaporates with the speed of rubbing alcohol.

"I'm sorry," I whisper. My voice is pleading, full of remorse. If only I could take those words back, suck them in.

"It's okay," she says softly, staring at her Diet Coke. She fastidiously eats another piece of muffin and takes a deep breath.

"You don't have to walk on eggshells with me, Cat. I'm your mother."

"I know that," I say quickly. "I just—that was stupid, that's all. I wasn't thinking."

"But that's life," she points out with a shrug. "Forget it. What are you going to do, censor yourself in front of me? I don't want that. Anyway, I need to get used to stuff like that. I can't get my back up every time someone, I don't know, makes a cancer joke or something."

"A cancer joke?" I stare at her, aghast. "If someone makes a cancer joke, you totally have the right to get your back up. What kind of person would do that?"

"Maybe that was a bad choice of words, but you know what I mean."

I take a sip of my soda. "Is there really such a thing as a cancer joke?"

She daintily finishes the muffin. I stare at her empty plate, and feel a twinge of hope.

"I have no idea." She starts to laugh, a true belly laugh, and I join in.

• • •

"What do you think of this?" Mom holds up a red-and-white striped top.

"For you, or me?" I eye the shirt warily.

"If you have to ask, then never mind." She hangs the shirt back up and continues rummaging through the sale rack.

We're out shopping together for the first time in months. It's almost weird to see my mother dressed, with makeup on, browsing around the racks of clothes. With her wig in place, she looks exactly like she did before. It's a bit unnerving; it's almost too easy to forget, when I catch a glimpse of her, the months of misery and suffering.

"This one is nice." I hold up a slinky black top with a bow. "It would look great on you."

"You think?" She takes it tentatively, holds it up against her. Her smile wavers. "I feel so ugly."

"You look great," I say, honestly. "You look exactly the way you always did."

"Only because of this dead animal on my head." She touches the wig gingerly and makes a face. "I hate it. I feel like everyone can tell." It comes out as a whisper.

"They can't." My voice is firm. "No way. It looks exactly like your hair."

"My old hair," she corrects me, softly.

I don't answer. I don't know what to say. Standard procedure, these days.

"So this top?" She takes it over to the mirror and stares, frowning. "Not too young?"

"It would look great on you," I say again. I mean it, too.

She shrugs and drapes it over her arm. "Okay," she says. "If you say so."

"Do you want to try it on?"

"No, at home. It's too much work." She looks tired, and, as if on cue, yawns.

"Is this too much? Being out?" I study her, anxious. "We can go."

"No! No." She shakes her head furiously. "It's so nice to be out like this with you. Like before."

It is nice. We wander through the store, stopping to try on shoes and sunglasses before we leave. I pass on footwear, but choose a funky pair of red plastic shades. Mom gets some cool new leather riding boots with buckles up the back and some retro-looking aviator glasses.

"Ice cream?" My voice is tentative, but hopeful. We always used to get frozen yogurt after a shopping trip. I wait for her to gag and make some kind of declaration comparing frozen yogurt to rotting bananas and moldy gym socks, but she just smiles.

"That sounds great." She reaches over and squeezes and my hand.

We enter Yo-Greats, and drop our parcels and jackets at our old table in the back right-hand corner, under the painting of a giant, gleaming strawberry. I peer over to see if Xander, the cute guy who used to work the cash, is still there, but he's been replaced by a sour-faced girl with a mouthful of braces.

"Have you been here before?" she asks, sounding bored.

"Yes," we say in tandem.

"It's self-serve, and you're charged by weight," she goes on, as if she hasn't heard us. "Toppings are over there on the left. Please use the spoons and tongs provided."

Mom and I exchange a glance and try not to laugh. I take two paper cups and hand her one. We each fill up with a swirl of chocolate and vanilla, then load on toppings: caramel sauce, sprinkles, and peanuts for her; crushed peanut brittle and whipped cream for me.

We dig in. It's as good as I remember—better, even. The whipped cream is thick and cool, and dissolves slowly in my mouth. Mom eats her yogurt cautiously, handling her spoon as if it's an explosive device that might, at any time, go off.

"How does it taste?" I ask, nervous.

She's chewing slowly. "Not bad, actually," she says, looking surprised. "Good enough to eat, anyway."

For a few minutes, we sit in a pleasant silence, enjoying our afternoon treat. A ray of late-October sunlight streams in through the window, illuminating the tiny dust particles in the air. Mom eats another spoonful and looks over at me.

"So," she says slyly. "Any boys in your life?"

"Boys?" I stare at her in disbelief. "Um, no. I haven't exactly had a lot of spare time. And not because of you," I add hastily. "It's just with the SATs, and all the AP classes—"

She cuts me off. "That's what I wanted to talk to you about." She stirs her frozen yogurt, frowning. "I'm worried about you. You're working too hard. You don't get enough sleep—"

It's my turn to interrupt. "I'm not tired," I point out, and it's true. I feel fine. "If I weren't getting enough sleep, I would feel tired."

"I'm worried about you," she says again. "You should be going out, enjoying yourself. Dating boys. Going to parties."

I groan. "No one *dates* anymore, Mom," I swirl my spoon

around, so that the candy, cream, and yogurt form a dense, sticky mess. "It's not like that. And I do go to parties." A fleeting memory of Rory comes to mind, and I flinch a little. That was the last party I went to; I've been making excuses ever since.

"I know when you're lying, Caitlin Marks." Mom folds her arms across her chest. "You haven't been to a party in ages."

I stab my dessert with my spoon, scowling fiercely. "You know, a lot of parents would be thrilled with a daughter who avoids parties and works hard." I scoop out some yogurt, let it drip from my spoon. "Would you be happier if I was smoking pot every weekend or whatever?"

"You know, there is a happy medium between pothead and social hermit," she points out. "I just don't want you to miss out on the fun stuff. It's important, too."

"It's fine." I lick my spoon. "I'll go out more. Let's drop it, okay?" I can hear the edge in my own voice.

"Okay," says Mom hastily. "I don't want to argue with you."

"I know. So let's forget it. Let's just enjoy our ice cream." I stare at the melting glop before me, trying to regain my appetite for the frozen treat. I take another spoonful, but it tastes off now, spoiled. Sadness is like cancer that way, an unwelcome guest that takes the body or the mind hostage, stripping the joy from even that most basic and human of sensory experiences—eating. I push away my dish.

Chapter 12

After

Melody is back in Barracks B. When the new crop of recruits arrived yesterday, she was booted back in with us. Her former bunkmates seem more than satisfied with the new arrangement. Even Sari, smiley guitarist of infinite patience, seems relieved to have her gone.

She's drinking a Diet Coke on her bed when we arrive back from the village, filthy and sweaty from a long and grueling day's work. Even Taylor is covered in streaks of mud: when the Internet went down, he had to crawl around in the dirt examining the cables. We're exhausted, hungry, and cranky. *Hangry*, Tess used to call it: a cross between hungry and angry.

"No," moans Taylor when he sees her. "You're still here. Didn't Jesus tell you? He would choose Barracks C."

Melody glares at him but says nothing, her gaze focused on her can of soda.

Margo throws her a disgusted look. "Do you just sit here all day?" She peels off her clothes and faces Melody stark naked, her hands on her hips. She has chicken blood stains on her arms and legs, making her look like a character in one of those low-budget teen slasher films that come out around Halloween every year. Melody shudders, and looks away, and I wonder what offends her more, the blood or the nudity. She changes in the bathrooms each day, even though Taylor makes a point of leaving the barracks before us to give her privacy.

"I'm outta here," says Taylor. He may be gay, but I don't think he's entirely comfortable with Margo's willingness to strip with abandon.

"Seriously," says Margo, grabbing her shower caddy and towel. "If you're going to just sit here all day, you might as well go back to Alabama, or whatever. It's infuriating to the rest of us who are busting our butts to see you crying in your pillow." She gives Melody a final dirty look before heading off to the showers.

I sit down on my bed and nod awkwardly at Melody. "You okay?" I ask hesitantly.

She stares at me, then nods slightly. I wait to see if she's going to say anything else, but when she remains silent I shrug and pull out a novel. The well-intentioned Sari thought it was a good idea to give me a copy of *The Fault in Our Stars* when she heard my mom had died.

"It's about *cancer*," she had said meaningfully, pressing the book into my hands.

The book of course is about *kids* with cancer, which is hardly uplifting to begin with, and worse, the medical references keep giving me flashbacks. Margo has threatened twice to take it away from me when she found me with book in hand, tears and mascara streaming down my face.

"Why are you doing this to yourself?" she'd demanded. "It's masochistic. Also, you look really ugly when you cry."

"Thanks," I'd sniffed. "But I have to finish it."

I have never abandoned a book. Not even in ninth grade when I unwittingly committed to reading *Les Miserables* for a book report, and the rest of my group went for the Cliff Notes. Besides, if I stop, how will I find out what happens to Hazel and Augustus? I curl up on my side, book comfortably tucked under my elbow.

"I'm sorry," says Melody suddenly.

Surprised, I turn around. "Sorry?"

"About the shovel." She sits up. "I didn't…I wasn't…" she grapples for words.

"It's okay," I say cautiously.

"No." She shakes her head. "I need to explain."

I wait. It's the longest I've ever heard her speak without either preaching or offending or irritating someone. I watch a fly buzz lazily around one of Taylor's granola-bar wrappers, looking for leftovers.

"Something…bad happened to me," Melody says finally. "To me and my sister. When we were younger. I have flashbacks."

"Right," I say. I'm not sure how to respond. She isn't looking at me; she's looking at her hands. Her fingers weave in and out of each other as she struggles to speak. I watch them wiggle in familiar motions: *This is the church, this is the steeple*…my mother used to play that with me in kindergarten.

"I wasn't…I didn't know where I was," she concludes quietly. "I'm sorry."

"I understand," I say automatically. She's still avoiding eye contact, so I stop trying. I look around instead at her living space. Taylor and Margo have decorated theirs with pictures of friends and family from back home, but mine and Melody's are stark, devoid of any kind of personal effects. I have a photo of me and my parents in a pretty pink frame that I brought with me, but I can't bring myself to put it out. Every time I pull it out of my backpack, I feel an ache for my mother so powerful it leaves me breathless.

She looks over at the copy of *The Fault in Our Stars*. "I'm sorry about your mom," she says. "My mom died too, but I was only five. I don't really remember her."

"That's awful," I say sincerely. My memories of my mother are precious.

"We—my sister, Jessie, and me—went to live with my aunt and uncle. My uncle…" her voice trails off, and I wait while she struggles to speak again.

"My uncle was the one who hurt me." Now she looks me in the eyes, and I feel my stomach turn. I know what she's about to tell me.

"He used to…touch me." Her voice trembles. "He'd come into my room at night. He said if I told anyone he would send Jessie to foster care."

"Jesus," I say, then bite my tongue. "Sorry, that was unintentional."

She keeps talking, shakes her head. "When I saw him start going into Jessie's room, though, I lost it." Her eyes have a faraway look in them.

I swallow. "What—what happened?"

"I went at him with a baseball bat," she says flatly. "The police came. He's in prison now, but Jessie and me, we ended up in foster care anyway." She laughs harshly. "I should have done it years before."

I don't know what to say to Melody. I feel almost the same way as I do in the village—that I am living a parallel existence in a kinder, more gentle, universe. Her story is the kind I've read in the papers or seen on CNN.

"Melody, I'm—I'm so sorry." Tentatively, I reach over and put a hand on her arm.

She flinches slightly, but she doesn't pull away. She takes a deep breath and reaches under her bed for something.

"Diet Coke," she says. "My sister and I would always buy one and share it on our way home from school."

I recall Taylor's earlier taunts and feel a pang of guilt. "Do you know where your sister is?"

"Yes." She brightens. "She got placed with a great family, and she's doing really well in school. Straight As." She sounds like a proud parent. She fishes a cellphone out from under her pillow and shows me a picture of a girl who is almost a carbon copy of herself, only with redder hair and several years younger. She's smiling in the picture, a genuine sort of smile.

"That's wonderful." We're both quiet as she tucks the phone back under her pillow and pops open her soda can with a crack and a hiss.

"Want a sip?"

I don't, really, but I don't want to refuse either at this point when we've made so much progress. "Thanks," I say, reaching for the can and taking a small sip before passing it back to her.

"I wasn't always religious," she says after taking a long swig. "When I was in a group home, I turned to God, you know? It was either God, or a bottle of pills. For Jessie's sake, I went with God."

"I guess," I say, though I don't understand. Any doubts I had about a higher being were confirmed when my mom died. Grief had not made me religious, and in fact had pushed me farther in the opposite direction.

"It helps," she says. "Like maybe this life sucks, but the next one—that'll be good. Like me and my mom and my sister will all be together again, in heaven."

I blink. I can't understand this kind of thinking. My parents weren't religious or even spiritual, and I've always thought that when you're dead, you're dead. *Finito*, full stop. But I guess we all think—and cope—in different ways. After all, most people probably wouldn't have dealt with personal tragedy by running off to the rainforest. Grief and its ensuing madness have many faces, I suppose.

"Do you…believe all that stuff?" I have to ask. I can't help it.

"I don't know," she says honestly. "Sometimes, yes. Other

times…I'm not sure. But I want to. I try to. Otherwise what is the point of it all? Why not just end it?"

I ponder this, wondering if perhaps Melody is lucky. Religion is a comfort to her, whereas I have no security blanket to cloak myself. I try to picture my mother as an angel in heaven, but don't know whether to laugh or cry. Mom would have snorted in ridicule at such an image.

"I'll try to tone it down," says Melody. "I know everyone hates me."

"We don't hate you," I say lamely.

"It's okay," she says. "You do. I sort of do it on purpose. I can't explain it. It's like it's easier to just have everyone hate me than deal with people and relationships and all the rest of it."

I wince. "That's really sad."

She shrugs. "I've lived in three foster homes. Trust me, it's easier this way."

I don't know how to answer, so I don't. Instead, I grab Margo's iPod, plugging it into her wireless speakers. I flip through her songs until I find what I'm looking for: "Let it Be," Paul McCartney's tribute to his own deceased mother. Melody and I lie together, silent, listening to his words, absorbed in the melancholy sound and our own sense of loss.

• • •

Rafael makes a special effort over the first week to ensure we are, as he puts it, "settling in comfortably," which annoys Margo.

"This isn't the Hilton," she mutters to me and Taylor as

we set back on the path toward the base. "He's acting like the concierge of a hotel or something."

"He's just trying to be nice," I protest lamely. I don't want to say too much, in case Taylor resumes his teasing.

On cue, Taylor snorts. "He likes *Catalina* here," he says, putting heavy emphasis on an affected Calantes accent. "He's trying to win her heart." He fakes a swoon, hands folded across his chest.

Margo coughs. "Win her heart?"

"Well, at least get into her pants," Taylor concedes with a smirk.

There's a rustling behind us and we all jump; everyone here has warned us repeatedly about jaguars, ocelots, and other stealthy and carnivorous creatures of the night. With dusk falling, our senses are alert.

"Sorry." It's Rafael. "I didn't mean to scare you. I was wondering if I could speak with Cat."

Margo and Taylor exchange a knowing glance. Taylor once again mimes a swoon, and I feel myself go as red as the passion flowers that decorate the rainforest like ornaments on a Christmas tree.

"Sure," I say. I motion at Taylor and Margo to go ahead. "I'll catch up."

I stand on the edge of the path, yanking my shirt-sleeves down as far as I can. It's best to expose as little skin as possible at night. The mosquitoes seem to be particularly vicious at dusk, as if the setting sun brings out the worst of their blood lust.

"Hi," I say, unnecessarily. Margo and Taylor are out of

earshot, and I realize it's the first time I've ever really been alone with Rafael. Feeling awkward, I gather my hair into a ponytail, just to have something to do.

He smiles. "Sorry to bother you." He pauses, as if unsure how to continue. My heart speeds up a bit as I watch him struggle for words. His hair is curlier in the evenings from the humidity, and it's extremely attractive.

"I was thinking," he says carefully. "That you might be interested in some Spanish lessons. As long as you're here."

"Oh!" I say, deflating. *I wasn't expecting this, but then what was I expecting? An invitation to a movie? Coffees at the local Starbucks?* "Sure. I mean, that's probably a good idea. For Taylor and Margo, too?"

"Oh. Um, yes. Of course." He fidgets with the sleeve of his windbreaker. "Would you like to go for a walk?"

My heart accelerates again, but I'm wary. "Now?" I gesture towards the tree canopy, which obscures the setting sun. "Isn't it dangerous?"

"Just to the water," he says quickly. "I'll walk you back to the base afterward. I know the path by heart, and I have a flashlight. And a knife," he adds.

A knife. I shiver, and ask myself how I ended up here, being courted in the jungle by a veritable stranger who admits to having a knife.

"Sure," I say, wondering if Margo and Taylor will know where to look if I don't come back. "Let's go."

Rafael leads me through a partially cleared path, taking my hand at times to guide me over tree roots and uneven terrain. The mosquitoes buzz hungrily about my face, longing to make a meal of my exposed cheeks. The ever-darkening jungle leaves me with a sense of dread and foreboding, but each time Rafael touches me, I forget about anything else but the feel of his calloused palms. It's electric, a pleasant rush like the drop of a roller coaster, and despite my natural instincts for caution, I long for more.

We reach the water. There's still enough light streaming through the trees to see the gentle waves ripping across the dark surface of the river. Rafael stops and settles down on a large rock, motioning for me to join him.

"I love the river," he says. "Knowing how long it is, how it links so many different places. I like to come here and just watch."

I don't say anything. I don't feel quite the same way. The water is murky and opaque, and I know from my reading it is full of hideous creatures—anacondas and piranhas. Feeling guilty, I stare harder, trying to capture for myself whatever sense of peace the river seems to bring Rafael.

"Do you feel it?" he asks, putting his hand on my thigh. "The river? Almost magical."

"Mmmmm," I say. The river isn't doing much for me, but his light touch on my leg is working wonders.

We sit in silence, his hand still gently resting on my thigh.

"Your English is really good," I say, when the quiet between us becomes awkward. "Did you learn it in school?"

Rafael turns to me. "No," he says. "My father is a history professor. He studied at Oxford, and he's always spoken English with me."

"Ah," I say. That explains the trace of a British accent and slight formality to his speech. "My dad is a professor, too. English."

"Really!" He looks pleased at this commonality. "Is he the absent-minded professor, like mine? Papa once left the stove on and went to South Africa for a conference. Mama and I were visiting relatives in Brazil. It's only due to luck the house did not burn down."

I laugh. "Not as bad as that, but he definitely has his moments." An image of my dad in the dark, clutching a bag of chips, comes to mind, though I desperately try to block it out. *Not now!* "He once almost went to work with no pants on."

"What?"

"Yes, he got all dressed in his suit jacket, tied his tie and everything, but somehow forgot to put on his pants. He was almost at the door before my mother stopped him."

Rafael looks amused. "He's lucky she noticed."

"Yes," I say, and feel a stab of guilt. *Who would watch over my father and make sure he was fully dressed, now?*

"When they came for my parents, I tried to fight them," says Rafael. The laughter has faded from his eyes. "I had a stick; they had guns and knives."

I recall his scars. "Is that how you got those?" I ask softly, gesturing.

"Yes," he says shortly. He runs his hand over the scar along his chin. Though faded, it is still visible, a thin red line, like the Amazon as depicted on a map.

We are both silent. I try to imagine having to fend off

armed men with a stick, but I can't. To me it's like a scene in a movie.

"*El rio*," he says then unexpectedly, pointing at the water.

I blink, confused, then realize he's started his Spanish tutorial. It's clear he wishes to change the subject.

"Even I know that one," I say with a smile. "My Spanish isn't that awful."

"*Siento*," he says, apologizing with a grin. "I will have to get a better idea of what you know and what you don't know."

The insects are out in full force now. It's almost like looking through a screen, only instead of mesh the screen is made up of thousands of tiny beings, all humming and fluttering wildly. Somewhere nearby, an animal howls, and some primal part of me becomes overwhelmed with fear. *What am I doing in the middle of the rainforest at night, with a stranger?*

"I want to go back now," I say abruptly, standing up.

Rafael looks surprised, but doesn't argue. "Of course."

He walks me back to the base in near silence. He's a perfect gentleman, touching me only to help me over tree roots or to hold back branches and vines. He asks repeatedly if I am okay, and I say yes each time, even though I'm not sure that's true.

When I'm safely back in my barracks, I collapse underneath my mosquito net, the fatigue setting in. I dread this time of day, when I am no longer busy enough to ignore the perpetual hollow ache that is my mother and the sadness that is the longing for my father. His perfunctory emails have become few and far between, and I wonder if he is still wandering from room to room with F. Scott in one hand and potato chips in the other. I stare at the net overhead until it is a blur of white, debating whether to email Aunt Caroline about his mental health. My thoughts are interrupted by a sudden loud snort: Margo, though she denies it, snores loudly. It's like sleeping in the vicinity of a noisy garbage truck.

I look around. Melody is absent. I know she showers at night when everyone else is asleep, so she can lock the door. She has been quiet since our unexpected heart-to-heart; she has reached a sort of cold détente with Margo and ignores Taylor entirely. She's civil with me, but she acts as if we never spoke. I don't know whether to engage her to bring out the good I know is in there or to leave her alone.

I look over at Taylor and notice that he is awake, and watching me.

"How'd it go?" he asks.

"I don't know," I answer honestly. I don't mention the internal turmoil of being drawn to and repelled by Rafael, or the fact that he led me out into the jungle with a knife.

"You okay? I'd have thought you'd be more excited, hooking up with Latin Loverboy."

I make a face. "We did not hook up. We just talked."

He shakes his head. "Pity. Better luck next time."

Before I can answer, Melody comes in, stealthily—like a jaguar stalking its prey. She's clutching her shower caddy and is fully dressed in leggings and a T-shirt, even though it's oppressively hot and the rest of us sleep nude or nearly so. She eyes us both but says nothing.

"Hey," I say casually. "How are the wells going?"

Melody has chosen well-digging as her placement. I don't think she enjoys it, but it's predictable work that doesn't require any emotional involvement or interpersonal interaction.

"Fine," she says softly. "How is the village?"

"Fine," I answer back, though nothing really is fine.

Taylor scowls, and even in the dark I can feel his animosity toward Melody. She must feel it too, because she stiffens and her face turns hostile. She crawls under her net and props up her bible before pulling out a flashlight.

"Could you turn that off?" says Taylor loudly. "Some of us are trying to sleep."

Melody says nothing, but yanks a blanket over her head to dim the glow. Taylor makes an angry sound and turns the other way.

I don't intervene. Instead, I think of Rafael's hand on my thigh. The feeling in the pit of my stomach has nothing to do with fear or caution.

Chapter 13

Before

"That'll be twenty-seven dollars and thirty-six cents." The woman at the counter waits expectantly while I dig out a couple of crumpled bills. She peers at me, frowning, from behind a large pair of red plastic glasses that clash with her eggplant hair.

"Here you go." I hand over the cash and grab the sweatshirt, sighing with relief as I shrug it on and zip it up. It's overpriced and tacky—"San Francisco" is scrawled across it in bright pink script—but it does the job. I hadn't realized it would be so cold here.

"I thought California was supposed to be warm," I complain, as my parents pass me a hot chocolate. They'd been at Starbucks while I was in line buying my tourist-trap hoodie.

Dad grins and sips his coffee. "Not in San Francisco. I did try to warn you."

He had tried. And I'd brushed it off as typical parental over-caution, the kind that inspires moms and dads everywhere to try to persuade their kids to pack gloves and hats in May. But in this case, he'd been right. San Francisco is cold. Not just cool—cold. Like, chilled to the bone, fantasizing about a blanket and hot shower kind of cold. I had been woefully unprepared, hence the impromptu sweatshirt stop.

Mom, thankfully, had listened to Dad and packed accordingly. She's dressed now in a woolen peacoat and cashmere sweater. She's knotted a mint silk scarf at her neck, and she's pink-cheeked from the cold; she looks healthy, better than she has in months. Her hair is starting to grow back, too. It's almost in a pixie cut now, and she's happily discarded the wig in favor of cute caps and hairbands. She's wearing a little cream knit hat now, with her new hair peeking out in the front. The new hair is curly, and lighter than her normal color.

"What's with these curls?" she asked last night, frowning at herself in the hotel mirror.

"They're cute," I'd said. "I'm sure they'll look great with a little gel."

"How do you grow this out, though?" She pulled at a tiny ringlet. "I'm going to look like Art Garfunkel."

"Who?"

"Old guy. Singer. Wild mass of curly hair."

"You don't have to worry. I read the chemo curl eventually goes away."

"Chemo curl?" She made a face and pointed at her mouth in a gagging gesture. "It has an alliterative name? Like it's cute? That's awful."

I had agreed, and we'd both laughed.

Now, she brushes a stray curl back under her hat and grins at me.

"Stylish sweatshirt." She nods at the window of the souvenir shop I just left. "Didn't you want the matching hat?" I turn to look where she's pointing; the mannequin in the window is wearing a decidedly uncool San Francisco baseball cap.

"Funny, Mom," I say, turning back to stick out my tongue. Inside, though, I feel a warm glow of happiness spreading from my belly all the way to my fingers and toes. Six months ago, I'd never dreamed we'd be on this trip. I figured if I wanted to go see Stanford, I'd have to go myself, or with Tess. Or, more likely, not at all. I'd even been rethinking Stanford entirely, looking into options closer to home. But things seem on the upswing now. Mom's latest mammogram was free of any suspicious lumps or bumps, and her strength was gradually returning. The trip had even been her idea: we would check out Stanford, visit San Francisco, and drive down the coast to LA. She'd always wanted to visit California, she said; she'd just never had the chance.

The college visit had gone even better than I'd expected. My parents were taken by the picturesque, quintessentially Californian campus, with its red-tiled roofs and solid sandstone buildings. The student-tour reps were bright and accomplished, but not too intimidating, and the professors we met were the kind of people that show up as experts on the six o'clock news. Even the dining halls were surprisingly impressive: the food was actually quite fresh and delicious. I had a burrito that was a lot tastier than anything I'd ordered at the local Mexican spot back home.

My high SAT scores would put me in the running for at least a partial scholarship; a good thing, too, since the tuition and fees were no joke. I made a stop at the financial-aid office to pick up applications for a host of scholarships and bursaries. My guidance counselor back in Ohio had informed me that there was plenty of money out there, you just needed to know how to find it, and she'd been right: there were funds available for all kinds of different groups, from religious and ethnic to geographical or hobby-based.

Once the campus visit ended, we'd made straight for San Francisco, where Dad had booked us a gorgeous hotel right near the Ferry Terminal. The terminal, to my surprise, was not just a place to catch a boat, but also something of a food paradise. So far, I'd indulged in some of the best Vietnamese and Mexican dishes I'd ever tasted, not to mention the delights I'd sampled at the farmers' market that set up shop in and around the building twice a week—fresh produce, artisanal cheeses, and a breakfast sandwich made with maple bacon and sourdough bread that I'd fantasize about for months to come.

Now, exploring the touristy, somewhat tacky, area around Fisherman's Wharf, watching the sea lions sunbathe on the floating docks, my dad happily snaps pictures of us on his new phone. He hasn't touched a potato chip since we boarded the plane. I don't think I'd been this blissfully content since a family trip to Walt Disney World, back when I was in fourth grade.

"What should we do now?" Dad asks, whipping out his

San Francisco guidebook. My mom and I glance at each other and simultaneously roll our eyes. Dad is literally attached at the hip to his book—he hasn't taken a step without consulting it first.

"It says the original Ghirardelli's is nearby," he announces. "Anyone up for a hot fudge sundae?"

"Does anyone every say 'no' to that question?" Mom looks over at me. "How about it? You up for brownies and ice cream?"

I groan and clutch at my waistline. "We just had shrimp! I'm going to need new jeans."

"Don't be a spoilsport," says Mom, elbowing me in the ribs. "We're on vacation. If we don't put on a few pounds, how can we claim to have had a good time?"

I follow my parents to the famous ice-cream parlor, where we take a number and get in line. Despite the freezing cold, we're surrounded by people either eating or waiting to eat ice cream. Everything looks and sounds delicious, but the thought of eating ice cream with the wind whipping at my hair, blowing it in every direction, chills me to my core. I rub my hands together and bob up and down in an effort to warm up.

Mom notices me shivering. "There's a woman selling hats over there." She fishes some cash out of her purse. "Go get something."

"I don't really need a hat, do I?" I glance over at the hat lady, skeptical.

"Most of your body heat is lost through your head," Mom replies authoritatively. "Trust me, I know. I was bald. It's freakin' freezing."

I grin. "Okay," I say. "I'll meet you back here in five. Don't go having any hot fudge without me."

She feigns indignation. "I wouldn't dream of it."

I stroll over to the vendor, who brightens considerably when she notices my lack of a proper jacket or other cold-weather attire.

"Chilly, isn't it?" She smiles toothily. "We have lots of nice hats. One for ten, two for fifteen."

I examine the hats. They're handknit, and most feature cartoon characters like Hello Kitty or SpongeBob. I pick a funky purple one that looks like an owl. Not my style, but perfect for Tess. I put it aside and comb through the rest of the collection until I find one that isn't too flashy or quirky, pale pink with a small yellow flower attached to one side.

I'm handing over a twenty-dollar bill when I hear a familiar male voice, shouting. Instinctively, I look over at the ice-cream line. There's a crowd around the shouting man, who is on his knees. I feel my stomach turn. My father.

I abandon the hats and the money and run toward him, oblivious to the protests of the vendor, waving my hats and a five in the air.

"Dad!" I cry. "Dad!"

"Oh, Cat," he says, seeing me, his voice breaking. "*Cat.*"

Mom is on the ground, unconscious and shaking.

Chapter 14

After

"You fix clothing?" Anna makes the hand motions of a needle and thread as a group of guys rushes past carrying a comrade howling in pain. He has a large gash to his upper arm that's quickly soaking the dirty towel wrapped around it with blood.

"Sewing, you mean?" I ask, confused. Then I realize what she's really asking.

"Oh—no," I say hastily, stepping backwards. "No, no. I can't sew a person. No."

Anna shrugs and gestures for me to follow. "Get the alcohol," she says simply.

I grab the alcohol, along with some cotton strips I'd just finished sterilizing. Praying Anna is a decent seamstress, I rush to the back of the tent where she is instructing the boys to lay the patient out on our makeshift gurney.

"What's his name?" I ask, forgetting to use my Spanish.

"Pedro." For the first time, I notice Rafael is among the group. Our eyes meet. "He was cut."

"Apparently." My eyes linger on the gaping wound as Anna yanks off the filthy towels, muttering to herself. She instructs me to clean the area. Gently, I dab at Pedro's arm with some damp cloths before swabbing the area with alcohol. I watch as Anna prepares a needle and thread, dipping the needle in the alcohol before turning to grimly face the patient.

"This is going to hurt," she warns him in Spanish.

Pedro says nothing, but he closes his eyes. I take his other hand and, thinking of old movies, grab a wooden ruler and place it in his mouth.

"Um, *mordisco si necesario*," I say lamely. My Spanish is improving, but it's still pretty rudimentary. Pedro's eyes fly open and he stares at me, uncomprehending, until Rafael mutters something to him. He nods, relaxes, and bites down on the stick as I thought I had suggested.

"Did I just tell him his sister married a cocker spaniel or something?" I ask, as Anna begins to stitch up the wound. I feel Pedro stiffen, so I squeeze his hand tightly. He squeezes back, trembling.

"No." Rafael tries not to laugh, given the gravity of the situation, but his eyes twinkle. "It was almost understandable. It's the grammar that presents issues."

"Si," I say.

"You must show patience," he says, not for the first time. "You are still a new student."

I have been studying Spanish with Rafael for about two weeks now—since that night by the river.

"You will learn from your work, too," he tells me. "Try to use your Spanish more."

I should, but I've been spoiled in the Infirmary. Anna speaks enough English that I'm able to be lazy about practicing. And she wants to improve her English, so when I do try to use my limited Spanish, more often than not she answers me in English anyway.

The village is grateful for our day-to-day help, but what I've learned is that they're mostly grateful for our trailer full of Western medications and first-aid supplies. Before we came, Anna told me, all they had was alcohol, distilled and produced right here at the camp, and a couple of bottles of expired Aspirin. That's what the raids and attacks on the base are usually about, Rafael explained. The rebel groups know we have supplies. Advil and Polysporin and antibiotics. Little miracles in little bottles.

"Aaaaah!" Pedro's legs kick reflexively as Anna pokes at his arm the way you might if mending a sock.

"Shhh," I whisper soothingly. I reach for a damp cloth and press it against his forehead. "It's almost over."

Pedro stifles a sob and bites down harder on the ruler. I guess the Victorians knew what they were doing with the wooden stick.

It's over within a few minutes. I hand Pedro some Aspirin and a small cup of water.

"You need to rest," I say. *"Necesitas descansar."*

Pedro stares at me, gaze flicking back and forth between my eyes, and I wonder again if I've told him something ridiculous instead of reassuring. Then he swallows the Aspirin and, without a word, swings his legs off the table and stalks out.

"Was it something I said?" I stare after him.

Rafael puts his hand on my shoulder. "He's just ashamed he was weak in front of a girl," he explains. "You should take no offense."

"None taken." I grab a clean sponge and begin mopping up the mess. There's a fair bit of blood on the ground and the gurney. "What happened to him?"

"He slipped," Rafael says simply. "Near the river. Cut his arm on the rock. We were on a trading mission."

"Trading mission?" I ask curiously. I know the village interacts with others, but the politics remain fuzzy to me. Anna's tried explaining some of it, but a lot of it is confusing.

"With one of the native tribes," he says, and I perk up, interested.

"Native tribes? Really?" I picture a row of men clutching handmade spears, clad only in loincloths fashioned from leaves and feathers. "Is that dangerous?"

He laughs. "No. They are not isolated. They have contact with the outside. They just maintain a more traditional lifestyle."

"Oh." I wring the sponge out. A mix of blood and water trickles into the sink. "So more like Native Americans on a reservation." I modify my mental image, swapping loincloths for shorts and Nike T-shirts.

"I would imagine so." Rafael grabs a cloth and bends to help me. "It is not like *National Geographic*, with spears." He grins slyly, as if he knows what I was thinking.

"Of course not," I say quickly, looking away.

"There are more isolated tribes, but not in this area of the jungle." He tosses the rag in the sink. "Not so close to San Pedro. There have been settlers here for years, on and off."

This much I know. Anna has managed to convey some details during our downtime together here. Between patients, she tells me what she knows, and in turn I tell her about America, and my mother. The village was built up around an old camp that was abandoned years ago, after the rubber trade collapsed. Initially cleared and built by European explorers and entrepreneurs, it was later used as the headquarters for a now-defunct Amazon tour operator. Since the war, it has operated as a village mainly for refugees from San Pedro and other nearby towns devastated during the civil war.

Rafael straightens. "I will see you later? I'm going to go after him," he says, gesturing in the direction Pedro had taken.

"Yes, sure," I say. "The usual time?"

"*Si.*" He smiles at me. "*Hasta luego.*"

Anna tears the red-stained sheets from the bed and smirks at me as Rafael disappears through the tent flap. "He is liking you," she says, winking at me.

"Oh, no," I say, blushing. "He's just trying to be nice. He's happy we're here to help."

Anna waves her hand dismissively and snorts. "It is romance," she declares. She grabs a mop and clutches it to her in a passionate embrace.

My cheeks burn as I turn away, busying myself with fitting the bed with new sheets. Behind me, Anna chuckles. She's only two years older than me, but it feels like a lot more. Her mother was a nurse and midwife, and Anna often went with her for deliveries and house calls. She's a wealth of both regular and traditional medical knowledge; when she learned of my IBS, she mixed me some kind of minty tea made from a local plant that works wonders on my nervous stomach. I've barely had an episode since I started drinking it regularly. She was studying to be a doctor when the war broke out. When I ask if she's sorry she couldn't finish school, she shrugs.

"I'm more useful here than I would be in school," she says, and it's true. The camp couldn't function without her. I wonder if things will ever improve to the point where she can return to her studies—and if she would even want to. It might be difficult to accept the inertia of the lecture hall once you've been out in the field getting your hands dirty for so long.

Anna has explained to me that many in the village were in the middle and upper classes before the war, including teenagers like her, who had been studying at university or in apprentice-ships before their lives were abruptly changed forever. "Probably not so different from you," she said in Spanish one afternoon as we rolled bandages together, taking turns with a small battery-operated fan to counter the stifling heat of the small hut. I listened closely, struggling to understand. "Only our neighbor-hoods had private *policía* to keep us safe."

Anna told me how her parents, along with most here, were professionals or merchants, and found themselves denounced and imprisoned—or killed, along with the government and its officials, when the president fell.

"That seems unfair," I said in a mix of English and halting Spanish. "They were just regular people. The government was corrupt."

Anna looked around and leaned forward, holding the fan between us. "The government was corrupt," she repeated slowly in English. Her voice was low. "And—how do you say? *Nos hemos beneficiado de la corrupción.*" We benefited from the corruption.

"There's corruption everywhere," I said, thinking of the newspapers back home. Daily headlines about insider trading, sleazy campaign financing, bankers getting rich off phony mortgages. "Is it that different, really?"

After that, though, she clammed up. "Do not say anything I told you here," she said quietly, grabbing my arm with her roughened hand, her eyes full of fear and guilt. "Please." I nodded and promised, wondering what would happen to her if someone overheard. *Who was she afraid of? Eduardo? Rafael?*

Now, I grin good-naturedly at Anna's love dance with the mop and lean into the sink to wash my hands. Anna goes to dump the bucket out back, where mosquitoes will lay eggs in the resulting pool. In this humidity, the water never fully evaporates. Unlike the others here, I don't have to live in fear that the fever will snare me. By an accident of birth, I have both access to and the funds for highly effective preventative medication. Many of our patients in the Enfermería are malaria sufferers, writhing and delirious, bellowing with fever. Once the parasite infects you, it can recur for life, stalking you like Captain Hook's alarm-clock-swallowing crocodile.

I glance outside. It will be time for dinner soon; I no longer have a watch or phone to rely on, but I've become much more adept at judging the hour by the position of the sun's shadows beneath the endless canopy, together with the day's increasingly predictable routine. Dinner in the village is often a communal event, served up in a grassy area near the canvas tents where many sleep. The Enfermería and other common areas are slightly farther along the clearing. Sometimes, Margo and Taylor and I stay for dinner.

The village is well run, and from what I've seen, Rafael plays a large part in that. It helps that many here are young, and united by a common cause. As Anna explained, most are war orphans, either literally or figuratively. Rafael's parents are alive, but they're in jail. His mother was a vocal human-rights advocate who criticized the new regime; his father was guilty by association. Anna's father was killed in the fighting; her mother remains missing. Anna's sure she's dead, but her brother Julio refuses to believe it. Julio is one of those entrusted with village security, patrolling the perimeter. Anna says she can't believe anyone would trust him with a gun, and that he used to be a mamma's boy who cried in the dark. It's hard to believe her, since Julio is well over six feet and two hundred pounds.

I've tried asking questions about what, exactly, Rafael's politics are, but it's tough getting a clear answer. From my conversations with Rafael, I can see that he sees the village not simply as a refugee camp, but as fertile ground for teaching the others political philosophy, the virtues of liberal democracy, and social welfare. However, many of the other young men here just seem angry, ready to storm buildings in the capital and shoot off rounds of ammunition. Anna's mentioned that the village is in talks with other, similar, groups across the country about forming a sort of network of opposition, but so far no one can agree on a unified message. I can imagine. Our student government back home had trouble uniting the student body, and all they had to do was get a bunch of privileged middle-class kids to show up at Homecoming.

That evening, Anna convinces me to stay for dinner, and I in turn pressure Margo and Taylor.

"I'm starting to think you guys like it here," Taylor grumbles at dinner that night. We're having chicken in some kind of spicy marinade made from locally grown peppers and herbs. It tastes like something you'd eat at a trendy restaurant back home, if you can genuinely call any restaurants in Ohio trendy.

Margo ignores him. "Do you like the chicken?" she asks. "I helped prepare it."

"Did you make this sauce?" I ask, using my flatbread to soak up some of the extra. "It's amazing."

"No," says Margo. "I killed the chicken."

"Jesus." Taylor shakes his head.

"My first on my own," she continues proudly. "Caught the bird and snapped its neck. Plucked the feathers myself."

Taylor looks nauseated. "Is that really necessary?"

Margo sniffs at him. "You're willing to eat it, no problem, but you don't want to hear where it came from. That is so typical."

"Typical what?" he takes another bite of chicken, resting his cutlery on his left leg. We eat our supper on the ground, in a clearing.

"Typical spoiled American. Did you think meat came from the grocery store?"

"Yup." Taylor grabs some bread from a plate nearby. Margo's group bakes it fresh every morning. "From the supermarket, on those little white Styrofoam trays. It's grown like that in labs and shipped out."

Margo scowls. "You're being ridiculous."

"Yeah, well, at least I don't think I'm at summer camp," he says under his breath.

"Excuse me?" Margo puts her plate down. "What, exactly, is that supposed to mean?"

Taylor shrugs. "Just that we're here in this shitty, war-torn country and you're cheerfully going on about killing chickens."

"I'm trying my best to help," she snaps. She looks angrier than usual; this is more than the usual Taylor-Margo banter. He's hit a nerve.

"Whatever. I'm just saying, this is fun and quirky for you, but for these people, it's their life. They don't get to go home after ticking it off their med-school application checklist."

"Excuse me." Margo stands up, looking furious. "At least I'm not afraid to get in and get my hands dirty. You're sitting at a fucking computer all day, for God's sake. What is it you do, exactly? Check your Facebook page?"

"Actually, I've learned a lot," says Taylor quietly. "From Eduardo, and from the social media work. These people are suffering."

"You don't think I know that?" Now Margo just looks upset. "They could live a month on your allowance, I'm sure, Hotel Heir Boy."

"You're full of shit, you know that?" He shakes his head. "Your parents are doctors."

"I'm Canadian," she shoots back. "Doctors there are practically civil servants."

I don't say anything. While they fire insults back and forth in a verbal match of Ping-Pong, I stare at my plate. Do I think I'm at summer camp, sneaking off behind trees with Rafael? Am I not doing important work in the infirmary? Does the fact that I get to leave, whereas Anna and the others have no way out, change the value of what I'm doing here?

Taylor is about to fire off another retort when Rafael eases into a spot next to me, holding a plate.

"Hi," he says. "I am not interrupting?"

I look over at him and blush as I think of Anna earlier, dancing with her mop. His longish hair is curling from the humidity, and his cheeks are dark with a five-o'clock shadow. He crosses his legs, and our knees touch, briefly. I feel a sensation in my belly that has nothing to do with the chipotles in the chicken.

"No," Taylor assures him. "We were just discussing... income inequality."

Margo snorts derisively and stalks off. Rafael pauses, unsure of what to say. "Is everything okay?"

Taylor and I exchange a glance. "Yeah," he says. "I was just telling Cat how much I've learned about Calantes doing the social media work."

Rafael brightens at this. "That is great," he says. He cuts carefully into his chicken, but doesn't begin eating. "That is what we need. Americans to understand, to get involved. We need change."

"Change?" Taylor asks casually, and I can see he's listening closely.

"Yes, change," says Rafael. His face glows as he continues speaking. "We are networking with other groups. If we can all get together, we could make a difference."

I'm finished eating, and push my plate aside. "What kind of difference?" I ask. "Like protests? Uprisings?"

"Yes!" he says, grabbing my hand excitedly. I'm surprised, but I don't pull away and neither does he, not even after he settles back down. I feel the warmth from his hand travel up my arm.

"Like the Arab Spring," he continues with enthusiasm. "It could work for us. We could overthrow the government! It worked in the Middle East."

Rafael's eyes flash with exhilaration; they are like lava in the light of the setting sun, bright and liquid and full of heat.

"Arab Spring ended in ISIS," says Taylor quietly, almost under his breath. He looks skeptical.

Rafael doesn't answer. His cheeks are flushed with excitement.

"But you aren't soldiers, Rafael," I say, worried. We are still holding hands, which at this point is both pleasurable and awkward. I look around at the village, at the disproportionate number of women and youth. This is not a military training camp. It's a place for the dispossessed, the sick, the hungry.

Rafael nods in agreement, his enthusiasm unchanged. "We aren't," he agrees. "But others—some of them are."

What others? I want to ask. *The ones who come to our base with guns in search of Pepto-Bismol?* I drop his hand, feeling uneasy, and notice my plate is crawling with insects. A swarm of ants cover the flatbread until it is unrecognizable, black and quivering and alive. I look away, nauseated.

"There's a meeting a week from today," he says. "We'll know more then. On the thirtieth."

"The thirtieth?" I say suddenly, doing the math. "So today's the twenty-third?"

"Yes." Rafael looks puzzled. "Why? What's wrong?"

The twenty-third. My mother would have been fifty today. I feel my insides churn. I picture her at her last birthday, which we had celebrated, thinking she was done with cancer. Her hair in a pixie cut, laughing happily over a cake that she had actually admitted tasted like chocolate.

"I'm going to go see Anna," I say, standing. "I don't feel well."

I rise, turning my back slightly to him as I look out into the vast expanse of the jungle. It's more familiar now, but no less terrifying. In the distance I catch sight of fast-moving creatures, too quick to identify as more than flashes of bright color. Somewhere, a bird sings shrilly and an army of cricket-like insects chimes in, taking up their song.

Rafael rises and hovers, uncertain. "Do you still want to study later? Spanish?"

My stomach cramps, and an image of my father floats in front of me, hunched over and dressed in black. The day of my mother's funeral. For reasons unknown, the worst memories come fast and furious when I'm in pain. "I don't think so."

"Cat," he whispers. He's close now—very close. I can feel his breath on the back of my neck, warm, even in the heat of the jungle air. His arms brush up against mine, our fingertips touching. No one has touched me like that in so long. For a moment, I forget everything but the sensation of his skin touching my own. Conflicting images sail across my mental vision like words on a teleprompter: Rafael, bending in to kiss me; my mother, bald, cold, and shivering in the throes of chemo.

The pain intensifies as I stumble away from Rafael. "I can't now," I stammer, even as my heart beats faster. Hugging myself around the middle, I rush for the safety of the Enfermería.

Chapter 15

Before

"Mr. Marks?" A guy in scrubs appears in the doorway of the waiting area. He doesn't look much older than I am, and is fidgeting nervously with a stethoscope so expertly placed around his neck that it actually looks staged. I figure he's probably an intern, a recent medical-school grad. I briefly wonder if he really needs the stethoscope around his neck, or whether it's more of a security blanket, making him feel like a "real" doctor. I don't judge him for this. I can't imagine it's easy getting people to believe you're a doctor when you look like you're a high-school student dressed up for Halloween.

"Yes?" My dad rises, clutching the ancient *Time* magazine he's been staring blankly at for the last hour. I slip my phone back into my pocket and stand up too, knotting my hands together behind my back.

"If you'll come with me, please." Intern Boy glances at me and straightens his stethoscope again. I resist the urge to grab it from around his scrawny neck as Dad and I follow along behind him.

"Just in here." He motions for us to join him in a small corner office with a breathtaking view of the Golden Gate Bridge. Even in my panic, it's a beautiful thing to see. The desk is cluttered with medical journals and, oddly, a copy of *Vogue*. I check the name on the door: Dr. Margaret O'Sullivan.

"I'm not Dr. O'Sullivan," he blurts out, noticing me reading the sign.

I raise my eyebrows. He's both male and Asian. "Clearly," I say, as politely as I can.

"Dr. O'Sullivan is away," he says. He lowers himself awkwardly into her chair, looking uncomfortable. "I'm David Lee, her Chief Resident."

"Chief Resident?" My dad looks surprised. Apparently I'm not the only one who's noticed the doc looks like he's barely old enough to drive.

"Yes," says Dr. Lee, somewhat defensively. Then he looks down at the desk and his face changes. His features soften and he looks up at us somberly. I wonder if they teach that as some kind of lame bedside-manner exercise in med school.

"So, as you know, the patient—your wife, Mrs. Marks," he begins, folding and unfolding his hands.

"It's back, isn't it," I interrupt.

Dr. Lee looks flustered—I've probably interrupted a practiced speech of some kind.

"The cancer," I say, my tone matter-of-fact. "It's back, and it's spread to her brain."

I've already come to this conclusion. I came to it hours ago, when they first wheeled away Mom for testing and left us sitting in waiting-room purgatory. I'm not a doctor, fine, but I do have a smart phone and Internet access. Seizures in a former breast-cancer patient almost certainly means the cancer is back, and not just in the boobs. I promptly vomited the shrimp I'd eaten earlier on the pier, a disgusting fishy pink mess. Stinking of old seafood, I'd then cried in the bathroom until my tear supply was exhausted. I didn't tell my dad, and he didn't ask why I was in the bathroom for an hour. I'm not sure he even noticed I was gone. At that point, I busied myself playing Solitaire on my phone. I avoided Google, so I could spend at least an hour or so in denial. I let the numbness sink in, anesthetizing my anxiety.

Dad makes a small noise that sounds like a mewling kitten. Dr. Lee looks increasingly panicked; this is not going the way he planned.

"Now, please," he says nervously. He's back to fidgeting with his stethoscope. "Please, let's all calm down for a moment."

"Am I wrong?" I demand, staring at him. He can barely meet my eyes.

"Well—"

"Am I wrong." I say it again, flatly, and lean forward on the desk. My eyes bore into his, and I refuse to look away.

Dr. Lee takes a deep breath and sits back in his—Margaret O'Sullivan's—chair. "No," he says quietly. "I'm so sorry. The CT scan shows there is evidence of tumor infiltration in the brain."

Dad slumps over in his seat. He buries his face in his hands and his entire body shakes with sobs, reminding me of the wobbling sea lions at Fisherman's Wharf. *Was that really only hours ago?* I shake my head. It feels like a lifetime.

"What next?" I ask tonelessly. I ignore my father and open up the notepad app on my smart phone. Someone has to be responsible here.

I type quickly as Dr. Lee runs through the list of treatment options and outcomes. He fidgets a lot through our conversation, repeatedly referring to the fact that we will need to confirm the diagnosis and treatment plan with our oncologist back in Ohio. He says it so many times I briefly consider telling him off or dispensing with words altogether and just throwing a pencil holder at him. I bet it must have something to do with fear of being sued, and that this is even a concern for him, in this moment, enrages me.

"Can you take us to her now?" I snap when he's done. "Is she awake?"

"We gave her a sedative to stop the seizures," he says. "She might be awake by now, but she's probably groggy."

"So she hasn't been told?" I grip the edge of the desk, hoping she didn't have to get that news alone in a strange hospital bed in a strange city.

"Not yet." He stands up. "We wouldn't give that kind of news to someone without proper social support."

Proper social support. This guy is definitely parroting Bedside Manner 101. His grades in college must have really been something, because he clearly didn't get into med school on his stellar people skills.

We trail behind Dr. Lee again as we navigate the hospital corridors. My mother is in a semi-private room, but thankfully the other bed remains unoccupied. She looks tiny under the thin, blue hospital blanket. I stare at the IV pole, the slow drip in the tube, and feel a sinking sense of déjà vu.

"Mom?" I kneel at the side of the bed, touching her hand. It's cold. Her wedding band feels like it's been dropped in snow. I reach for another blanket from the bedside table and gently place it over her.

"Cat?" Her voice is hoarse. With a considerable effort she struggles, and fails, to sit up.

"Careful," I say, reaching over to support her. "They had to give you a sedative."

She blinks, looking fearful. Her eyes dart back and forth. "I don't remember," she says helplessly. She turns her head slowly and notices Dr. Lee. "We're in a hospital," she says, and I watch as her expression changes from one of puzzlement to resignation.

"Tell me," she says, gripping my hand. "Please."

I break the news, and she says nothing. Beside me, my dad begins his stifled crying again. Dr. Lee lurks awkwardly by the wall, wearing his best Sympathy Face. I ignore him.

"Lie with me here, Cat," she says finally.

I crawl into the narrow hospital bed and gingerly settle in beside her. "I love you," I whisper, flinching as my arm brushes the IV catheter. *Don't leave me*, I add silently. *Please.*

We lie there together for ages. Through her thin hospital gown, I feel my mother's heart beat against me, and I grip her tighter. Neither of us cries.

...

I sit outside the doctor's office and fidget with my phone, repeatedly hitting the refresh button on CNN.com and then not reading any of the headlines. I haven't told Tess about this appointment; even my mother doesn't know. It was Mrs. Marino, the school guidance counselor, who gently but firmly insisted I seek counseling, and I resentfully agreed. Not that I'd had much choice, of course, if I wanted to avoid suspension. Turns out smashing a hockey stick into pieces by repeatedly thwacking it against the concrete gym walls is frowned upon at Warren G. Harding High. Who knew?

It was Alison Dean who set me off. Not that she had any way of knowing I was going to go all Incredible Hulk on the gym equipment, but she just wouldn't *shut up* about her shopping trip to Chicago with her mom. On and on, while the rest of us were just trying to get through gym class, chasing a blue plastic ball while half-blind in a pair of sports goggles. When she mentioned going to buy an American Girl doll "for old time's sake," I lost it completely. I don't really even remember what happened. One second I was pretending to be guarding left wing, hoping Mrs. Fox wouldn't notice I wasn't actively participating, and the next, I was near the bleachers where they hang the banners and pennants, gleefully smashing the hockey stick against the wall. Over and over again, I hit it, enjoying the sensation as the wooden stick eventually cracked and splintered. At some point, I vaguely recall Mrs. Fox blowing her stupid whistle and shouting my name, but apparently it took three people to forcibly remove the fragmented remains of the stick from my hands.

I shake off the memory and cross and uncross my legs, wondering if I have time for another trip to the Ladies' room. Hospitals didn't used to send me running for the nearest bathroom stall, but since my mom's diagnosis, they evoke a flight-or-fight response. Just the smell of the place—that unmistakable aroma of antiseptic mixed with microwaved meatloaf—is enough to make me reach for the Imodium.

Since returning from San Francisco, I've been here with Mom four times, all to meet with different specialists and consider what the experts call the "options." Referring to them as options is a bit of a joke, imbuing them with a false sense of hopefulness, or promise. It's like choosing between the chicken or the fish on an airplane—they're both going to make you scramble for the airsickness bag, so why not just drop the illusion of choice?

"Ms. Marks?" The secretary, an older woman with a kind smile and Little Orphan Annie red curls, pokes her head out. "The doctor will see you now." She gestures towards the door, motioning for me to go ahead and open it.

I pocket my phone and take a deep breath as I reach for the doorknob. Dr. Shapiro comes highly recommended from my family doctor. She says he's one of the top adolescent grief psychiatrists in the state. I wonder how many "adolescent grief psychiatrists" there could possibly be, but I don't say anything. I imagined Dr. Shapiro would look like old sepia-toned photos of Sigmund Freud: grave, stern, and smoking a pipe.

Dr. Shapiro is none of these things. I can't say for certain he doesn't smoke a pipe—smoking is not permitted at the hospital—but he looks as though he's definitely smoked something in his time. His thinning curly hair is scraggly-long, and he sports a bushy beard. He isn't wearing a suit, like I'd pictured, but instead a tie-dyed shirt and jeans. Something about the shirt annoys me, like he's trying too hard on the one hand—doesn't he know tie-dye hasn't been cool in, like, fifty years—and is not being serious enough on the other. My mother has cancer; why the hell is this fool dressed like a Ben and Jerry's commercial?

"Come in, Caitlin," he says, adopting what I'm sure he thinks is a teenager-friendly tone. I comply, shutting the door behind me with a wordless click.

"Have a seat." He points across from him at a leather couch, and I try not to smirk. *He actually has a couch.*

I sit stiffly and place my bag next to me. I fold my hands neatly in my lap and look at him, expectant.

"So, Caitlin." He smiles pleasantly. I don't like it at all. "It's nice to meet you."

What is this, a dinner party? I stare at him, silent.

Dr. Shapiro shuffles some papers around on his desk. He's a large man, considerably overweight, and with the door closed the office air feels thick and humid, like a microcosmic rainforest in the middle of the hospital. I watch a drop of perspiration trickle down his temple and look away, mildly repulsed.

"I'm sorry about your mother, Caitlin."

I bristle. I hate that word, "sorry." *Why is he sorry? Did he give her the cancer? He doesn't even know her.* I consider walking out, but instead I exhale and shift in my seat.

"It's Cat," I say.

"Cat, then." He scribbles something on the clipboard in front of him. "Can you tell me a bit about what brought you here today, Cat?"

"You mean you don't know?" I frown. "Shouldn't it all be in my file? I told it all to Dr. Kelley so she could arrange the referral."

"I'd like to hear it in your words." That phony, fake-pleasant smile again.

"My words?" I feel the surge of adrenaline that of late has come to mean I am about to imminently lose my shit. I furrow my eyebrows at Dr. Shapiro. He's lucky there are no hockey sticks in his office.

"Please." He picks up one of those squishy stress balls from his desk and hands it to me. "This might help."

I don't say anything, but I take the squeeze ball and feel an immediate and surprising release of tension as I grasp it tightly in my right palm.

"My mom is dying," I say. My tone is matter-of-fact. "No one will come out and say it, but it's true. Breast cancer spread to her brain. Treatment options are all different forms of torture and won't cure her."

"And how does that make you feel?"

"Seriously?" I stare at him. "You guys really ask that?"

"Sometimes it's helpful to put your feelings into words."

"Fine. How do I feel? I feel livid. Distraught. Devastated. Lonely. Broken." I glare at his beard. Something about it disgusts me, like there could be tiny bugs nesting in there and I'd never know.

"Very descriptive words." Dr. Shapiro is writing furiously.

"Well, I rocked the SAT," I say snidely. I stretch out my legs so that they almost hit the battered maple coffee table that separates us. "I have a very broad vocabulary."

"Yes," agrees Dr. Shapiro. He flips a page. "I see here that you managed to achieve very high scores on the SATs, despite your mother having been in chemo at that time."

I don't reply. I examine my nails, which have little white lines on them. I wonder if these are a sign of some kind of nutritional deficiency. I can't say I've been eating all that well. With Mom out of commission and Dad back on the Frito-Lay Diet, I've been mostly fending for myself. *How long can one survive on grilled-cheese sandwiches and celery sticks?*

"It also says here that you're doing well in your classes, many of which are Advanced Placement."

"Yeah."

"Do you have any hobbies?"

"Not anymore." I think back to my old life. I used to occasionally get involved backstage in school productions. Making costumes, helping with makeup, that sort of thing. I once built an enormous, man-eating plant out of papier-mâché and a pair of old green curtains for the sophomore production of *Little Shop of Horrors*. People talked about it for weeks afterwards. Now, I can't imagine why I'd ever bother with anything so pointless.

Dr. Shapiro makes a noise. I can't tell if it's intended to be sympathetic or disapproving, or if he's just clearing his throat.

"So you don't do anything to relax?" He pushes his glasses back up his sweaty nose. His pores are huge.

"Sometimes I bake." I feel impatient, and glance at the clock. Ten minutes have already passed. *Shouldn't he say something useful at this point? Why do you have to go to medical school to do this job?*

"Do you?" He leans forward in his chair. "What do you bake?"

"I don't know. Cookies. Cakes. Pies." Last week, after we'd been to see the oncologist, I went down to the kitchen after my parents were asleep and baked two batches of brownies and a lemon meringue pie. I took them to school and dropped them off at the staff room. I knew neither of my parents would be eating them. I relay this story to Dr. Shapiro.

His head bobs up and down as he nods, his pen flicking back and forth across the page at a mile a minute. "So you tend to bake a lot of things at once."

"I don't know. Sometimes, I guess. It relaxes me."

"That's interesting."

"Why is it interesting?" I challenge him.

"Because it could be considered hypomanic behavior. As could excelling in your classes and acing the SATs during such a difficult time in your life." He puts down the clipboard and looks directly at me.

"Hypo what?" I'm caught off guard. "Did you say manic?"

"Hypomanic," he clarifies. "Not quite manic, but with signs of mild mania."

I bristle. "What are you saying?"

"There's something called Bipolar II disorder," he explains. "It's not quite bipolar. It's much milder, but with symptoms of hypomania and depression."

"Bipolar?" I jump out of my seat. "Are you kidding me?" I think of Tess's Aunt Suzanne, who has bipolar disorder, or as it used to be called, manic depression. She once pulled Tess's cousins out of school in the middle of the day and drove them across three states in a brand-new Porsche she'd bought that same day. They were almost at Disneyland when the authorities caught up to her.

"Calm down," he says. "Sit."

Shocked, I sit. "I really don't think I'm bipolar," I say quietly. I stare down at my lap, not sure whether to get upset or furious. I wish I'd never thrown that hockey stick. I know I've got some issues, but this guy has me at an eight on the crazy scale, and I figured I was hovering somewhere closer to four.

"You shouldn't think of it in terms of labels," he says. He pushes his glasses back up again, and I envision myself punching him squarely in the face, taking pleasure in the mental imagery of shattering glass and broken plastic. "You should think of it in terms of trying to get better."

"I really didn't know I was sick," I say.

"Often a stressful life event, like a parent's illness, can bring on a hypomanic episode," he says. "I'm concerned that, once this passes, you'll find yourself in a depressive episode."

"I'm sorry, but I feel kind of depressed right now." I shake my head, baffled. "My mom is going to die. I cry all night. If I was hypomanic or whatever, wouldn't I feel better than this?"

He nods knowingly. "You're probably shifting right now. Which is why it's a good thing you're here."

"I'm here because I smashed up a hockey stick in gym class," I point out. I'm starting to feel pretty seriously pissed off. "Where does that fit in?"

"Irritability and outbursts can be seen with Bipolar II," he says authoritatively. He clicks and unclicks his pen. "I think we should try some medication." He reaches for a prescription pad. "I think we should try Abilify."

I will myself not to grimace at the peppy name. "Abilify?"

"Yes. I think it would really help you, Caitlin. Cat." He riffles through my file and pauses. "Your family doctor—Dr. Kelley—has you on sleeping pills. Do you need a refill?"

Finally, something useful. "Yes!" I say quickly. "Please."

"Do you have trouble falling asleep, or staying asleep?"

"Both, I guess." I figure adding that I often simply don't sleep at all would be redundant.

"It's possible the Abilify might help with that too, but I'll refill this until we get a better hold on your situation. It's common to have sleep problems during a time of crisis."

He scribbles something on the pad and hands it to me. "Start it right away, and you'll see me again next week."

I stand up. I guess our appointment is done. I can't say I feel any better now than when I arrived, though I suppose that may be the point of the drugs. I wonder what Dr. Google will have to say about Abilify.

"I'll see you soon, Cat." He opens the door for me, and I catch a faint whiff of salami on his breath. My stomach heaves;

it takes almost nothing to set me off these days. I don't say anything as I walk quickly past him and down the corridor, the rubber soles of my shoes squeaking against the freshly cleaned tiles.

Outside, it's bright and ruthlessly sunny. I squint in the sunlight as I take a deep breath, making a valiant effort to relax, to compose myself. It's too late. With a groan, I grasp the sides of a nearby trash can, and vomit.

Chapter 16

After

The sun has set, and the jungle air rings with the sounds of what I call the night crew: the insects that provide our bedtime lullaby. The songs, croaks, and hums are distinct from those of their daytime brethren, an entirely different soundtrack. I picture an assortment of ants, bees, and mosquitoes retiring for the day, turning things over to their night counterparts like human shift workers. In fact, the security crew in the camp works much the same way; the daytime watch hands their rifles to the night watch shortly after the sun goes down.

Rafael has a small campfire going, and we sit together, conversing in his mother tongue. I don't know what to think. Sometimes it feels as if there are two Cats—the one who longs for love and companionship, who's lonely and desperate for affection, and the other one, who's desperate and desolate and pushes people away, almost determined to stagnate in her grief. Sometimes I enjoy Rafael's excuses to touch me, and that he stares at me with longing brown eyes. In spite of everything I find myself responding. I seek him out in crowds. I brush my leg up against his when he sits down beside me. It feels reckless and wrong and right and exciting, all at the same time. Best of all, it makes me forget. When I am with Rafael, I don't think of my mother. I live only in the present, able to drown out the last year in a rush of endorphins and the cacophony of jungle sounds.

My eyes water from the smoke, and I try to ignore the sting as I conjugate Spanish verbs.

I can tell Rafael is trying not to laugh at my appalling accent, and I stop, embarrassed.

"You're laughing at me," I pout, tossing my hair. I know I'm flirting, and it empowers me. I run my hands through my long hair.

"I'm not," he protests. "I would never." But then he starts to laugh, and so do I.

"Maybe we should take a pause," he says.

"Break," I correct him, happy to play the teacher for once.

"Right," he agrees.

We're both quiet for a moment, then Rafael turns to me, looking serious. "What do you think of this place? Of Calantes?"

I hesitate. I don't know, really, what I think. How to sum up an entire country in a few words, especially one as complicated as this? "It's beautiful," I say carefully. "But obviously

there are a lot of problems. Look at the village, the poverty…"
My voice trails off. I'm not sure what he wants to hear. "I want
to think I'm doing some good here, but I know it's silly to think
I can change anything in a few months."

"Exactly," he says, nodding, but it's not clear what, pre-
cisely, he's agreeing with. He puts his hand on mine. "I'm glad
you see it. We need change."

I wonder if he is still thinking about soldiers and weapons
and fighting. If that is what change means to him. "Change?"
I say carefully.

"Change," he says fiercely. "It's time for some real change."

But before I can press further, Rafael freezes. He motions
for me to be quiet and puts a firm hand on my arm.

"What's wrong?" I ask fearfully, in English. "What is it?"

Rafael says nothing, but there is terror in his eyes. Before I
can turn to follow his gaze, he reaches past me with both arms,
grabbing at the ground. There's a loud hissing sound, and I gasp
at the sight of the snake writhing in his bare hands.

He clutches the furious beast near the head and the tail as
it thrashes, a long, thin creature of shimmering orange, white,
and black. It is at once both beautiful and horrifying.

I whimper and jump back, nearly tripping into the fire. I
steady myself and watch, fascinated, as Rafael flings the angry
snake deep into the bush. When he turns to face me, he is
shaking.

"Coral snake," he says abruptly. He sits back down, looking dazed. I stare at him and realize I'm shaking too. "Pretty.
Venomous."

"Thank God you saw it," I say. I wonder what would have happened if I had been bitten. *Would I have died?* I know we don't have any antivenom here—we don't even have adequate mosquito repellant. *Would there have been time to get to a hospital somewhere? Would they have even taken me?*

"You're shaking," observes Rafael. He cautiously draws his arm around me and, despite myself, despite everything, I thrill at his touch. "Are you very afraid of snakes?"

An image of my mother recoiling from a boa constrictor at the zoo pops into my head. "Not really," I say. My heart is still pounding. "I mean, I don't like them, but I'm not phobic. Not like my mom. She is—was—completely freaked out by snakes." *Is. Was.* The words hit me in the stomach like a lead-filled sock.

"Was?" The fire snaps and crackles as Rafael tosses in a long tree branch.

"She died. She had breast cancer." I avoid looking at him. I don't think I could stand the Cancer Face right now. I haven't mentioned my mother to him before.

He's silent for a moment, and then speaks up. "I had a cousin. Emilia. She was seven." He pauses, breaking another branch in half.

"She had the most beautiful hair. She wore it in two long braids at either side of her head. I used to pull on them when she made me angry." He smiles faintly at the memory. "She kept having fevers. Nosebleeds. Bruises in odd places."

Tears spring to my eyes. "Leukemia," I whisper. *Cancer of the blood.*

"Yes." He nods. "The doctors said there was treatment.

But the treatment was worse than the disease. When she died, she was nothing like Emilia. She was empty, and her braids had fallen out. Emilia had died long before."

I think of my mother in her last days, bald and hollow-eyed, her arms and legs so skinny they looked wasted. I take Rafael's hand.

"I know," I say. "I know."

Rafael pulls me close to him and strokes my hair. He kisses the top of my head, a gesture I appreciate for its kindness, for its sense of giving without the expectation of return. I snuggle closer to him, my head against his chest. I can hear his heartbeat.

When he moves in to kiss me this time, I don't fight him.

• • •

"I think there is something going on between Taylor and Eduardo." Margo glances pointedly in their direction, where they're engaged in an intimate-looking tête-à-tête. We're both on a break from work, taking fifteen to cool off and hydrate. As outsiders here, we have that luxury. "I've seen them together like that a bunch of times recently."

"You think?" I observe the pair, noting the way Taylor's head snaps back in laughter when Eduardo whispers something. "Maybe you're right."

"I usually am," says Margo. She smiles. "Of course, you might have noticed yourself if you hadn't been so... preoccupied."

"What's that supposed to mean?" I ask, even as I feel the color creeping into my cheeks.

Margo snorts. "Oh, please," she says. "Everyone knows about you and Rafael."

My face—my entire body—feels hot. "I don't know what you're talking about."

She gives me a knowing look. "Please."

"I *don't* know." She's right, of course; so what if people know? But part of me resents the intrusion, wants it kept private. I'm not sure how I feel, or what I'm doing. At the same time, I'm not sure I care. I left the logical, intellectual Cat behind in Ohio, shed her like one of the jungle snakes sheds its scaly skin. The new Cat—the bold stranger who runs off to South America instead of starting college—is happy to let Rafael kiss her and run his hands along her back. That Cat is falling hard and fast.

I reach for my canteen and take a swig of water. I wonder what Dr. Shapiro would think of my feelings for Rafael. *Pure hypomania taken to its logical conclusion? Or something to do with my broken relationship with my father? Both, probably.*

"I can't believe you're both hooking up with people while I'm off killing chickens," Margo gripes. "Maybe Taylor's right. It is like we're at summer camp or something, the way everyone is carrying on."

I take another look at Taylor and Eduardo, who appear considerably more serious now. Taylor's forehead is creased with worry, as Eduardo speaks rapidly, his hands flying in every direction. I wonder if Margo is right, or whether something else is going on.

"You think we act like we're at camp?" I toy with the lid on my canteen, screwing and unscrewing it. "You don't think we're helping?"

She gives me a look. "Come on. Who are you? Sari? You really think you can parachute in here for a few months and save the world?"

I frown. "No," I say, struggling to find the right words. "But when I'm in the infirmary, I do sort of feel like I'm help-ing. And I—well, it helps me forget. You know?"

"I do know," Margo says, nodding. "I get it. But really— are we doing it for them? Or is it really for us? Sometimes it's not clear to me."

We sit in silence, contemplating each other's words. *Was Margo right? When I mended someone's wound or offered them relief from pain, was I helping them, or was I helping myself? And did it matter?*

"I miss home," Margo announces, out of the blue. Startled, I drop my canteen into the dust. I watch as grains of sand and bit of dirt stick to the spout where it was still wet, and curse inwardly.

"That's not like you," I reply carefully, reaching for the canteen. It's not like Margo to admit any kind of weakness, any kind of vulnerability. Especially not when it comes to her life and family back in Toronto.

She wraps a strand of dark hair around her index finger. "It was my mom's sixtieth birthday yesterday."

"Oh," I say, not knowing how to respond. I think of my own mother's birthday, several days back, and feel the familiar ache. I don't look at Margo, instead focusing on a bright orange-and-black beetle bobbling though the tall grass. The pattern on its back reminds me of one of my dad's uglier ties.

"My dad has been planning this huge surprise party for-ever," she continues. "It meant a lot to him. He was crushed when he realized I'd still be here."

"I thought they wanted you to come out here," I say. "For your résumé."

"They did," Margo says. She breaks a branch off a nearby tree and snaps it in her hands. "But I timed it so I would miss the party."

"Oh," I say again. I'm still not sure what to say.

"I just—I wish I had done things differently," she says. She uses the longer piece to scribble in the sand, drawing abstractly. "I wish I could have been there for the party."

"Yeah." *My mother will never have a sixtieth birthday party.*

"Anyway." Margo tosses the stick aside and straightens. "Maybe Taylor's right. What good is killing chickens really doing for these people? Do they need us here? What they need is money."

Margo swats irritably at a mosquito. The little pests have become more active recently. Rafael says it's the start of the rainy season that brings them out in swarms.

"But we are helping," I protest. "You're helping feed peo-ple. I'm helping heal them." I think of earlier today, when I helped set a girl's broken arm. When Anna forced her dislocated shoulder into place with a satisfying snap, I had felt empowered. I tell Margo this, as she goes back to her doodling.

Suddenly, Margo slaps violently at her forearm, hissing loudly. We both watch the little fountain of blood that spurts forth: she must have caught the annoying insect mid-feast.

"The problem is," she says quietly, "that not all problems are like a broken arm, where you can set them. Some are like—" she stops abruptly, flushing.

I'm puzzled at first, but then I realize what she was going to say. "Some are like cancer," I say flatly.

"Sorry," she says, abashed. "I didn't mean that."

"It's okay." I shrug irritably. "You can say cancer in front of me. I'm not going to break. Cancer, cancer, cancer!" I shout loudly, to prove my point. My voice reverberates around me in the stillness of the jungle.

Overhead, there is a flurry of brightly colored feathers as a bird makes its escape, frightened into flight. Margo stares at me warily.

"Sorry," I say. I kick at the ground, accidentally sending the beetle flying. Margo and I both watch as it lands on a log nearby. I wonder if it's scared, and I feel guilty.

"It's true, though," she says. "This place has huge problems. It's going to take major changes to fix it."

"Like?"

She shrugs. "Taylor says Eduardo talks a lot about elections. Getting the UN in here to supervise, like in Ukraine."

"Uh-huh," I say. "That sounds reasonable."

Margo snorts. "The president isn't reasonable though, Cat. He's a military lunatic."

I think of what Rafael has been saying, about uprisings and guns and armies. "But a peaceful resolution—"

"There is no such thing," she cuts in flatly. "And Rafael knows it, I think. Taylor says that Eduardo says Rafael is talking to militia groups. And Eduardo is worried."

Taylor says that Eduardo says…it sounds like high-school gossip, like the game Broken Telephone that we used to play as kids. I don't say anything.

"Has Rafael said anything to you?" she asks. "Or do you two not do much talking?"

"Funny," I say. I hesitate before answering, but then I see no reason not to be honest. After all, Rafael certainly isn't keeping his thoughts under wraps. He'll tell anyone who will listen.

"He talks about change," I say carefully. "And he's mentioned uprisings and whatever."

"Uh-huh," she says. Her lips are pursed and she looks worried. "Maybe you should talk to Eduardo."

Now I'm annoyed. I'm not tattling on Rafael, who's been so kind to me. Who's made such an effort, who has been the first good thing to happen to me in ages. What do I care what his politics are?

"I'm not talking to anyone," I say flatly. "Rafael is just trying to do good work for people here, and so am I." I take a final swig from my canteen and screw the cap back on. "I have to go now."

Margo calls after me as I stalk back to the Infirmary, but I ignore her.

. . .

"That feels good." The words escape my lips involuntarily, and I cringe, realizing how silly they must sound in context. Rafael is applying insect repellant to my exposed shoulders, rubbing it in carefully so there are no gaps. He chuckles softly and brushes my hair to one side with his hands.

"You're easy to please, Catalina," he says softly. His breath is hot and tickles my ear. He bends in closer and bites it, gently. "Now only I can bite you." I shudder with desire and lean into him. My entire body feels useless, as if it has turned into a quivering mass of jelly.

Rafael's hands slip under my T-shirt, and he very lightly strokes my stomach with just the tips of his fingers. He hesitates at the bra line, but I shake my head.

"It's okay," I whisper. "Please. Yes."

Encouraged, he explores my breasts with the same delicate touch. I close my eyes, and wonder how they can be the source of both such pleasure and such pain.

Rafael can sense my change in mood. "Are you okay, cariño? I will stop."

"No," I say, feeling frustrated. "It's just—it's my mother."

"Oh," he says. His arms fall to his sides and he reaches to take my hand in his. "Let's sit down."

It's night, and Rafael and I are alone. We've taken to meeting like this when we can. Margo and Taylor don't even bother asking me to walk back to the base after supper. Rafael and I always meet here, in this same spot by the fire, once the others have gone. Our spot. We don't pretend we're studying Spanish anymore.

Wordlessly, I allow Rafael to lead me over to a fallen tree. He pulls me down next to him and touches my cheek. "It's okay, Cat. I understand."

"Margo and Taylor keep telling me to be careful," I say suddenly.

Rafael stiffens, but doesn't pull away. "Why is that?" he asks.

I sigh. "They're worried you're talking about uprisings and stuff. Weapons." I pull back and look at him, my hand on his chest. In the moonlight, his eyes are even darker, barely distinguishable from the blackness of the night around us. I can feel his heart speed up under my hand, the beats closer together now.

"I just want to do what is best for my country and its people," he says. He sounds angry, and I regret bringing it up, spoiling the mood. Somewhere out in the darkness, something shrieks. It's eerily human-sounding, even though I know it must be a bird or a monkey. My skin is riddled with goosebumps.

"We have tried peaceful negotiations. Envoys. Nothing works. Do I let my parents rot in prison forever?" He's nearly shouting now, though he pulls me closer, his hands now tightly grasping my wrists.

I don't how to respond. He's told me this before. "I know," I say finally.

Rafael exhales loudly and loosens his grip. "There are two

camps among us," he says. "Some, like Eduardo, still think this can be done peacefully. But I'm past that."

"What will you do?" I whisper. I take his hand, feel his fingers entwine with mine. I'm not sure I want to know the answer.

"We need help. Money," he says grimly.

"Money." Unwittingly, I picture Rafael emptying a piggy bank, counting quarters and stacking them in little piles. "For weapons, you mean."

Rafael doesn't answer, and I feel my heart sink like a stone tossed into the river.

"Are you still in touch with others?" I ask hesitantly.

"We have—" he pauses, a look of hesitation on his face, "other groups assisting us with this."

"Other groups?" I repeat warily. "What kind of groups?"

"We are not the only group unhappy with the current government," Rafael says carefully.

I can tell he's uncomfortable with this line of discussion. He busies himself with tending to the fire.

"But aren't you afraid?" I pull my knees up to my chest and hug them. "The other groups may have a different agenda. How can you trust them?"

"They have better connections with the outside. With government," he says, not answering my question. "More experience."

"More experience," I say, frowning. "With what?"

He still doesn't look at me. "With this sort of situation."

"You mean war. Weapons. Violence." My voice rings hollow.

Rafael cringes at the word "violence." He touches my cheek, then tucks a loose tendril of hair behind my ear. My mind is brimming with questions. I think of what Margo said earlier: there's no such thing as a peaceful revolution. *Is she right? Is this the only way forward? Is that the real way to do good?* I don't know what to think.

Rafael moves to kiss me again, but the moment is over, the mood spoiled. It feels different, more clinical somehow. Like I'm analyzing kissing for a science project. I don't pull away, but Rafael can sense it and stops.

"I will take you back now," he says. He waits for me to respond, but I just nod, staring at the ground.

• • •

"You were out late last night," Taylor says pointedly. He's already dressed, poised to leave the barracks, when I wake up. He looks so different from when we first met. His hair is almost long again now, and like the locals here, he's sprouting a full beard.

He grabs his canteen and waits, glowering, for me to answer. I look around for Margo, but she must have left early to feed the livestock. Melody, of course, is nowhere to be found. I meet Taylor's fierce gaze and feel a wave of resentment.

"I didn't realize you were in charge of curfews," I snap, fussing with the twisted mosquito net. I try not to tumble head first out of the hammock.

"You were with him, I guess?"

"Rafael? Yeah." I frown. "Why do you care?"

Taylor hesitates. "I'm just worried about you," he says carefully. "Eduardo told me some stuff about him. He can be a bit of a fanatic, with the idealism. He knows Rafael from growing up."

"And?" I say, feeling impatient. I don't like being lectured by Taylor.

"And he didn't deal well when they took his parents, that's all. Eduardo says he's getting restless here. Wants to do more."

I think of his words last night, about his plans to join with more militaristic groups. I don't say anything to Taylor.

"Maybe you just don't know what it's like to lose your parents," I retort instead, my voice trembling.

"Rafael's parents aren't dead," he says patiently. "They're in prison."

"Which I'm sure is a really nice place to be in this country," I shoot back.

"The point is, Eduardo is worried that—"

"Oh, Eduardo," I interject, my voice heavy with sarcasm. "Enough. I don't want to hear any more about wonderful Eduardo."

"Huh?" He stares at me.

"So your boyfriend is trustworthy, but mine isn't?" I'm on my feet now. It's hard to stand in the tent—even at my height, the top of my head skims the rough canvas.

"Boyfriend?" His tone is shocked, defensive. "What the hell are you talking about?"

"Margo told me all about you and Eduardo. I find it really interesting that it's okay for you to get involved with someone here, but there's something wrong with me seeing Rafael."

"Margo doesn't know what the hell she's talking about," snaps Taylor. His face is bright red, as if he's been sunburned.

"I saw you with him yesterday."

"I don't know what you think you saw." He doesn't look at me. "Eduardo is engaged. To a girl," he adds for emphasis.

I watch Taylor's shoulders sag slightly as he conveys this news.

"But you're in love with him," I whisper.

"Don't be stupid." His tone is sharp, but he still won't look at me.

"Then why are you so convinced he's right, and not Rafael?" I sit back down on the edge of my hammock, but I'm still angry.

"Rafael has big plans, Cat. He has other loyalties, responsibilities. I'm not saying he doesn't really like you, I'm just saying you should be careful."

"He wouldn't hurt me." My voice is firm. "And maybe I agree with him. Have you thought of that?"

Taylor stares at me a long moment. He opens his mouth to say something, then closes it, turning to leave. He lifts the tent flap and then changes his mind turns back once more. "Be careful, Cat," he says quietly. He leaves without another word.

I sit staring at the blank tent canvas for ages after that. Anna is waiting for me at the Enfermería, but I remain paralyzed, spooling Taylor's words in my head over and over.

Chapter 17

Before

"I don't want any more chemo." Mom's voice quakes, and she shrinks back in her seat. "It's not going to do anything. I don't expect a miracle. I just don't want to suffer."

"But sweetheart," Dad pipes up, his face ashen. "Shouldn't we at least try? How can we say for sure it's not going to do anything?" He clutches the sides of his chair like a security blanket.

"I have brain cancer." She stares at him flatly. "There is no good outcome here."

We're in the oncologist's office. She's a good doctor, smart without being patronizing or condescending. Instead, she's frank and practical, and doesn't wear a stethoscope around her neck like some sort of status symbol. She's sitting now on the examination table, her legs dangling. She's a bigger woman:

not fat, but broad-shouldered and big-boned, and seeing her like that is disarming.

"I understand," she says now. "I wouldn't want to do it, either."

My father glares at her, his jaw clenching.

"What do most people do?" I interject, before Dad can say anything. I am calm; the Abilify, clearly, is working. I am vaguely aware that this is the sort of conversation that, a week ago, I would have found upsetting. Instead, I just feel numb.

"It really depends." Dr. Allport shrugs slightly. "Some people will try anything—they'll go for the clinical trials as a last hope. Others don't want anything. It's very personal."

"I will not be a guinea pig," my mother quails. The clinical-trial option scares her. She pictures herself as a lab rat in a cage, being injected with glow-in-the-dark poison or whatever. I've tried to explain it's not quite like that, but she's adamant it's not something she wants to pursue, and really, who can blame her? Statistically, the chances of a clinical trial being of any value are probably less than winning the lottery, and the side effects truly suck.

"I can't believe we have to make this decision." My dad is on his feet now, pacing the tiny room. "You're the doctor!"

Dr. Allport's eyes brim with sympathy as she watches him walk the perimeter of her office. "It's a terrible thing," she says simply. "I wish there was an easy answer."

I interject. "What about radiation?" I've done my googling; radiation could be an option here.

The doctor nods, her blunt hair bobbing. "It can be useful

in shrinking the tumor a bit so that the side effects of the brain mets aren't as severe. It wouldn't be curative, but it could help."

I blink at the word "mets." Metastasis. You don't have to be a doctor to know that's a bad word. It should devastate me. I should feel sick at the very word. Intellectually, I know this, but am unable to feel it properly in my medicated haze.

"What are the side effects?" Mom looks wary. She was exhausted during radiation last time, and the skin around her breast became so swollen and inflamed, it looked a bit like she'd grown a third boob.

"You may experience nausea and seizures," Dr. Allport begins, and my mother cuts her off.

"I'm already experiencing those," she says sharply. "How is that helping, then, exactly?"

"That's a fair point," the doctor concedes. "You don't have to do anything right away. You don't have to do anything at all."

"I don't know." Mom buries her face in her hands. "I just don't know what to do."

This isn't the first time we've been here, dissecting our options. We came right away when we got back from San Francisco, and Dr. Allport presented the various possibilities and gave us some reading material. The three of us have been waffling ever since, unsure of what the right thing is. If there is a right thing at all.

"There isn't a right or wrong choice," Dr. Allport says gently, as if reading my mind. "You can also play it by ear. If the symptoms start to get worse, you can always opt for the radiation."

"Maybe that's the best thing," I say. With a considerable effort, I wrench myself out of my Abili-fog and reach over to squeeze Mom's arm. "Maybe we should just wait and see."

Mom looks up. She's tearing up again, the kind of tears that make your eyes large and luminous. She looks so beautiful in a delicate, vulnerable, sort of way, like a character in a Dickens novel suffering from consumption. *As if being eaten from the inside could make you beautiful.* I shudder at the thought.

"I'm sorry, Cat," she whispers. "You shouldn't have to be the one in charge."

"I'm not in charge," I say automatically. I don't want to be in charge. "I'm just trying to help."

"My wonderful little girl." She reaches over and smoothes my hair out of my eyes. "You've been so brave."

I don't want to be brave, either, I want to say. I want to rage and scream and cry and smash everything in this office, starting with the large ceramic pink ribbon hanging on the wall. Pink ribbons make me sick. As if the struggle and suffering of millions of women can somehow be represented by the favorite color of five-year-old girls everywhere. It's infantile and it's silly and I hate the ribbons and all the other pink cancer crap. Breast cancer sucks, and pink spatulas and other assorted kitchen tools and appliances demean the experience of having your breasts lopped off and your hair fall out. But I don't say anything. I try to conjure the rage, just to see if I can, but nothing happens. I don't like it. *Where is the girl who smashed the hockey stick?*

Dr. Allport's eyes follow mine to the ceramic ribbon, and

she gives me a knowing look. "A patient made that for me," she says. "In some kind of pottery class, I believe."

I imagine a thin, frail woman, her bald head bent in concentration as her IV bag thumps against a pottery wheel, and shudder. Relieved at this normal emotional response, I take a deep breath.

"We'll think about the radiation," I say to Dr. Allport. "We don't want the chemo or the clinical trials."

"But—" Dad looks panicked, but Mom stands to face him, taking both his hands in hers. "I'm sorry," she says. "I love you, but I can't do it. I just can't."

He chokes on a sob and collapses against her. She cradles his head and whispers in his ear. I can't hear what she's saying, and I don't want to.

"I'll go make a follow-up appointment and pull the car up front," I say, looking away from them. *I don't want to be brave*, I think again. Calmly, I get out my phone and go out to face the receptionist.

Later, I overturn the bottle of Abilify into the toilet. I want to feel my rage, I know now. I want to grieve and scream and cry. It's my right. With a certain satisfaction, I pull the lever and watch the tiny blue pills as they are forcibly pulled down the drain.

• • •

"The dissection kits are at the front. Please take only one per pair to ensure we have enough." Mrs. Carlisle motions wearily towards the chalkboard, where thirteen little black-leather cases are neatly stacked on a rolling cart. "And make sure you wear your lab coats."

I button my lab coat and roll up the sleeves, while Tess eyes the fetal pig in front of us with an expression of blatant disgust. "I don't know if I can do this," she says weakly.

"It's fine. I'll handle the actual dissection. You just make the notes." I nod toward Mrs. Carlisle. "Go get us a kit."

"Yes, boss." Tess snaps a salute and makes a final face at the pig before turning away towards the front of the room, where the rowdier boys are cracking loud and obnoxious jokes about bacon. Mrs. Carlisle tells them off, going on about respect for the porcine specimens, but her comments fall upon deaf ears.

I examine our own pig, trying not to think of how it came to be lying here in a shallow pan before me. A quote from English class—we've just finished *Macbeth*—comes to mind. Something about being untimely ripped from a mother's womb. I stare at its tiny piglet face, its eyes closed, never to open, and feel a wave of sadness.

"Why does it look like that?" Tess is back. She drops the dissection kit on the lab bench with an unceremonious thud and pokes at the pig with the back of her pen.

"Like what? A pig?"

"Like it's plastic. Or rubber." She pokes it again. "It feels kind of rubbery, too."

"It's probably from the formaldehyde," I say. "Or maybe because it's a fetus. I don't know."

"I feel kind of bad for it." Tess points at the head with the pen. "Look at the little ears."

Tess is right: there is something sad about the tiny, pointed ears. I have a sudden, bizarre urge to pat it on the head, like a kitten.

"Stop," I say instead. "It's bad enough without having feelings for the pig."

"Sorry," she says. "I just…I won't talk."

I reach for the scalpel, my hands shaking slightly. Coming off the Abilify hasn't been easy—especially since I'm doing it without medical supervision, ignoring the warning on the bottle. Taking a deep breath, I follow Mrs. Carlisle's instructions and make a small incision at the head and continue down the spine. The skin cuts easily; it's like slicing into a pie. I peel back the flaps of skin and peer inside. The air reeks of formaldehyde, and I try not to gag.

"Okay," I say, businesslike. "Do you see the vertebrae?"

"I guess," Tess answers, swallowing hard.

Mrs. Carlisle walks by and peers over my shoulder. "Nice incision, Caitlin," she says approvingly. "You're a natural."

Natural what? I wonder. *Dead pig desecrater? Butcher?*

"Future surgeon, perhaps," she goes on. She leans in. "Do the cranial region next, before you turn the pig to examine its ventral side."

"Okay," I say, carefully pulling the skin back from the pig's head. "Tess, I need you to hold this back."

"Oh, God." Tess takes an instrument from the kit and places it where I'm gesturing to keep the skin away. Her fingers tremble, and she looks distinctly like she might pass out at any moment.

"Just don't look," I say, impatient.

I press harder, to delve into the cranial area. I insert the scalpel to lift out the brain and place it cautiously in the pan. We stare at the squiggly ball of mush. Tess's eyes are still open; she's repelled and drawn to look at the same time. "Brains," she whispers, shuddering.

I inhale and cut into the brain. We've been instructed to slice into it, so that we can examine the various regions: the corpus callosum, cerebellum, cerebrum. I poke around, trying to decipher which is which.

Across the room, Brian McAlister holds up his pig brain in triumph. "Look at this, Stephenson!" he shouts. "I bet it's twice the size of yours!"

Brad Stephenson gives him the finger. "And its schlong is twice the size of yours, McAsshole."

"That's enough!" Mrs. Carlisle raps a desk with a ruler. "Respect! Next person who shouts out goes directly to Mr. Stanley's office."

The class quiets down, and I turn back to the task of labeling the brain. It's a challenge: the brain is so much softer, so much more delicate, than I would have guessed. Given its important role, I always imagined it would be tough and hardy, but it isn't at all. It reminds me of Jell-O.

I make another cut and then pry gently at what I think is the cerebrum. Suddenly I wonder where Mom's tumor is, and I struggle to ignore the thought. Instead, I grab the clipboard with the instructions and diagrams and try to compare those with what is in front of me.

It's no use. I imagine an octopus-like creature—a childish but still somehow terrifying image of Ursula the Sea Witch from *The Little Mermaid* comes to mind—with tentacles snaking through my mother's brain.

"Are you okay, Cat?" Tess peers at me, anxious.

"Fine," I say quickly, but I am not fine. My hands are shaking again. I make another incision and my hand slips, chopping the brain clear in half at the completely wrong angle.

"Damn!" I drop the scalpel with a clatter. I've ruined our specimen. "I screwed it up!"

"It doesn't matter." Tess gestures around her. "People are messing up all over the place. We just have to do the best we can."

"No!" I retort. I stare at the ruined brain before me, full of despair. "It has to be perfect!"

"It really doesn't." Tess looks worried now. "Are you sure you're all right, Cat? Maybe—"

"I ruined it!" My voice is louder now, shrill. "I wrecked the brain!"

Tess's lower lip trembles. "I'm going to get Mrs. Carlisle."

I stand motionless, my eyes fixed on the unraveling mass of gray matter before me. There's no going back; it's ruined. Spoiled. Destroyed. There's no putting a brain back together once it's come apart. Slowly, I lift my scalpel and, with a noise that is half-scream, half-moan, I bring it down hard on the remnants of the pig brain. Again and again, I stab at it, enjoying the sensation of the knife as it cuts like butter through the cerebrum and cerebellum and whatever else. My entire body is shaking now, and I can feel the tears stream down my face, hot and sticky.

Tess is crying beside me, her hands on my shoulders. "Cat!" she says, stifling a sob. "Please, Cat. Stop."

I am vaguely aware of the rest of the class watching me, silent and open-mouthed, as Mrs. Carlisle rushes over and gently coaxes the scalpel out of my hand. She puts an arm around me and ushers me out of the room. In the office, calls are made for someone to come and get me, but there is no one to come. Mom is no longer allowed to drive, and Dad is teaching today. Finally, Mr. Stanley, the principal, comes out and softly speaks my name.

"Am I suspended?" I ask in a small voice.

"No, Cat." His eyes are full of pity. "I'm here to drive you home."

• • •

"So you attacked the brain." Dr. Shapiro touches his beard. "How did that make you feel?"

"Honestly?" I sit back on the fake-leather couch with force and cross my arms. "I don't even really remember it."

"Is that so?" He leans forward. "Can you explain that a bit more?"

"Um…no." I stare at him. "I just went sort of crazy."

"Like with the hockey stick?"

I shrug. "I guess."

Dr. Shapiro looks at me intently. It's unnerving, so I shift my gaze to the wall, where his medical degree hangs next to a copy of Vincent van Gogh's *The Starry Night*.

I nod at the painting. "Like van Gogh."

"What do you mean by that, Cat?" He rubs his beard again. This time, I picture birds mistaking it for a nest and laying their eggs deep inside. Maybe I just prefer thinking about Dr. Shapiro's beard rather than all the things that bring me here.

"Didn't he go all crazy and cut off his ear?"

The doctor frowns. "I wish you would stop using the word crazy."

I shrug, indifferent. "Whatever you call it, it's still crazy."

"Crazy is a pejorative term," he says primly.

"Whatever you call it, that will end up being the bad word eventually," I say, scowling now. "Hysterical and insane were the proper words once upon a time. One day people will say the same thing about 'mental illness.'"

"Interesting point." He nods appreciatively. "But let's get back to the dissection incident."

"I'd rather not." I lean forward, cupping my chin with my hands. "It was pretty humiliating. People are avoiding me at school now like I have Ebola."

"I imagine that's very difficult for you." He scribbles something on his clipboard. "High school can be a pretty unforgiving place."

"Well, it would be a lot worse if I actually cared," I admit. "Fortunately, popularity is way down on my list of concerns right now."

Dr. Shapiro slides his glasses back up his sweaty nose. "How is your friend Tess?"

"She's been amazing," I say truthfully. "She's always there for me."

He nods. "Social support is very important. You may want to consider talking with a group, with others like yourself. They can be very helpful."

"What, a support group for kids whose parents are dying of cancer? No, thank you." I shudder at the thought. My own grief was almost too much to bear. I couldn't take on anyone else's right now.

"You'd be surprised at how much better you might feel if you spoke to someone your own age who's experiencing the same thing."

"No." I shake my head adamantly, my ponytail flying back and forth. "I can't handle their stories. I don't want to hear them. Not now."

He sighs and writes down something else. I wonder if he's describing me as uncooperative.

He does the glasses thing again and turns back a page in my file. "How's the Abilify going so far?"

Down the toilet, with gusto, I answer silently. It didn't help. Not only did I not feel better, I felt nauseous and slow and had already put on two pounds. Watching the pills make their way down the drain was one of the first enjoyable moments I'd had in weeks.

"Fine," I say. "It makes me nauseous and slow and fat."

"Fat?" He frowns and begins flipping through my file. I

don't have to be clairvoyant to know he's searching for evidence I have an eating disorder.

"I'm not anorexic," I say, exasperated. "I just don't want to put on weight for no reason. If I'm going to pack it on, I want it to be because I ate, like, sixty Reese's Peanut Butter Cups."

"But it's not 'no reason.'" Shapiro is still frowning. "You're taking medication, to help you."

"Yeah, yeah." I don't say anything else. *If I complain too much, he might realize what I've done with the pills.*

He consults his notes again. "How is the irritable bowel syndrome?"

I shift in my seat, slightly uncomfortable at discussing poo with this aging hippie. "The same."

"So you're still experiencing the diarrhea."

"Yeah. But it's fine. It's under control."

"There's a new drug—"

"Forget it," I snap. "I'm fine with my Imodium. I don't want any more new drugs. It's enough."

"I'm only trying to help," he says calmly. He makes another note, and I'm sure he's writing that I have an anger-management problem and am difficult to control. I hope my file is confidential.

He continues talking. "How is the sleep?"

"What sleep," I mutter. Which isn't exactly fair; I do sleep, only I can't manage it without the meds, which I'm not sure really counts. It doesn't feel the same as normal sleep, but it's better than the alternative of lying awake all night, wondering what it will be like to bury my mother under a heap of dirt.

"The pills don't help?" He looks surprised.

"They do. It's just that I can't sleep without them." I look over and notice for the first time a picture on his desk of a young girl, about my age. It must be his daughter. She looks surprisingly normal. Pretty, even. She looks happy.

He follows my gaze. "That's my daughter, Stephanie," he says. "Her mom died when she was six. Brain aneurysm. That's how I got into this field."

I feel myself go hot with shame, as if I've stuck my head in a hot oven. "I'm sorry," I murmur.

"Thank you." He nods, and pulls out his prescription pad. "So, more of the sleeping medication, then?"

I nod silently, taking the slip of paper and pocketing it.

"I'll see you in two weeks," he says.

I turn to leave, but he stops me. He's on his feet, rummaging around his messy desk.

"Here's some information on those support groups," he says, pressing a pamphlet into my hands. "Just in case you change your mind."

"Okay," I say. "Thanks."

Outside, I intend to toss it into the nearest trashcan, but when I reach one, I don't. I hold it over, ready to drop it in, but at the last second I change my mind. I shove the pamphlet into my bag.

Chapter 18

After

"Maybe Taylor's just jealous," Margo says thoughtfully. We're swimming together, in the river. It's a murky brown, a bit like chocolate milk, and while we were initially terrified of the river and its collection of things unseen, we like to rinse off midday when we can. We bring soap from the village. It's homemade from some sort of local palm oil, and smells strongly of violets.

She passes me a small sliver after rubbing some in her own hair. "He's clearly in love with Eduardo, and unfortunately Eduardo doesn't swing that way." She pauses to dunk her sudsy hair in the water, careful not to expose her eyes. Margo has come a long way, but she's still wary of parasites in the water. "They burrow into your eyes," she's informed us grimly on many occasions. "Eat them from the inside out."

I lather up as best I can with the soap; it's not exactly Ivory or Dial. I skip my hair. Margo's hair is naturally shiny, but washing my hair with soap leaves it dry and dull and flyaway.

"Not," adds Margo, grabbing a torn piece of cloth as a makeshift towel, "that I don't think Rafael is kind of crazy. Sofia says he's got great intentions, but he's talking to the wrong people."

I think of Rafael's conviction that you can't have change without some sort of major upheaval, even if that means violence. But then I think of the doctors who enthusiastically pumped my mother's veins full of poison. I know all about good intentions, and the road to hell. Sometimes, it can be hard to know what is the right path to take.

"They're middle-class kids here, mostly," Margo goes on. "Most of them don't have the stomach for violence and the rest of it."

"Rest of it?" I scan the water warily for snakes before quickly dunking my head beneath the water. It's a bit like bathing in warm coffee. I squeeze my eyes and mouth shut.

"Drugs," she says when I resurface, as if it's obvious. "Hasn't Rafael told you?"

"Apparently not," I answer carefully. I wring the water from my hair.

"Drug trafficking," she explains. Her tone is matter-of-fact. "Cocaine. Whoever controls the trafficking routes controls Calantes."

"I know a little bit," I say, thinking of Anna's history lessons. "What about it?"

Margo wriggles into her clothes, skin still damp. She's in a borrowed pair of pants and an ancient looking T-shirt from one of her chicken-murdering friends. Both are too big on her. In oversized clothes and makeup-free, she looks much younger. With her hair wet and loose, she could pass for fourteen.

"To get ahead, they'll need to link up with one of the rebel trafficking factions," she explains. "And that means dirtying their hands. Drugs. Weapons. This isn't a fight that's going to be won through televised debates and tax-break promises, and our friends here are afraid."

I remember Rafael's comments about other groups. *Is that what he was referring to? Drug traffickers?* Despite the warm water and humid air, I suddenly feel cold. The medication-seeking raiders seem tame in comparison to professional drug cartels. *Do I tell Margo?*

"Have you done it yet?" asks Margo, abruptly changing the subject.

"Done what?" I ask, guarded. I'm still in the water, naked from the waist up, trying to French-braid my hair. I don't look at her.

Margo rolls her eyes. "It," she says meaningfully. "You know. With Rafael."

Oh. I blush so hard my whole body feels like it's turning pink. Embarrassed, I drop down in the water to my chin. "No," I mutter.

Margo quickly twists her hair into a knot and studies me. "You've never done it, have you," she says.

"No," I admit.

Margo raises her eyebrows. "Are you waiting for something in particular?"

I shrug. "Yes. No. I don't know."

Margo continues, grinning. "A date at a five-star restaurant? Jewelry? Violins?"

"Violins?"

"Yeah, you know." Margo mimes playing the violin. "Like, music in the background. Serenading you out of your pants."

I stick my tongue out at her. "Very funny." I frown, trying to find the right words. "I just haven't done it yet. No reason. I haven't had a lot of time for guys the last couple of years. You know, with my mom." At the thought of my mom, I feel the usual crushing pain in my chest. It burgeons there, before slowly spreading to my shoulders and radiating down my arms. I read once that these are the symptoms of a heart attack, and I wonder idly if whoever coined the term broken heart suffered from a grief-related cardiac arrest.

"Shit. That really sucks."

"Yeah, well." I shrug. I don't feel like talking about it. "What can you do."

I stand up again and finish my braid, then emerge from the water. When my clothes are back on, I sit down next to Margo, who is drawing in the dirt with a stick. I peer over her shoulder.

"It's a macaw," she says. She moves the stick lightly across the sand, shading. "I saw one earlier. It landed right near me, but then it flew away."

I watch silently as she works, her eyebrows furrowed in concentration as the stick moves back and forth expertly.

"You're really talented," I tell her, awed by the delicacy of her work. "That's beautiful."

"I love to draw," she says quietly. "I wanted to be an art major."

"Why didn't you?" I watch her deft hands work their magic, her eyes alive and focused.

"I have to go to medical school, Cat." She smiles bitterly. "I can still paint, right? I'll paint after surgery, my mom says. No big deal."

I feel a wave of sadness for Margo, trapped between what she wants and what her parents expect. I don't know what the right answer is. Once upon a time, I would have said she should follow her art, and her dream, but dreams don't always come true. Usually they don't come true. Would Margo be happy as a starving artist? Now that we've seen starving—real starving—does it seem less romantic? I pose the question to Margo, who seems startled.

"Maybe you're right." She freezes mid-sketch and stares at me.

"I'm not trying to be annoying," I add hastily. "I just—"

"No, you're probably right." She shakes her head. "All this time here, and I'm still a privileged brat. Think Anna would whine about going to medical school?"

"Maybe it doesn't have to be medical school," I suggest. "Maybe there's a way to compromise."

Margo resumes her drawing. "Maybe," she says with a shrug.

"You've done a lot of good here," I add, trying to be encouraging.

She snorts. "I kill chickens, Cat. It's hardly brain surgery."

You're the one doing the important work. Have you thought about medicine?"

Medicine. I don't think of the Enfermería; I think of the doctors and hospitals that dominated my life over the last two years. *Could I do that? Be one of them?*

Margo finishes her sketch. It's beautiful, so lifelike. I touch her arm. "It's wonderful," I say, my breath catching. "It looks so real. Like it could take off and fly away."

Margo looks at me, and then stands. She sweeps her bare foot across the drawing, erasing it.

"Why?" I manage, stunned.

She shrugs. "It flew away," she says. "Let's go."

. . .

"Why do you braid your hair?" Rafael tugs on the elastic holding the end of my braid, releasing it. He runs his hand through the plait, unraveling it slowly. "It is so beautiful around your face like this."

I smile self-consciously as he tucks a still-damp wave behind my ear. He's been to the river too, and his curls are damp and smell of soap and something else that is uniquely Rafael. I inhale deeply, intoxicated by his scent. We are alone together in his tent. It's my first time here; usually we head to the fire late at night to chat privately, but it is raining tonight, and he suggested I come here. Unlike most, he has his own space. It's much like the one Anna and I use as a makeshift hospital, only smaller and with little personalized touches—a picture of his family tacked to the top beam and a pile of books in the corner. I glance at the one on top. It's Dostoevsky, in Spanish.

"Any news?" I ask casually. "Talk to any other groups today?"

Rafael shakes his head, and takes my hand, bringing me a bit closer. "Not yet," he says. *Do I push?* I wonder. *Do I ask about the drug traffickers?*

"You smell nice," Rafael says softly, moving toward me. He lifts a strand of my hair and twists it around his finger.

"I was just thinking that about you!" I watch as he releases the hair, which still holds the shape of his finger.

"What do I smell like, Catalina?" He puts a hand on my waist and draws me closer to him.

"Like soap and…like you." I struggle to describe it. "Like wood smoke and peppermint and spices. Cloves, maybe."

He laughs, burying his face in my neck. "You have…how do you say it? A way with words, cariño."

I blush, feeling silly, but quickly let it go as he nibbles at the space between my neck and shoulder. I gasp, feeling it in every square inch of my body.

"I wish to kiss you on all the places of your body," he whispers. He bends and lifts my shirt, dropping tiny kisses all over my belly. I moan softly as his mouth moves across my navel.

"Don't stop." Thinking of my earlier conversation with Margo, I pull my T-shirt over my head and toss it aside.

He looks at me, hesitant. "You are certain?" he asks. His hands travel up to my shoulders, and he runs his fingertips gently down my arms.

I shiver with pleasure. "Yes," I say firmly. "Yes."

He leans in to kiss me. I wrap my arms around his neck, and allow myself to be lowered onto his makeshift bed.

There are no violins, but I hear music all the same.

• • •

When I awake, I expect to feel different. Changed, somehow. I stare at my naked arms as if my skin should show some tangible evidence of last night. However, with the exception of a few extra mosquito bites, I look the same.

Rafael is no longer beside me, but sitting at the foot of the bed, staring at the tent wall. He looks deep in thought. I crawl over and put a hand on his shoulder.

"Hey," I say softly.

He jumps slightly, then relaxes, placing my hand over his. "Cat."

His voice sounds strained.

"Is something wrong?" I ask, concerned.

He exhales loudly. "The president executed a group of prisoners last night." He buries his face in his hands. "I think my father might have been one of them."

"Oh, Rafael." I curl up into his back and wrap my arms around him. His skin is cool, despite the morning humidity. "How do you know? Are you sure?"

"I need to speak with Eduardo," he says, rising abruptly. "He can check the newsfeeds. I only know what's been on the radio."

He pulls on a shirt and pants, and I become acutely aware of my nudity. Feeling awkward, I grab the sheet from the edge of the mattress and pull it up to my shoulders. "Is there anything I can do?" I ask lamely. I'm reminded of people's response to my mother's cancer, the meaningless and oft-repeated "let me know if I can help." I feel useless.

He stares at me a moment. "Maybe," he says. "Cat, if you could, would you help me? Would you help Calantes?"

"Of course," I say. I think of the children on the side of the road, of Anna's bravery, of Rafael himself. "Of course I would."

He squeezes my hand and runs a lone finger down my arm. "I will see you later," he says, turning away to pull on his boots.

He's partway out the door before he turns back and drops a perfunctory kiss on my forehead. Confused, it is some time before I slowly dress and make my way to work.

• • •

I'm with Rafael again the next night, and the one after. Taylor is full of disapproving glances and warning words, but I ignore them. Rafael needs me. His father is on the lists that have appeared on the Darknet. He has spent the days shut in his tent in near-darkness. The nights he spends with me, attacking me with a passion and ferocity born of grief.

"I know," I whisper, clinging to him. I run my fingers through his hair, which is slick with sweat, and shush him the way I would a baby. His weeping is unpredictable, starting and stopping with no obvious pattern. I remember that feeling acutely. In the days after my mother's death, I would be calm and reasonable, speaking with funeral directors and choosing a headstone. Then the reality would set back in and I would find myself huddled in the shower, screaming as the water rained down. I vividly recalled clutching a pink Bic razor and wondering if it was sharp enough to inflict the sort of damage that would end the pain. At those moments, the suffering seemed too much to bear, like it would be easier to just give in and stop it.

"They will pay," repeats Rafael, over and over. "They will suffer, like I have."

"Yes," I say soothingly, because I don't know what else to do. I have the experience to know that words are meaningless when you've reached a certain level of utter despair. Instead, I bring him closer to me.

He mutters something in Spanish that I can't quite understand, then switches back to English. His accent is more pronounced when he's upset, and at first I don't catch what he's said.

"The only way to stop him is to play his game," says Rafael grimly. Warily, I stroke his chest.

"Don't say that," I say softly. "You don't want to sink to his level."

Rafael laughs harshly. "Sometimes," he says ominously, "one cannot afford to take the moral high ground."

Uneasily, I lace his hands through mine. *What does he mean?* I start to ask, but before I can form the words, the weeping starts again.

"Come here, Cat," he says, pulling me to him almost roughly. "Help me make the pain stop."

Wordlessly, I move closer.

Chapter 19

Before

"We don't have to do this," I say, eyeing my mom warily through the mirror. I watch as she carefully applies her eyeliner, hand trembling ever so slightly. "Not if you're not up for it."

"Don't be stupid, Cat." My mother grins and reaches for a plum-colored lipstick. "This is finally something I want to do. I wouldn't miss this for anything."

We're going shopping together for a prom dress. I want to tell her I don't want to go to the prom, that it now seems trite as well as inappropriate, that I don't have a date, because everyone at school is afraid of me, and, most importantly, that I am no longer capable of having fun. But I don't say anything, because she is so excited about this, and I don't have it in me to disappoint her.

"I see you in a delicate fabric, like *peau de soie*," she says dreamily. She brushes her hair gently with a tiny comb. It's still soft and fine, like a baby's, but it's hers. The wig is at the back of her closet, tossed haphazardly on a shelf. I try not to go in there, as it scares me. It's like seeing my mother's disembodied head lying there with the sewing kit and her flip-flops.

"I don't know what that is," I say warily. "I don't want you to spend a lot. We don't have to drive all the way to Cleveland. We can go to Miranda's—"

Mom makes a face. "My daughter is not getting her prom dress at Miranda's," she declares, dismissing the local dress shop with a wave of her hand. "We're going to Cleveland, and we'll spend an absolute fortune if we have to. And you can't argue with me, because I have cancer."

I don't know whether to laugh or cry. I grab a lip gloss from her vanity and apply some. It's tinted a raspberry shade, and tastes of vanilla.

Mom studies me critically. "That doesn't suit you," she says, handing me a tissue. "Try this one." She rummages around and pulls out a sheer pink lipstick.

She's right; this one is much better. It brightens my skin and brings out the blue in my eyes.

"See?" she says smugly. "I always know these things."

Don't leave me, I want to scream. *I need you. I don't even know how to choose lipstick. I don't know what* peau de soie *is!* But this is a happy day, so I don't cry or shout. Instead, I lean forward and kiss the top of my mother's downy head.

"You look beautiful," I say. "Let's go."

...

The drive to Cleveland takes us a little over an hour. Mom puts on her favorite classic rock station, and we roll down the windows and sing along to familiar tunes by the Beatles and Eric Clapton. I drive; Mom voluntarily relinquished her license when we returned from San Francisco. It feels weird to be in the driver's seat. When I first got my learner's permit, I accidentally drove up on the curb and nearly crashed into a post, with Mom in the passenger seat, shrieking. She refused to drive with me after that, leaving my driver's ed to Dad. Since getting sick, though, she hasn't made any negative comments about my chauffeuring abilities, other than to ask if she can have control over the radio. It's as if our roles have reversed, with me as the parent, and her as the teenaged daughter, lounging in the passenger seat and complaining about my crappy choice in music.

"How do you think you'll wear your hair?"

"Huh?" My eyes flicker to a sign on the freeway indicating we're two exits away from our destination.

"Your hair." Mom reaches out and touches it gently. "Were you thinking up or down?"

"Uh, I hadn't really thought about it." *I haven't thought about any of this*, I add silently. *Because I don't really want to go.*

"I think you should wear it down," she says. "It's so pretty down. You have your whole life to wear it up, but you can really only wear it long like this when you're young."

"Okay," I say automatically. "I'll wear it down, then."

"We can put rollers at the bottom, if you want," she offers. "Give it a Kate Middleton look."

"Sure," I say. "Do you think you could get it to look like that?" "For sure," she says eagerly. "And I'll do your makeup. We'll make your eyes look huge and glamorous."

"Okay," I say, smiling. For the first time, I feel a small twinge of excitement. When I was little, I'd beg her to put makeup on me, to make me look like Ariel or Cinderella, and sometimes she would agree. I would be almost breathless with excitement as she'd delicately apply the tiniest bit of eye shadow or lip gloss. Afterward, I'd stare in the mirror, mesmerized at my transformation, while my dad muttered about gender stereotyping to Mom and she rolled her eyes in his direction good-naturedly.

I park as close to the door as I can—Mom is tired these days, and I don't want to wear her out before we even get to the mall. It's a handicapped spot; we got the permit a few days ago. It feels strange, but neither of us says anything.

It's a surprisingly fun morning. I try on dozens of dresses in a handful of stores, while Mom examines me critically from all angles, snapping photos and making notes on her phone. "We'll try on everything, and then we can go through and pick the best one," she explains, as I pose in a lavender taffeta gown. She circles me and frowns. "Not your color," she says. Relieved, I unzip it. It made me feel like a parade float.

We stop for frappuccinos, which are my mom's absolute favorite thing. I order her a huge one, topped with whipped cream and drizzled chocolate.

"I can't manage this whole thing!" she protests when she sees it. "Look at all that whipped cream!"

"Eat it," I say. "Who cares?"

I've ordered myself a smaller one, but tell the barista not to spare the whipped cream on mine, either. Worrying about calories became less of an issue for me watching Mom unable to eat during chemo. The day may come when I can't eat, and I don't want to waste my life skipping out on all the little treats that bring me a taste of happiness day-to-day.

We sip our drinks slowly, people-watching in the huge mall food court. Our town has a mall, of course, but the whole place is about the size of the Neiman Marcus in this one. When I was a kid, I used to love coming here. I'd save my allowance or birthday money to buy myself a new book or pair of ear-rings, carrying it in my little purse, feeling impossibly excited and grown up. My favorite part was handing the cashier the money myself, just like an adult. I smile at the memory and use my straw as a spoon to scoop up some of the remaining whipped cream.

"Doesn't that girl go to your school?" Mom nods and points discreetly a few yards away, where Kayla Moffat is walk-ing with her mother and younger sister. Kayla and I aren't friends; she's the Pep Squad type, and I'm the sort who sneaks out or fakes sick during pep rallies. Her mother and I make eye contact and she nudges Kayla, whispering. I groan inwardly. I don't want to talk to her.

"Cat!" Kayla rushes forward, a smile plastered across her face. "How are you?"

"Fine," I reply. I stare down at my frappuccino, stirring it unnecessarily.

Mrs. Moffat and Mom exchange phony pleasantries, while Kayla and I stare at each other, awkward. Every so often, Kayla's eyes flicker in my mother's direction. Her eyes are full of pity.

"Bye, Caitlin," Mrs. Moffat says after a moment, pulling Kayla along with her. "Nice to see you both." My mom waves politely, but I don't look up. Instead, I poke angrily at my cup.

"You didn't have to be so rude," Mom says mildly. "Do you not get along with Kayla?"

I shrug. "I don't really give a crap about her either way."

"Cat." She looks at me, surprised. "What's wrong?"

I push my drink away. "I hate the way they look at us!"

Mom's expression softens. "They're just trying to be nice," she says quietly. "People don't know what to say."

"I wish they'd just leave us alone!" It comes out louder than I expected. A group of middle-schoolers next to us move their chairs farther away. "I don't want their pity."

"Forget it," says Mom. She reaches over and squeezes my hand. "Let's not ruin this. I'm having such a good time."

"I'm sorry," I say, angry at myself for upsetting her. "Of course."

I pick a safe topic—shoes—while she finishes her drink. She brightens immediately, chattering cheerfully about how killer I'll look in a pair of high heels. I flinch at her choice of adjective, wondering how she does it. *How can she shut the big C out of the picture with such swiftness and ease. I envy her.*

Our last stop is Cara's, a pricey boutique that sells bridal and evening wear. I don't want to go in—the dress on the mannequin looks like it might have cost the same as our car—but Mom pulls me in, drawn to the silk dress in the softest of pinks.

"Oh, Cat." She fingers the hem, breathless. "Look at this."

I find the tag and cough. "Mom," I say, showing it to her. "We can't afford that."

"It's just money," she says sharply. She reaches up and retrieves a dress in my size, holds it against me still on the hanger. "It's perfect," she says. She thrusts it at me. "Try it on."

Obediently, I grab the hanger and enter the change room, expertly stripping down. I've done it so many times today, I can now shed my jeans in a record thirty seconds. Carefully, I slip into the dress, open the door. Mom's face transforms when she sees me.

"Oh, Cat," she says again. "This is it. It's perfect."

I stare at myself in the mirror while she zips me up. The bodice is strapless and clingy, with inverted pleats at the waist. The bottom is full and swishes gently when I move. I look beautiful, but it's more than that. It's a special dress, and I look special in it, not just like a teenager headed to prom.

"Please tell me you like it." She looks at me, pleading. "You have to like it."

I can't stop staring. "I love it," I manage. "It's beautiful."

"You're beautiful," she says. She grips my hands, her eyes full of tears. She's looking beyond me, and I turn around to see the display of veils.

"I'm sorry," she says quickly. "I just—"

"Don't," I say quietly.

We stand there, gazing at my reflection, at the lovely pink gown. I start to cry, and then she does too, and then neither of us can stop. A saleslady comes over, but then thinks better of it and backs away.

"Careful," Mom says. She snorts with a mixture of laughter and tears. "Snot is notoriously hard to get out of silk."

We take the dress. The saleslady packs it up for us warily, clearly uncomfortable at our tandem outburst. My mom pays and hands me the bag, eyes shining with happiness and tears.

"For you, Cat," she says. "Thank you for today."

I take the bag, hugging her tightly. I didn't know it was possible to feel so happy and so sad at the same time.

• • •

Tess watches as I slam my locker shut. It's perpetually messy, overflowing with books and papers and unwashed gym clothes, so it usually needs a good bang to get it properly closed. She leans against Morgan Masterson's locker, and regards me critically.

"So you let your mom spend a fortune on a dress and you have no intention of going to the prom." She frowns, her arms crossed against her chest.

"She won't know," I say feebly. "I'll get dressed and stuff as if I'm going, and then I'll, like, go hang out at Starbucks or something."

"Or you could, you know, just go to prom." Tess shakes her head and lowers her voice. "Have you talked to Dr. Shapiro about this?"

"No." I'm annoyed now. "What does he have to do with any of it?"

"Caitlin." Tess uses my full name, which is a sign she means serious business. "You're planning to lie to your sick mother about going to the prom, then hide in a coffee shop for five hours in a party dress with your hair done."

"I could change." I don't look at her.

"Not the point, and you know it." She sighs. "Why don't you just come to the damn prom? You can come with me and Jake."

Jake Rothman is Tess's prom date and on-again, off-again boyfriend. Right now, they are off, but have agreed to attend prom together for practical reasons. He's a decent enough guy, but has a tendency to neglect Tess in favor of his fantasy football league, which is both rude and kind of sad and depressing, all at the same time.

"I don't want to be a third wheel," I say, even though my reluctance has nothing to do with her and Jake.

Tess shakes her head vehemently. "As if," she says, making a face. "I am never letting that idiot touch me again. We're going as friends."

I don't say anything. I guarantee that, by the end of prom night, Tess and Jake will be hooking up at some lame after-prom party.

"I mean it this time," she says, as if reading my mind. "Just friends."

"Uh-huh." I glance at my phone. "I'm going to be late for English. See you later?"

"Okay. But think about it. You should come with us."

. . .

I settle into my desk in English class, wedging my backpack under my seat. I nod hello at the teacher and at Kevin Chang, who sits next to me and who also always does the readings. It's an AP class, but there are only a handful of us who seem to actually read the books and the plays. Everyone else is happy to rely on Cliff Notes and Wikipedia.

Mrs. Arnold claps her hands to get our attention, and leans at her podium with a battered copy of *Hamlet*, which we've been studying for weeks. I love Shakespeare, and *Hamlet* is by the far my favorite of his plays. My dad being an English professor, I've been a Shakespeare devotee since before I could even read.

"As I'm sure you've noticed, one of the themes of *Hamlet* is madness." Mrs. Arnold flips open her book and begins to read: "O, that this too too solid flesh would melt / Thaw and resolve itself into a dew! / Or that the Everlasting had not fix'd / His canon 'gainst self-slaughter! / O God! God! / How weary, stale, flat and unprofitable, / Seem to me all the uses of this world!"

Someone in the back snickers, and Mrs. Arnold taps on the podium. "Mr. Seligman," she snaps. "Care to explain why you find that particular passage so humorous?"

I turn around. Matt Seligman, football quarterback and unabashed dumb-jock caricature, shrugs his shoulders. "It just sounds, you know, really crazy."

"How so?" Mrs. Arnold presses, waiting.

"Well it sounds like he wants to kill himself or something." Matt shrugs again. "That's pretty crazy, right? Only crazy people kill themselves."

The teacher nods, looking thoughtful. "Does anyone want to comment on that?"

No one puts up a hand, so I do.

"Miss Marks?" Mrs. Arnold points at me.

"He's upset," I say sharply. "His father just died, and his mother isn't much help. He's in mourning, and he can't help but wonder what it's all for, why he should bother going on. Why is that crazy?"

"Interesting, Caitlin." Mrs. Arnold nods encouragingly. "Continue."

"Well, everyone always wants to know: was Hamlet crazy, or was he faking it." I frown, trying to find the right words. "But what's so crazy about what you just read to us? He just sounds depressed. He's experienced tragedy. He feels alone. Is it really madness to think about death when your father's just died?"

"Depression is kind of crazy, though, isn't it?" It's Matt Seligman again. "I mean, those commercials for Prozac or whatever. They say it's a disease, right?"

Mrs. Arnold starts to say something, but I cut her off. "So if someone is unhappy about something really crappy in their life, that's a disease now? What isn't a disease, then?" I'm on a roll now. "When did grief and sadness and anger become medical conditions?"

Everyone is staring at me. There are people whispering—I can see Kelly Ellerton murmuring something to Tad Schaffer.

Obviously they're talking about my mom, and about me, and the hockey stick and the pig and whatever else. But I don't care.

"I mean, it's like *Catcher in the Rye* all over again." I can't make myself stop talking. "Holden's brother dies of leukemia, and he's depressed and angry and full of angst, all which seem pretty normal to me, and then there's all this is-he-or-isn't-he about being "crazy," whatever that means." I make little quotation marks with my fingers when I say crazy. I'm starting to hate the word, which makes me feel like Dr. Shapiro.

Mrs. Arnold looks a bit wary—I'm sure there's a picture of me with a big "warning" sign in the staffroom—but also excited. She rarely gets us engaged in any real discussion. "That's an excellent comparison, Caitlin," she says. "Hamlet and Holden have a lot in common. Both experience great personal tragedies, and both react to it in such a way that we, the readers, are left to wonder about their sanity."

Kevin Chang speaks up. "I agree with Cat," he says, looking at me. "We've hit a point where we medicalize, like, everything. Like the commercials Matt mentioned. Sure, some people have severe depression, but I'd bet a lot of the people who take those drugs don't fall into that category. I mean, when did feeling shitty start needing a prescription? Shouldn't you feel bad if someone in your family dies?"

I expect Mrs. Arnold to chew Kevin out over "shitty," but she doesn't mention it. Instead, she looks thoughtful. "I think the question is, when does it cross over from normal grief into something else? Something more, something—pathological?"

"But that's the point!" Roiling with frustration, I practically leap out of my seat. "What is normal grief? Who gets to decide how bad someone should feel when their little brother died? Or their dad?"

Next to me, Kevin nods fervently. Even Kelly has stopped whispering and is looking at me with interest.

"It's true." Tad Schaffer speaks up. "I mean, how can anyone look at another person and say, I know how you feel? Because how do they really know? They can't."

We debate the point for the rest of the class. While some feel like Matt—that to even think of killing yourself means you're crazy—most seem to agree with me about the personal nature of grief and the subjectivity of human experience. For many, it's the first time they've participated in class all semester. I can tell Mrs. Arnold is both surprised and thrilled.

The bell rings, and I bend to pack up my things, almost knocking heads with Kevin.

"Thanks for your support," I say. "That wasn't easy, at first."

"You don't have to thank me." He shrugs. "You're right." He pauses, and I can tell he wants to say something else. His cheeks flush, and I wonder if it's about my mom.

"Cat," he begins. He fumbles with the belt loops on his jeans. "Do you want to go to the prom with me? Just as friends," he adds quickly. His face is so red now it clashes with his orange shirt.

I blink at him. "Prom? Really?"

"Yeah. I mean, if you're already going with someone—or you don't want to—"

"Sure," I say, surprising myself. "Sure, I'd love to go with you."

"Oh, great!" He looks immensely relieved. "I have a calculus quiz now, but I'll text you later, okay?"

"Sure. Thanks, Kevin." I smile as he dashes out of the room, fumbling in his bag for his scientific calculator.

I can't believe I just accepted a date for prom. I shove my notebook inside my bag and pull the strings shut. Now I'm going to have to actually go.

The funny thing is, it doesn't feel as absurd an idea as it did an hour ago. I picture my mother's face when I tell her I have a date, and I grin inwardly, knowing I've done the right thing.

Chapter 20

After

It is night, and I am with Rafael. He traces the outline of my spine with his fingers and whispers things to me in Spanish that I only half-understand. I luxuriate in the pleasure of the moment, in feeling and not thinking. Too soon, it will be morning again and we will be forced to face our demons.

Suddenly, Rafael changes his tone, the anguish apparent in his voice as he begins to speak of his father.

"He was a wonderful man, Catalina," he says. He buries his head in my shoulder, and I can feel his tears, hot and wet against my skin. "You would have loved him."

"Shhh," I say softly. "I understand."

"I know you do," he says, fierce now. He clutches at me. "How will I bear it?"

I blink as he looms over me. Even in the darkness, I can see the shadow of pain in his eyes.

"I'm not the person to ask," I say quietly. "My doctor thinks I have a mental illness." I roll over onto my side. I wonder what Rafael and Dr. Shapiro would make of each other.

"Mental illness." Rafael snorts. "Because you are sad? Of course you are sad. I want to tear the world in two."

I picture an anguished Rafael clutching a map, ripping it to shreds. I recognize the anger and reach out to take his hand.

"Being with you has helped me," I say. "It's made me feel alive again." And it's true. When I'm with Rafael, I can forget. The love and intimacy have dulled the pain, masked it. Helped give me a reason to get up in the morning and greet the day with hope.

"I don't want Papa to have died in vain," Rafael says, clenching his fists. I don't know if he's even heard me.

"He died for his country," I say half-heartedly. I know how Rafael will respond.

"This isn't his country," he says bitterly. "Not anymore. And it's not mine, either."

I sigh and prop myself up on my elbows. I want to help Rafael, but grief and idealism have become muddled within him. He can't think of his father without thinking of Calantes, and vice versa. In his mind, they have become intertwined.

"We need to do more," he says. It's become his mantra. "It's time to raise the stakes."

"But the drugs, Rafael," I say. "You can't. You can't align yourself with drug traffickers."

"Why is that any worse than anything else?" he asks, slamming his fist into the worn mattress. It sags at his touch, and fails to rebound entirely. "Why is it worse than oil? Your government has no problems carrying out wars over oil."

I stiffen. "I've never voted," I say. "What the government does is hardly my fault. And I don't necessarily agree."

His face softens. "Of course not. I'm sorry, Cat. I'm just frustrated. Drugs are not ideal, certainly, but there is demand. Why not capitalize on that demand? Take the money, use it for good? To help Calantes?"

I shake my head. "I don't know," I say. "It doesn't feel right. Dirty money."

His face darkens. "It must be nice to have the privilege of turning away money," he says coldly.

I don't answer. I know how it is to be so tormented by loss that you say and do things you may not mean.

"Think of the violence, then," I suggest calmly. I gather my hair and braid it, desperate to get it off my neck. Even at night, the heat is oppressive, and the strands I grasp at are damp with sweat. "What happened to a peaceful solution?"

"There can be no peaceful solution," he says firmly. "Do I want to work with the *narcos?* Is it my first choice? No. But how can we have peace when they execute our families? They have chosen violence."

I feel a mosquito buzz lazily at my cheek, the irritating sound amplified by its proximity to my ear. Even with the nets, the beasts are inescapable. I slap at it, and there is a spurt of blood. Rafael notices and reaches forward to wipe my face with the corner of the sheet.

"You see?" he says, showing me the red stain. "You don't negotiate with the mosquito. You don't try to come to a peaceful arrangement. You crush it." He mimes with his hands.

"It's a bit different," I say, frowning. "People aren't mosquitoes, Rafael. They—"

I'm cut off by shouting. It's Margo, banging her hand against the tent frame.

"Get your clothes on, Cat. Anna needs you. Valentina is having her baby."

"Valentina?" I scramble for my T-shirt. "But she isn't due for another four weeks."

"Well, I guess the baby doesn't know that." Margo pokes her head in as I pulled on a pair of leggings. "Come on!"

Rafael, unconcerned at his nudity, squeezes my hand as I make for the tent flap. "Good luck," he says, and I see the worry in his eyes. If the delivery doesn't go well, we may not be able to get Valentina to the hospital in San Pedro in time.

I rush out of the tent, close on Margo's heels. "Is she in a lot of pain?" I ask nervously. There are no anesthetics in the infirmary. It'll be the stick for poor Valentina.

"Well," says Margo. "She was shouting at her boyfriend— what's his name?—that she was going to kill him in his sleep for doing this to her."

"Juan," I say grimly. "He's so nice, too. Always talking to her belly, kissing it."

Margo mimes gagging. We hear a piercing shriek from the direction of the infirmary and pick up the pace.

"Cat, thank goodness," says Anna when I arrive, looking

immensely relieved. "Valentina is going to have her baby today. She is almost fully dilated."

Margo, who is hovering at the door, looks revolted. "Ugh," she says, shuddering. "I'm out of here. Good luck."

"What can I do?" I ask, going to wash my hands. I scrub at them fiercely, attacking my fingernails with soap. Slipping into a makeshift gown, I glance at Valentina, who is pacing the tent. Every few minutes, she stops to howl in pain, grasping at her watermelon-like stomach in agony.

"Time the contractions for me, please," says Anna, handing me an old plastic Timex stopwatch. "They started last night after dinner, and have been slowly getting closer together."

"Okay," I say, taking the watch. I pause. "The contractions—that's when she's screaming?"

Anna raises her eyebrows at me. "Yes."

"I'm sorry," I say, feeling silly. "I've never seen a baby being born. Not in real life, anyway." I think of birth scenes in movies, where labor and delivery are edited down to a five-minute montage of dramatic water-breaking and a bit of shouting before a Gerber-type baby emerges. Anna has warned me it isn't like that in real life. That labor can go on for days, and that newborns are wrinkled, with weirdly shaped heads and covered in goo.

I dutifully time the contractions, which are now less than two minutes apart. Anna motions for Valentina to climb back on the gurney. Juan hovers nearby, looking frightened.

Anna pulls on a pair of gloves and examines Valentina, who doesn't seem to mind that she is spread-eagled on a table for everyone to see. I recall my mother's words about pain: that it is all-consuming, all-encompassing. That when you are in the throes of it, you lose sight of everything and everyone else.

"The baby is still posterior," Anna says grimly to me, in English. For the first time, I notice that she is unnerved. I watch as a bead of sweat trickles down the side of her head, caught in the crease of her slender neck. "I thought it would turn itself, but it hasn't."

"What does that mean?" I ask, trying not to look alarmed. Clearly, Anna doesn't want Valentina or Juan to know.

"The baby is upside-down," she explains. "It is face-up. To come out, it should be face-down. I'm going to have to go in and try to turn it around." She's breathing heavily, and I can tell she's frightened.

"Go in?" I stare at her blankly. "Go in where?"

She raises her eyebrows at me again.

"Oh," I say, realizing. "*Oh*. I didn't…" I don't complete my thought, which was that I hadn't ever thought of the vagina as a *place*, somewhere you can go in and carry out various objectives. I nod faintly at Anna, who is now instructing Valentina in Spanish to prop up her knees.

I grab some wet rags and my wooden stick for Valentina to bite on, sensing it may prove useful during this exercise. "It's okay," I babble at her in a soothing tone. I lay a rag across her forehead, dabbing at her hairline. Her long, dark hair, usually a mass of sleek, dark curls, is matted with sweat. Her eyes, hollow with pain and exhaustion, are shadowed by the dark circles that come from a lack of sleep.

Anna leans forward, and despite myself, I watch,

fascinated, as she maneuvers her hands, a look of steely deter-
mination on her face.

"I helped my mama do this once," she whispers.

"And?" I say in a low voice. I replace the cloth on Valentina's
forehead as her body goes rigid with another contraction.

"It should work." She grits her teeth, and I notice
Valentina's belly changing shape. Sections that were flat seem
rounder, and rounder sections seem flat.

"I think it's working!" I say under my breath. Valentina
lets out another moan, and I place the stick between her teeth.

"Bite on this," I tell her, feeling foolish. "It helps."
Thankfully, she doesn't throw the stick back at me, though her
eyes narrow to slits.

There is a flood of water then, and I gasp as it soaks the
bed, Anna, and the floor.

"Her waters have broken," announced Anna, looking
pleased. "Things will move faster now."

"There's so much water," I say stupidly, staring at the growing puddle.

"Yes," agrees Anna. "Birth is very messy."

I think of my mother's final days, of the sweat-soaked
sheets, the IV bags, and dirty bedpans. Getting into and out
of this world, it would seem, is a messy business.

I look down again and feel my heart seize with fear.
"Anna," I say hoarsely, gesturing. "What is that?"

Anna glances down, and her eyes widen. "She's crowning!"

"What does that mean?" I ask, panicked. I drop one of the
used rags to the ground.

Anna laughs. "That's the baby's head!" She claps her hands together and grabs a fresh pair of gloves. "Valentina, *Estás lista?*"

Valentina makes a strangled sound in reply.

"You have to push now," Anna instructs her in Spanish. "Push!"

Valentina screams so loudly that it's all I can do not to jump. My hands shaking, I dab at her head and clutch at the stick, urging her to bite.

"Push!"

It takes several tries, but eventually the baby slides out whole, a slippery bundle covered in red and white slime. Anna grabs it and whacks it on the back. Promptly, it begins to cry.

"It's a girl," says Anna softly, placing the baby on Valentina's chest. "*Es una niña.*"

Valentina, laughing now, reaches to grasp her infant. Juan, who has been cowering in a corner with half-closed eyes, beams now, his hand on Valentina's shoulder.

"Anna," he says firmly, motioning toward the baby.

Valentina smiles and nods, cradling the baby in her arms. "Anna Catalina."

I blink, startled. "Me?"

The couple smile and nod at me. They don't speak much English, but their meaning is clear. They are naming their baby for me and Anna, to say thank you. I am stunned into silence, marveling at the small perfection of the newborn as she stares into her mother's eyes.

Chapter 21

Before

"Dad?" My voice is hesitant. I'm dressed and ready for school, but my father, who usually leaves at the same time and has been known to give me a ride, is dressed in his boxers and a ratty old Cincinnati Reds T-shirt that I think predates my birth. He's seated at our breakfast bar, half slumped over a bowl of Lucky Charms. There is no milk in the bowl.

"What's up, Cat?" His voice is full of forced cheer as he directs a spoonful of cereal to his mouth.

"Don't you have work?" I watch as he chews, waiting for his reaction to the lack of milk. He doesn't react, and digs back in.

"Term's over," he says quickly. "My assistants are doing the grading."

I frown. "You always go in," I say. "Summer classes? Admin

work? Writing?" I don't know why I'm forcing it, but something doesn't feel right.

He avoids my stare. "I'm taking a break," he says finally.

"A break?"

"Time off." He puts the spoon down. "Stress leave."

"Oh." I sit down hard at one of the kitchen table chairs, wincing as the hard wooden seat raps my tailbone through my skinny jeans. "When did that happen? Why didn't you tell me?"

"Well, I didn't want to worry you," he says, trying to sound casual. He picks his spoon up again, moves the little marshmallows around. "I'm fine, really, but the dean thought it might be best."

"The dean?" I narrow my eyebrows. Something is up. My dad is not ordinarily on the dean's radar.

"There was an issue, with some papers," he says lamely. He scoops the marshmallows out and lines them up on the counter. One, two, three, four. He reorganizes them according the to the spectrum of the rainbow.

"Jesus, Dad." I bury my face in my hands.

"Don't worry about it," he says brusquely. "I'll be fine."

"But—"

"I have insurance for this. I'm still being paid sixty percent of my salary."

Sixty percent? That doesn't sound like a lot—not when the medical bills are piling up like snow during a February storm. I feel like going over and smacking him. Where is the Dad who blasted my sixth-grade teacher for removing certain books from the classroom library? Who told off the overnight camp director on my behalf? Who spent upwards of four hours with me pouring over *The Sound and the Fury* when I had dissolved into tears, sure I would fail tenth-grade English?

"I understand," I say instead, trying to remain calm. "Are you seeing a doctor?"

"Me?" He looks blank.

"For the stress," I say tightly. "The insurance company will want some kind of proof, I'm sure. Documentation." *So we can get the money*, I add silently, gritting my teeth.

"Oh." He looks surprised. "I guess I should go over the paperwork." He gestures somewhere behind him, even though all that's there is the stove.

I exhale loudly. "Do you want me to look it over?" I ask.

"No, no," he says quickly, at least having the decency to look abashed. "I'll do it later."

"Right," I say, even though we both know he isn't going to do it. "Just book the appointment. We can't afford to lose the benefits."

"Okay," he says. He stares down at his bowl of cereal. "I forgot the milk."

"I know," I say. Even though I am already late for school, I retrieve the milk from the fridge, carefully filling his bowl so that the Lucky Charms bob up and down like little buoys.

"Thanks, Cat," he says gratefully. "What would I do without you?"

He absently pats my back as I leave, my book bag heavier than usual over my shoulder.

• • •

A memory.

I am five years old, and my father is driving me to kinder-garten. We're early, and he drives around the side streets and cul-de-sacs near the school, killing time.

"Want to drive?" he asks me suddenly, a mischievous gleam in his eye.

"Drive? The car?" Five-year-old me is beside myself with excitement. "The real car?"

"Well, you've already driven the pretend one, so I think you're ready." He pulls over and unbuckles me from my booster seat in the back and helps me into the front onto his lap. I am giddy with anticipation. It's a beautiful day in early fall, and the leaves have just started to change from green to amber and red and gold.

"I can't reach the pedals!" I kick my tiny legs in dismay.

"I'll do that part," says Dad, smiling. "You steer."

"How?" I ask, suddenly nervous.

He shows me. Left, right. Hand-over-hand. Ten and two, like a clock. I cannot tell time, but I wear a Cinderella watch, so I know what he means. I beam with importance.

"Ready?" Dad turns the key in the ignition and the radio comes back on. I remember it clearly: "The Ketchup Song" was on. Big hit back when I was rocking preschool, I guess.

"Ready!"

It starts out well. I wobble a bit, left, right, but then I've got it. I'm clutching the wheel at ten and two and the car is heading straight. "I'm driving!" I shout, my voice full of glee. "I'm driving."

Then my hands slip. I try to recover, but the wheel turns too far to the right, and before I know it, we are up on the curb. There is a tree nearby, a stately old maple.

My father moves swiftly. He grabs the wheel and quickly rights the vehicle. He stops the car and gives me a rueful glance.

"We should probably go to school now."

My heart is pounding. I stare at the tree. "I almost hit the tree."

"No," says Dad firmly. "I would never let that happen."

I bury my head in his shirt. It smells like him, like dry cleaning and Clorets gum. "I'm scared."

"Don't be scared," he says, kissing the top of my pony-tailed head. "I'll take care of you, always, I promise. I'll be there."

It was our secret. We never told Mom, not even when she noticed the tire looked damaged.

Dad, I think silently now, as I sit at the back of my chemistry class, not hearing a word. *Where are you now?*

· · ·

I'm right, of course: my dad does need to see a physician to maintain the stress-leave benefits, so with my help—in between helping my mom and studying for algebra and geometry class—I arrange for him to see his family doctor.

"What happened?" I ask as he leaves Dr. Bender's office clutching a piece of white paper. I have accompanied him to this appointment to ensure he actually goes. I don't trust him not to end up at a movie theater. Last week, instead of filing the insurance paperwork, he went to see *Monsters University*.

"He says I'm depressed," answers Dad, looking affronted.

I exhale with relief. "Thank goodness."

"I'm *not* depressed," he mutters as he clicks the car's remote keyless entry. "I'm just grieving. My wife has cancer. How *should* I be? Why do I need to take pills?"

"Dad," I said patiently. "Think about the chips. About *Monsters U?*"

"I still don't see what the big deal with *Monsters U* is," he grumbles. As if I'm being ridiculous for thinking it's odd that a grown man would spend his afternoon at a Disney movie.

I open the driver's side door and slide in. He frowns. "You're driving?"

"Yes," I say with a sigh. "I'll stop at the pharmacy."

"I can go tomorrow."

"No, Dad." My voice is firm. "I'll drive. Get in."

The doctor has prescribed an antidepressant. "It takes six to eight weeks for it to work," says the pharmacist. She reels off a list of side effects that include sleepiness and weight gain, two changes my dad doesn't need. I press them into my father's hand, praying that his adventure in prescription drugs is more fruitful than mine. I picture my little blue pills swirling down the toilet, and ask the universe for the meds to work.

"Did Dr. Bender suggest that you see someone?" I ask him later. Mom is asleep again, and the two of us are picking at a Hawaiian pizza. "A therapist?"

"He did," answers Dad, not looking at me. He takes a bite of pizza and chews it with deliberate slowness.

"And?" I tap my fork against my plate expectantly.

"And I said no," he says bluntly.

"Dad—"

"You hate that therapist of yours. Why should I go?"

I pick at a chunk of pineapple. "I don't *hate* him."

"You do. You said even his beard makes you nauseous. Something about birds hatching."

"Yeah, but…" my voice trails off. He's right, of course— I don't like seeing Dr. Shapiro. But is it useful? Could it be? Might it be for him? I don't know.

I change the subject. We talk about the weather, school, municipal elections. We don't mention Mom, depression, psychoactive medication, or therapy. At times, I feel like we are reading from the script of a play about a normal family.

Dad takes another slice, his fifth. I want to tell him to take it easy, that rapid weight gain is only bound to make his problems worse at this point, but I stay silent. I am picking my battles now, and I am not done with therapy, at least not as it pertains to Dad, however hypocritical that may be. What's one more slice of pizza, anyway, when you're living on chips and licorice?

Battle-picking, hypocrisy, fretting over nutrition. I feel like a parent, I realize. I stare at my father and feel a surge of anger.

You said you would always take care of me, I want to shout. *That you would be there.* Frightened and full of despair, I stuff the rest of my slice into my mouth.

Chapter 22

After

My exhilaration over the baby's delivery is quickly tempered by Rafael's impassioned speeches about how tiny Anna Catalina deserves to grow up in a free and safe society, not a poverty-stricken village in the jungle. I listen patiently, trying to be objective, still wary of the narcos and the promise of violent rebellion.

"She cannot even get to San Pedro for vaccinations," Rafael says one night, gripping my arm. "Valentina's brother is wanted by the government—she would be arrested. Should a baby in this time die of diphtheria?"

I've spent the day helping Valentina with caring for the new baby, changing her dirty diapers and rocking her to sleep when she cried. I picture the tiny, swaddled infant sick with a fatal and preventable illness and cringe. "Of course not," I say.

I'm worried, now. "SWB knows about the baby. They'll call Doctors Without Borders, I'm sure—"

"Even if she gets the vaccines," he continues, cutting me off, "what hope is there for her? Growing up like this? What will become of her?"

I sigh. "There's always hope, isn't there? *You* have hope, or we wouldn't be discussing this." I stretch out on his bed, yawning. Overhead, I stare at the mosquitoes fighting to pass through the net, lured by the smell of our warm flesh.

He doesn't answer. His father's death has embittered him, and a dark and tortured version of Rafael has replaced the buoyant idealist I first encountered outside the base. I think of myself before and after The Cancer, and work harder to understand his pain.

"Look," I say. I prop myself up on my elbow and tuck a loose curl behind his ear. "I know how hard it is, with your father. I've been there, Rafael, I *know*. With my mother—"

"How can you stand it?" he cries out suddenly. He grabs me, and his skin is hot, almost as if he is burning with fever. "How can you stand it, when you remember?"

He kisses me roughly, preventing me from answering. Haunted by my own memories, I yield willingly, melting into him. His hands wander over my body, stroke my cheeks.

"I want you with me," he says, his hands weaving in and out of my hair. "You could help me. We could be a team, like they say on American television."

A team? Confused, I lean against him. "I don't know, Rafael." I run a hand along his arm. "The traffickers—"

"Don't worry about the narcos," he says dismissively. "Leave that to me. You can do good work. Deliver more babies. Help more sick people."

I sit up straighter. "Are you asking me to stay?" I ask, stunned.

"Yes," he says simply. "You belong here. With me."

Stay. Not go back to Dad, to college. I think of the joy on Valentina's face when she held her baby for the first time; of Rafael's hot skin against my own; of escaping my own past, leaving the demons behind indefinitely. Forever.

"I don't know," I say softly.

"Think about it," he says, pressing his lips against the back of my neck. "I love you, Catalina."

I love you. No boy has ever said that to me before. "I love you, too," I respond, my breath catching. And at that moment, I mean it.

He pulls me down, his mouth hard on mine. I give in to him, reveling in our twosome, as my mind is wiped temporarily clean of its slate of worry and grief.

. . .

I feel something crawling on my arm and flick it away with a shudder. I don't look to see what it was, sparing myself that particular horror. Margo, Taylor, and I are on our way from the village to the base—tonight, I've decided not to stay with Rafael. I need some time to think, some space.

The evening air is thick with insects of every kind, creatures

I have never seen or even read about. I catch sight of one that looks exactly like a leaf—green and shiny and shaped like a spade—only it has nearly-hidden legs and constantly whirring antennae. The noise is astounding, a veritable symphony of bugs with the occasional bird or other unidentifiable, but definitely not human, sounds mixed in.

"Everything okay?" asks Taylor politely. We've been overly formal with each other since our argument, speaking only in stiff, prim tones. Margo rolls her eyes; she's not one for formality, no matter what's transpired.

I shrug, pulling the sleeves of my shirt down over my hands. I can feel the mosquitoes hovering hopefully nearby, and hate the feel of bites on my fingers: they are the hardest to scratch.

"How come you're coming back with us?" asks Margo bluntly. "Trouble in paradise?"

I don't answer immediately, searching for the right words. "No," I say slowly. "No, the opposite."

"Opposite?" Margo frowns, then covers her mouth in horror. "You're not pregnant are you?"

"Pregnant? No!" I shake my head furiously. I brush aside a leafy branch, flinching as an angry bird swoops suddenly down, squawking in indignation at the disruption.

"Then what?" Margo stops, her hands on her narrow hips. "What's going on?"

"He's asked me to stay," I admit. I don't look at her.

"Stay?" Taylor pipes up, his voice tinged with horror. He adjusts the cap he's wearing—a makeshift mask made of a mosquito net attached to a visor. He looks ridiculous. "*Stay?* Cat, have you lost it?"

"I'm not like you," I retort. I'm still not sure myself if I want to stay or not, but I don't like being judged by Taylor. "I'm not going home to a hotel fortune. My mom is dead, my dad is useless, and here I have the chance to help out."

Margo stares at me open-mouthed. I want to warn her that actual flies may get in, but she reaches over and grabs my arm, tight.

"Cat," she says, sounding alarmed, "you're not thinking rationally."

Rationally. Manic. Bipolar II. Denial, anger, acceptance… I feel something inside me snap.

"Why should I be rational?" I shout back, and I hear my voice echo in the overhead tree canopy. Somewhere, a macaw answers me back, cawing loudly. "Where does it get you, really, in the end?"

Taylor and Margo are looking at each other the way my classmates did after the hockey-stick incident. I bristle defensively, avoiding eye contact.

"This thing with Rafael," Margo says carefully. "It's just a thing. It's hot, but you're, like, seventeen. Think about what you're saying."

"It's not just Rafael," I protest. "When I helped Anna deliver the baby—"

"A baby that is lucky to be okay, given that she did not have access to any kind of health care," Margo answers calmly. "Did you know babies are supposed to get stuff when they're born? Eye drops and shots and—"

"I get it," I snap. "Which is why I should stay. Help get the country back on track."

"Not to sound like a shrink," says Taylor, speaking up, "but it isn't your job to save the world, Cat."

Margo nods. Her eyes are full of sadness, without the hardness I've come to expect. "I know you lost your mom," she says, "but that wasn't your fault. And neither is Valentina's baby, whatever happens to her. Or Calantes, for that matter." She gestures around her. "This place is a bigger problem than we can fix, any of us."

I think about her words. Calantes is poisoned as surely as if the narcos were spilling their drugs directly into the Amazon. Just like the cancer that took my mom, that destroyed her body. *Is there, again, no way for me help? No way to stop the poison?*

Margo gently places a filthy hand on my arm. "It's not your fault," she says again. "I understand why you're here, and why you feel that way. But you couldn't save your mother, and you certainly can't save this place. What if you died, Cat? Rafael wants to align with the drug traffickers. How would your mother have felt about that? Is that what she would have wanted?"

I bristle again at this reference to my mother, what she would have wanted. Margo didn't know my mother.

But she's not wrong, a little voice whispers in my ear. I try to brush it off, like a pesky insect, but it persists. *What would Mom have wanted?* My thoughts wander to my mother in her last moments, how angry she would be with me if I died now, how disappointed. It feels like a knife being twisted deep into my gut, and again I feel lost. *Why?* I want to scream at her. *Why did you leave me?*

"I don't know," I mutter, kicking at the dirt. It puffs up in little clouds around my boot, disturbing the insects living beneath it. I notice some kind of spider scurry out of the way, something that would ordinarily frighten me. Now, I just stare at it with distaste. I don't have the energy to be afraid of spiders anymore.

"Look, Cat." Taylor's voice is hard—none of the gentleness that Margo has affected. It's like they're playing a game of good-cop bad-cop with me. "We come here, we try to do a little good, we leave. It's shitty, but that's how it is. Call me jaded, call me whatever you want, but when my time is up here, I'm out. This isn't my war."

I say nothing, walking faster now, ahead of my friends. I can imagine the worried looks they're exchanging behind my back, and I feel tears of anger and frustration prick at my eyes.

Margo jogs to my side. "Cat," she says worriedly, "you don't...you don't *want* to die, do you?"

Dr. Shapiro's words come back to me, something about grief and the desperate desire to join a lost loved one. I don't believe in that, but the thought of dying doesn't repulse me the way it probably should. *If I died, who would miss me? Would my father notice? Who would mourn me, the way my mother would have?*

Back at the base, I nod goodnight at Melody, who is lying awake in her cot, staring at the ceiling. She hasn't opened up to me again since that night, but we have a tacit understanding between us, an unacknowledged sisterhood of pain and loss. When she notices me watching her, she whispers her goodnight in return and rolls over onto her side, away from me.

When I fall asleep, my dreams are twisted and full of confused imagery: I lie on the jungle floor in the throes of labor, Rafael at my side. Margo and Anna work together to deliver the baby.

"It's a girl!" cries Margo, handing me a swaddled infant. I look down at my baby, who has the face of my mother before she died, complete with a little knit chemo cap. Heart pounding, I awake with a start. It's still night, but I don't fall back asleep.

Chapter 23

Before

"Close your eyes," says Mom, carefully dusting my lids with shimmery eye shadow, pale pink to match the dress. "This is going to look fantastic. I watched a video on YouTube." In front of her is a neat row of brushes in all shapes and sizes. The vanity looks like an art-supply-store display.

"I can't believe people take the time to post these things," I say, trying to remain still.

"You sound like Dad." Mom shakes her head. "How old are you again?"

"Ha." I try not to move as she pulls out an eyeliner pencil. "Careful with that thing."

She looks brighter, more alive, than she has in ages. Her cheeks are flushed with color, and her eyes have their old light in them. Her forehead is crinkled with lines of concentration.

"When I'm done with your makeup, I'm going to do mine like this, too," she says. She steps back and examines her work critically. "We'll take some pictures. I'll put on that black dress I wore to Lily Fowler's wedding."

"Really?" I smile, remembering how lovely she looked then, before the cancer and the chemo and the rest of it. She's still beautiful, of course, but it's not the same. The memories of before, it's almost like they're of someone else.

"Yes. I want some nice pictures of us tonight. I don't want to stand next to you in these disgusting yoga pants. God, I miss getting dressed and going out."

I don't say anything—I'm rendered mute as Mom reaches for a pinkish lipstick and applies it liberally to my gaping mouth. It feels weird to have someone else do this. I try not to drool.

"There!" she says triumphantly. "You look like a model."

I turn towards the mirror. My face is transformed: my eyes are bigger and more luminous, my cheeks pink, my lips full. My hair is thick and loose in soft waves about my shoulders—Mom set it in rollers and carefully brushed it out, lovingly combing each curl. I look like someone else, someone older and elegant and sophisticated.

"Thank you," I whisper. I can't stop staring at my reflection. "It's amazing. How did you do this?"

"Don't be silly," she says, waving her hand dismissively. "You provided the raw material." She rises slowly from her seat opposite me at the vanity, using the table to steady herself. She is frail these days, unwell. She tries to hide it from me, but I can see the gasps for air as she executes even the simplest of tasks; the little winces of pain when she thinks I'm not looking; the hollowed-out cheeks and dark circles around her eyes from not eating or sleeping. And the seizures. I've gotten used to a lot, accepted things I never thought I could. But the seizures I can't get used to. Each time, I want to cry, scream, hide from her.

When things started to get really bad, Dad convinced Mom to give radiation a shot, just one more time. Just to see if it helped. Almost immediately, her hair began to shed again, to release a little bit at a time. Not like with the chemo, but we'd notice more hair on her pillow, on her hairbrush, in the shower. After the third treatment, she put her foot down.

"I'm dying," she said flatly. "There's nothing anyone can do about it. And if I'm going to die, I want to die with hair. I only have a little dignity left."

We didn't argue. Dad wanted to, I could tell—I know a part of him still irrationally believes that she's not beyond hope—but even he knew better than to say anything. She's on some pretty heavy painkillers now, to cope with the pain, along with some other stuff: anti-seizure drugs, anti-anxiety meds, sleeping pills. Dad doles them all out to her daily in three shifts. He's got one of those little pill-organizer boxes with dates and times on them.

"Let's go get your dress," she says now. She takes my hand for support and retrieves the delicate pink creation from its hanger. Carefully, I step inside, and she zips me, brushing my hair out of the way so it doesn't catch. I hold her hands as I step into a pair of her high heels, teetering precariously.

"Caitlin." Her voice catches as she stares me up and down. "You look beautiful. Beyond beautiful."

I check my reflection and do a double-take. I look like I've been Photoshopped; the transformation is remarkable. Mom's face is radiant.

"It's even better than I imagined," she whispers.

I glance at my phone: it's four o'clock. Kevin is picking me up in less than half an hour. Against all expectations, I am getting excited. I feel a flutter in my stomach, like a thousand butterflies are trying to escape.

"I'm going to do my makeup now," Mom says. I help her back to the vanity. "We'll take some nice pictures before Kevin gets here."

I watch her carefully powder her face, then highlight her cheeks with blush. I used to love watching her put on makeup as a kid. When I was really little, I used to stand on a step stool, studying intently as she dusted her eyelids and puckered her lips. It occurs to me that this may be one of the last times I have the privilege of observing this ritual, so I stare unabashed, committing her face and actions to memory.

When she's done, I brush her hair, twisting the front back with a small barrette. I find the dress she's looking for, and it's my turn to help her into it. Standing next to me in front of the full-length mirror, she beams at the woman looking back at her.

"There I am," she says quietly. She turns to me. "I hate being ugly."

"You could never be ugly," I say firmly. I squeeze her hand and direct her attention back to the mirror. "Look at us. We should be in, like, a magazine."

"We do look pretty hot," she agrees. She goes over to her dresser and rifles through one of the drawers for her camera. "Let's get some pictures."

She beckons loudly for my dad, who is downstairs, reading. He emerges, looking taken aback at the pair of us.

"You look stunning," he says, his voice catching. "Both of you." He smiles tenderly at Mom. "What a great idea."

"I thought it would be nice to get some pictures," she says, handing him the camera.

We snap a variety of shots—some serious, and some decidedly not, as we stick our tongues out or strike humorous poses. We all laugh easily, something that hasn't happened in months. Finally, the doorbell rings, and my dad answers it.

"Hi, Mr. Marks," says Kevin shyly. He's wearing standard guy prom-wear, a rented tux. He looks nice enough, if slightly awkward, clutching a wrist corsage.

"Hi, Cat." He smiles at me, relaxing slightly. "You look great." He offers me the corsage, his cheeks flushing deeply. "I hope this is okay. My mom picked it up."

"Thanks," I say, slipping the white rose onto my wrist. "It's perfect."

We stand somewhat stiffly as my parents take a variety of traditional prom photos. It's all a bit weird, but my mother looks so thrilled, I can't help but grin back.

"Have fun!" she says brightly. "Don't hurry back. Stay out as late as you want!"

I smile good-naturedly. "Thanks," I say, grabbing my purse. "But I doubt we'll be out all that late."

Kevin shuffles his shiny shoes against our hall carpet. "I have a midnight curfew," he mutters. "My parents are really strict."

"Totally fine," I say, relieved. I have no intention of partying into the wee hours. "Let's go."

. . .

The prom is well under way when we arrive. I find Tess and Jake, and the four of us snag a table well away from the dance floor where we enjoy some canapés and fake champagne.

"What is this?" I ask, making a face. "It's awful."

"Non-alcoholic sparkling wine," says Jake knowingly. "My uncle has a drinking problem. We buy this for him on New Year's Eve."

"I think I would have preferred a soda," I say, putting my glass down. I look around. Everywhere, students in their finery revel, dancing enthusiastically to loud, cheesy dance music I can't identify and snacking on bacon-wrapped scallops. Some have clearly been trading the fake alcohol in favor of the real thing: a surprising number are surreptitiously sneaking sips from concealed hip flasks. There's a rumor, of course, that someone has spiked the punch, but it's not clear whether that's true or not. Not many people are drinking it, regardless; it looks less like punch than runny ketchup.

As if on cue, Jake pulls out a small silver thermos. "Anyone want to join me in making this crap actually drinkable?" he asks.

Nervously, Tess scans the area for teacher chaperones. "I don't want to risk it," she says finally, shaking her head. Jake sighs loudly and pours himself what looks like vodka. This is why they're always breaking up: Tess is so risk-averse she drives under the speed limit, while Jake yearns for excitement at any cost. They once had an epic fight in line for a roller coaster. I think that was breakup number four.

Kevin and I also decline Jake's offer. Kevin drove us here tonight, and I haven't touched the stuff since the debacle at Marianne's. Jake sighs, screwing the cap back on. I can tell he's mentally counting down the days until he's off to Ohio State, where I foresee he will spend most of his freshman year cozied up to a keg. I hope he and Tess have the good sense to permanently break things off by September.

"Let's dance," says Kevin suddenly, giving me a questioning look. "It's the prom. We should dance."

I want to say no, but he's right, so I follow him to the dance floor. He's a surprisingly good dancer, and I sway in time to the music, trying not to feel self-conscious. I look around at the school gym, which has been done up in painstaking detail by the Prom Committee to look like a New York nightclub—or at least what small-town Ohio envisions a New York nightclub to look like. There are lots of stainless-steel cocktail tables, rented white leather stools, and weird lighting in different shades of blue and purple.

"I heard you got early acceptance to Stanford," Kevin shouts above the music. "That's awesome."

"Thanks," I say. The letter arrived a week ago. Mom insisted we all have dinner together to celebrate. She didn't eat much, and we just ordered in Thai, nothing fancy, but it was nice. Both my parents were thrilled, though they also insisted they were not surprised in the least. I was happy, I guess, but not as happy as I'd thought I would be. I stared at the words on the page and felt only disenchantment and a sense of something like claustrophobia.

"I'm thinking of deferring a year." The words are out of my mouth before I have a chance to reflect on their meaning. I hadn't even considered putting college off for a year until this very second.

"Really?" Kevin looks interested. "That's really cool. What are you going to do, travel?"

"Maybe," I say. "I haven't decided."

The music slows down. We stand there, awkward, until Kevin puts out his arm. "May I have this dance?" he asks dramatically. I can tell he's overcompensating for the sudden weirdness between us.

We come together, his hand resting on the small of my back. "I'd love to take a year off and travel. Go see Europe or something." He looks wistful.

"Why don't you?"

"My parents would never go for it." He shakes his head. He's silent for a moment, then changes the subject. "Your mom looks good. Is she doing okay?"

I flinch at the unexpected shift in conversation. "Not really," I say softly.

His face colors with embarrassment. "I'm sorry," he mutters, looking away. "I didn't know."

"It's all right," I say quickly. I'm used to this by now. I've learned there's no good way to talk about cancer. It makes people uncomfortable no matter how you do it.

"Is she…in treatment right now?" I can tell he doesn't know what to say. His face is approaching the color of the possibly-spiked punch.

I shake my head. "Just pain meds," I answer. "She didn't want any more chemo or radiation."

Kevin is silent for a moment. "I'm really sorry, Cat," he says finally. "I don't know how you do it."

"Do what?" I frown.

He shrugs slightly. "I don't know. Cope. Deal. I don't think I could. You're brave."

"I have no choice." It's my turn to shrug. "I don't feel brave at all, but I think I understand what you mean." The song ends, and the music picks up again. I don't feel like dancing anymore, so I walk back toward the tables, Kevin at my side. "Before this happened, I would have thought that, if my mom got cancer, I'd just, like, totally fall apart and lie in bed all day. But it doesn't work like that. The rest of the world goes on as normal, and you kind of have to, too."

Kevin is silent. I can tell he's processing what I've said—his eyebrows are furrowed in concentration. "I get it," he says finally. "It's like Holden Caulfield and Hamlet, again."

I blink, confused. It's not what I was expecting. "What do you mean?"

"They're just trying to get by, even though they're, like, drowning in grief. And maybe part of the reason they act kind of crazy is that it must be infuriating to have the world go on like everything is okay when it's not for you." He stops, looking embarrassed. "Am I making any sense?"

"Absolutely," I say. My voice is quiet; Kevin's captured it well. "I wasn't going to go to prom."

"For that reason?"

"Yeah." I lean against a post. "It seemed infuriating, like you said. It's a good word. Like how can there be this big, stupid party when my mother is dying?"

"I get that." He nods, then pauses. "Why did you say yes?"

"For her." I look down at my dress, at the full skirt skimming the dance floor. "It meant so much to her, the prom. Buying the dress, getting ready, all of it. I didn't want to let her down."

"Are you having a terrible time?" His face is red again.

"No," I say, and it's true. "I'm actually having a pretty good time. My mom was right."

"Moms often are," he says, smiling. "Want to dance some more?"

I do, and we join up with Tess and Jake on the dance floor. After a few songs, Tad Schaffer and his band, Broken Windshield, get up on stage. They're a popular local act—they once competed in a major Battle of the Bands in Cleveland or Cincinnati, I can't remember which. They have some decent music of their own, but at gigs like this they generally cover classic rock.

"Hello, Graduating Class!" shouts Tad, and the crowd cheers. Mandy Bloom shrieks so loudly I'm afraid she might shatter the spotlights. She clearly has not been limiting herself to the non-alcoholic wine.

"Do you know how to rock?" he yells.

The crowd shouts back.

"I can't hear you!"

The response is deafening. Even I find myself bellowing out "Yes!" at the top of my lungs. The band strikes up "Come Together," from the Beatles, and everyone cheers again. Even I wave my arms enthusiastically.

"You're having fun!" Tess yells at me, an I-told-you-so expression on her face. "Aren't you glad you came?"

"I am, I admit it," I shout back, holding up my hands up in defeat. "You got me. You were right."

"I love the sound of those words!"

We both laugh, and impulsively, I grab her into a hug. She's been granted early admission to UCLA, and even if we're both in California together next year, it won't be the same as it was. We'll have different stories, different friends. Different lives.

The song ends and Tad's back at the mic. "I know it's prom, and we're supposed to play dance music." He pauses and adjusts the strap on his guitar. "But we're going to do a couple more rock covers before we let DJ Dave here have his stage back."

People clap appreciatively. Pretty much all of us have come out for Tad and his band over the years, and we're happy to support them one last time.

"Let's hear it for the Rolling Stones!" shouts Tad, and the rest of Broken Windshield strike up again.

It takes me a moment to identify the song amidst the hollering and foot-stomping of the crowd. Someone grabs my hand, and suddenly I'm part of a long chain of fellow prom-goers. The entire senior class, it would seem, is now one long chain.

"It's 'Paint It Black,'" I say to no one in particular. I freeze, but am propelled along by the chain, my high-heeled feet moving against their will.

Tad sings about looking inside himself and finding a black heart inside, and I stare at him, mouthing the words.

It's an odd choice for the prom, but then Tad and his buddies probably didn't give it that much thought. Most likely Brad Johnson just wanted to show off that he can play the sitar. Sure enough, when I look over, the spotlight is on Brad, who's swapped his guitar for the unusual instrument. His blond hair is mussed, and he's undone his bow tie and the first two buttons of his shirt. He beams at the crowd's attention.

The song goes on, its dark lyrics captivating me. My parents like this song; my mom always mentions how she used to know how to play it on the piano. I once read it's about a girl's funeral. Tad leans into the microphone, bellowing, and I sing the words under my breath. No one else even seems to hear them; they probably don't even recognize the song. The cheering is for Tad, for the end of high school, for the excitement of the night. I'm not sure there are any Stones fans in the room other than those on the stage, and perhaps me.

Tad goes on, spouting lyrics about one's whole world being black. My breath catches as I absorb the words. The band soon switches to a more light-hearted tune, but that phrase snags in my mind, repeating itself over and over as I try to ignore it, joining my classmates for a final dance.

. . .

Kevin walks me to the door just before midnight. The spring air is warm, but with a chill underneath that won't abate for at least another month.

"Thank you," he says, putting his hand on my shoulder. "I had a great time."

"Me too," I say, my voice sincere. "Thanks for asking me." I hesitate, then lean over and peck him on the cheek. Predictably, he turns pinker than my dress.

"I'll give you a call this summer," he says. "Maybe we'll catch a movie or something." His tone is casual, but I can tell he's nervous by the way his mouth twitches slightly.

"Definitely," I say. I don't feel that way about Kevin, but I'm happy to go to a movie all the same. He's a good guy.

I wave a final time as I twist my key and turn to open the front door. I expect the house to be dark and silent, but the hall light is on and my dad is seated on the stairs, his head in his hands. He's dressed in only his boxers and a ratty T-shirt.

"Cat," he says, relieved. "Oh, thank God. You're back."

"What is it? What happened?" My heart hammers inside

my chest. Frantic, I kick off my heels and they land, askew, at different places in our front hallway.

"Mom is very bad," he says. He stifles a sob. "She's waiting for you."

The rest of the world fades to black as I dash up the steps.

Chapter 24

After

When they come, I am in the infirmary. I hear only the shouting, the gunshots. Startled, I stumble, knocking over a stack of bandages I've just spent an hour sterilizing. I watch as they tumble to the ground. They'll be filthy now, caked in mud.

"Do not just stand there!" cries Anna, grabbing me. "Get down!"

I let her pull me underneath our makeshift gurney, and we hide there, under a pile of unwashed linens. I feel Anna inch closer to me as we huddle together. The shouting voices are getting closer. Rafael has said these raids don't generally end in violence—that supplies are all anyone is looking for—but it's hard not to be frightened. Especially when you're located in the same space as valuable supplies like iodine and Imodium.

I strain to hear what is being said—shouted—but I can't

make out the Spanish. Anna, however, gasps. Then I realize the voices are not all unknown.

Among them is Rafael.

"What is it?" I whisper urgently. "What's going on?"

Anna crosses herself, something I have not seen her do before. Until now, she has not demonstrated any signs of religious observation.

"Someone is hurt," she says. She looks frightened. "Shot."

Shot? But the raiders never shoot anyone. My heart beats faster. I hear a familiar cry and I freeze. It's Melody. What is she doing here? And what has happened to her?

Suddenly, Rafael bursts through the door, flanked by two unfamiliar men with guns. Soldiers, I think. Or terrorists. I wonder briefly if there is a difference in this case. They are older than Rafael, and harder looking. Multiple scars that were not properly attended to. Numerous tattoos.

A third comes in. He is dragging something. Someone. Someone who is bleeding, and screaming.

It's Melody.

"She's been shot," shouts Rafael in English. "Anna? Cat?"

We emerge from under the table with our hands up. Anna is shaking. She says something in Spanish to Rafael. He doesn't answer. I stare at him, but he avoids my gaze.

Melody is placed on the table, and I see right away the damage that has been done. She has been shot below the waist, and the blood seeping out around her body is considerable. I groan, wanting to close my eyes, to look away, but I can't. There is a sound from Melody like crunching peanut shells, and I realize she's trying to breathe.

Rafael's face is white as he surveys the damage to Melody. He says something in rapid-fire Spanish to Anna, who goes to Melody, leaning over her. The crackling noises persist as Melody's chest caves in and out, laboring with the effort. Tentatively, Anna rolls Melody onto her side, looking for an exit wound.

"The bullet is still inside," she says grimly. "She needs to go to San Pedro."

One of armed men shouts something, looking angry. Rafael cowers slightly and shakes his head at Anna.

"What is going on?" I ask, my voice trembling. "Who shot her? And why can't she go to San Pedro?"

Another of the soldiers shouts at me in Spanish to be quiet. I stare at Rafael, waiting for an explanation.

"She had another…panic attack," he says carefully. His voice is shaking as well. "They passed her coming into the village. She would not stop screaming."

"So they shot her." I feel faint. I watch as Anna tries, unsuccessfully, to staunch the bleeding. It spurts out with force as she presses against the wound with bandages, splattering us all. I gasp involuntarily as I feel the wet and warmth against my cheek.

"They say they tried to shoot her in the knee, but she dove to the ground." Anguished, Rafael looks hopefully at Anna, who shakes her head. I stand by, paralyzed with fear and shock.

"Melody?" I whisper, leaning in. I grab her hand, which is limp and tinged blue, like the rest of her. "Melody, can you hear me?"

She gasps, and the ensuing gurgling sound makes me cringe. Reflexively, I pull back, but I feel her squeeze my hand slightly.

"Cat," she manages, gasping again.

"Melody!" I grasp her hand again, this time with both of mine. "Don't worry, Anna will help you. We'll—"

Melody shakes her head, and I can see what an effort it is.

"I let them," she whispers. She turns to look me in the eyes. "I didn't—I couldn't—"

"Shhh," I say. Her lips look as if they have been stained with indigo dye. "Don't talk."

"No." She struggles again to move, and I feel the weak pressure in my hands that must mean she is trying to squeeze mine.

"I let—" she gasps, a horrible sound like cardboard tearing. "I let them shoot me."

"What?" I stare at her, stunned.

"I couldn't—" she wheezes loudly. "Do it anymore."

"No," I say again in disbelief.

She's trying to say something else, but I can't understand her. I move in closer. Her body is wracked with spasms as she tries to breathe and speak.

"Sister," I hear. "I am...sorry."

Tell my sister I am sorry, I realize. Tears prick at my eyes.

"I will," I promise. "I swear."

Her eyes fill with relief and her body relaxes on the table. She's quickly losing consciousness; the lack of oxygen and rapid blood loss are overwhelming her injured body. I let go of her hand and turn to Anna.

"Is she going to die?" I can barely speak. It comes out as a whisper. "Can't we do something?"

Anna squeezes my hand. Hers are covered in blood, there having been no time for niceties like sterile gloves. "I can't help her."

I flash back to the oncologists' pronouncements that my mother's cancer was effectively incurable. *They couldn't help her. I can't help Melody.*

I stare at Anna, who has stepped aside, her eyes downcast. "She is gone," she says quietly.

I turn my gaze to Melody, who looks no different than she did a moment ago, only now she is no longer a person, but a body. I shudder. *Body.* It so utterly fails to convey the life force of the person that was Melody. I guess that's the part Melody would have called the soul. I'm not sure what I would call it.

Rafael is whispering anxiously with the armed men, who appear unconcerned at Melody's violent end. I fumble for a blanket, which I pull over her, gently covering her face. *Goodbye,* I say silently. I'm too shocked to cry. I stand over Melody, swaying back and forth. I don't notice at first when Rafael puts his hand on my arm.

"Cat?" His voice is tentative.

"They killed her." My entire body is trembling. "You said no one ever gets hurt during the raids."

"They don't," he says carefully. "This—this wasn't a raid."

In the corner, Anna makes a small, choked sound. She is searching for something, and I notice her hands are shaking, too.

"What do you mean?" I watch Anna unearth an old sheet, a basin, and some sponges.

"It wasn't the raiders. It was a different group." Rafael isn't looking at me, or at Melody. He's studying the tent frame very hard.

"I don't understand."

"I—I invited them here." The words come out in a rush. "I did not know this would happen, Cat. You must believe me. I—"

"These are the drug traffickers," I say, realization dawning. "The narcos."

"It was an accident, Cat. Melody was out of her mind. You know how she can be."

I shake my head. "Not now, Rafael."

"But—"

"No." Firmly, I turn to Anna, who is hovering anxiously.

"We should clean the body," she says softly. "Sew the wounds." She holds up the basin. "Will you help me?"

"Of course," I answer. My hands shake as I hold them out towards Anna. "What do I do?"

Rafael places another tentative hand on my shoulder. "Cat," he says, his voice pleading.

"Not now," I say roughly, pushing him away. "There are more important things now, Rafael!"

He backs out of the tent, stumbling as he leaves. Anna pulls back the blanket and we get to work, tenderly sponging Melody's fair skin. Anna stitches her abdomen, while I dab at her hair with my sponge, cleaning away the blood that has made its way into her golden curls.

My thoughts wander, and my stomach knots with grief. *I should have made more of an effort, after our talk*, I think, as guilt overwhelms me. *Maybe she wouldn't have done it. She bared her soul to me, and I was too busy with Rafael.*

Anna speaks up quietly. "I'm so sorry," she says. "She was your friend?"

I struggle for the right words as I wash Melody's delicate shoulders. "She was a roommate," I say lamely. I don't feel I have the right to call her my friend.

Anna shakes her head. "So much violence," she says, sounding tired. I wait for her to say more, but she busies herself with Melody, trying to put together the pieces of the broken girl who will now never quite be whole.

• • •

I don't seek out Rafael that day, or the next. The SWB camp is in mourning over Melody, the administration caught up in a nightmare of bureaucracy as they try to arrange for the body to get back to the States. I spend the days instead with Valentina and her baby, comforted by the scent and feel of the infant against my chest. Valentina is grateful for the reprieve, and I am grateful for the distraction. With the baby, I feel hopeful; at the base, I am consumed by the guilt and fear and grief that is Melody's tragic, violent end.

Margo has been holed up in the tent since the death, curled in a ball and speaking in monosyllables. She had been on her way from the base to the village when the narcos arrived with their guns, making her a witness to Melody's shooting. It was hours before Sofia found her, hidden behind a clump of trees, rocking back and forth. Since then, she's barely said a word. Taylor, who has been busy since the shooting dealing with the media fallout, says Trish and the rest of the administration want her to go home. They're worried about post-traumatic stress disorder. They want me to go, too.

Back in the tent for the evening, I sit gingerly on the edge of Margo's cot, and tentatively offer her a Milky Way. "Chocolate?"

Margo rolls over and pulls out her earbuds, eyeing the candy bar warily. "Sure," she says finally, propping herself up. "I'll split it with you."

Hiding in the barracks for days without a shower or change of clothes has taken its toll on Margo. Her hair is frizzing at the ends, and there are trails of mascara down each cheek, like tribal war paint. She takes half the Milky Way, but doesn't eat it. Instead, she stares at it in her hands as if it's some foreign object.

Taylor walks in then, carrying an armful of junk food: cans of soda, bags of chips, candy bars.

"I see you had the same idea," he says, nodding at Margo. He dumps the load of chocolate, pretzels, and other snacks next to Margo and collapses on his own bed. "She needs to eat something."

"Don't talk about me in the third person, like I'm not here," snaps Margo, glaring in his direction. "I'm not that far gone."

"Well then, eat," says Taylor flatly. "You haven't eaten in two days." He glances sharply at me. "You're eating, right?"

"Yeah," I say with a shrug. My appetite has been substantially whittled down by memories of Melody's end, coupled with anxiety over Rafael, but I did have some flatbread earlier with Valentina. "More or less." I take a bite of the chocolate bar. It's ordinarily a favorite of mine, but it doesn't taste as good as usual.

Taylor opens a soda and takes a long swig before speaking. "I know it's nothing compared to what you guys are going through," he says. "But I can't stop thinking about how mean I was."

He pauses, looking miserable. "I was such a jerk to her. Over everything, even soda. And now she's *dead*." He flinches as something lands on his shoulder. He bats at it, frantic; its wings are large and transparent. Before we can identify it, it flies away with surprising speed.

I don't answer, but Margo does. She's still clutching at the chocolate, now rapidly melting between her fingers. "It's not your fault," she says quietly. "No one could have guessed she was going to get shot like that."

I could have, I wanted to shout, to confess my guilt to the entire rainforest. *She let them shoot her.* "We could have been nicer to her," I say instead, lamely. "We could have made more of an effort."

"We weren't nice because she was a proselytizing fanatic, who thought Taylor was an abomination." Margo's eyes are hard. "She didn't deserve to die, but it wasn't our fault. And she isn't some saint now that she got shot."

"Wow, you are cold, girl." Taylor shakes his head. "Even this heat can't melt you."

"I'm just a realist," says Margo. "If you want to paint me as the ice queen, go ahead. Nothing I haven't heard before."

"I'm sure," replies Taylor under his breath. He takes another sip, checking the rim of the can first to make sure it's free from flies. We've all come to learn that a can of soda in the jungle is an inadvertent insect trap. "But then, if you don't care about Melody, why lie here in the fetal position?"

"I'm not a monster," she snaps. She takes a bite of chocolate, accidentally smearing it across her cheeks. "I didn't want her dead. And I certainly didn't want to see her *shot*." At the word shot, Margo flinches and her eyes go blank, as if she's gone somewhere else. Seconds later, she blinks, shuddering.

"It was awful," she says, her voice choking slightly. "But I don't feel guilty."

I don't join in their conversation. They're both right: it's not entirely our fault, sure, but the guilt remains all the same. We—I—could have tried harder. And while illness, injury, and death don't make saints of otherwise ordinary people, I know as well as anyone that the shadow of impending death veils people's imperfections, renders them incapable of criticism. Melody could be awful, but she had been a victim, too. Who's to say how any of us will emerge after a tsunami of grief and trauma?

"Melody told me she let them shoot her," I say, before I can stop myself. "Before she stopped breathing."

"Let them shoot her?" Taylor looks baffled. "What do you mean?"

I wonder if it's breaking her confidence if I tell her secrets now, but I keep talking. "She had been sexually abused," I say. "By her uncle. Then she was stuck in the foster system. She told me one night." I start to tear up, the events of the past forty-eight hours overwhelming me, pulling me under like a powerful river current. "She said some things about heaven, about death being peaceful."

Margo groans loudly. "Jesus," she says.

"I didn't realize she meant it," I say, choking. "It's all my fault. I didn't bother making more of an effort with her. If I had—"

"Don't," says Margo, cutting me off. "It was *not* your fault."

"But—"

"Melody was battling some serious demons. You barely knew her. Befriending her wasn't going to cure whatever hell it was she endured."

I'm crying now, full, wracking sobs. For the first time since I watched Melody's life fade from her, I let the tears flow. "I came here to help," I say, gasping. The chocolate falls to the ground, and I ignore it. "I thought—I thought I could make a difference. And I couldn't even help one girl, and she's *dead*, she was *shot*—"

"Melody died because Rafael cut a deal with the narcos," interrupts Taylor. His face is hard. "If he hadn't invited them, Melody wouldn't have had the chance to let them shoot her, or whatever happened." He stands and reaches down, unflinching, to retrieve the dropped Milky Way, now host to a small family of burgundy ants. He wraps it in a tissue and puts it aside.

"Well, Cat is thinking of joining them," says Margo sarcastically. The chocolate has energized her, given her back some of her caustic wit. "You heard her last week. She wants to stay here with Rafael. Soon she'll have her very own rifle."

I don't say anything. I haven't faced Rafael since Melody's death. What will I say to him?

"I don't get it," says Taylor, shaking his head. "How can you even consider it? Do you *want* to die?"

I start to retort angrily, but then pause, considering. Dr. Shapiro's voice again nags in my ear, going on about "joining" loved ones. *Do* I want to die? I ponder the question. Was that the real reason I had come to Calantes? To end it all? Was my world like Hamlet's, weary, flat, stale, and unprofitable?

I think of the way I felt with Rafael, and when I helped deliver Anna Catalina. I think of prom night, and Tess, and school, and California. I think of my dad, Gatsby and all. And then I picture my mom's face the night she died.

"No," I say aloud. "No, I don't want to die."

"I don't want to die, either," Margo's voice is small now, the burst of energy and sarcasm gone as quickly as it had come. "That time I tried to kill myself—they blamed it on the Paxil, but I don't know. I really thought I wanted to die, but it was stupid. I don't. I don't want to die. That's why I'm so freaked out, I guess. It was sad and scary, for sure, but it's more than that. When I saw Melody get shot, all I could think of was, please, don't kill me, I don't want to die. I want to go home, see my family."

She looks impossibly young as she confesses, her cheeks

pink with heat and fear and shame. I reach over and squeeze her hand. "It's okay," I say. "It's okay to feel that way."

"You're not going to stay here, are you, Cat?" She looks serious now, her eyes wide. Taylor's eyes are also concerned, questioning.

"No," I say, quietly, and, as I say it, I realize I've made my decision. "No, I'm going home."

Chapter 25

Before

I take the stairs two at a time. Mom is waiting for me, still dressed in the little black evening dress. She hasn't washed the makeup off, and her hair remains perfectly coiffed. She's sitting in her bed, propped up with several pillows, an IV in her arm.

"Mom," I burst out breathlessly. "What happened?"

"Cat!" Her smile is wide. "How was it? Tell me everything."

"It was a lot of fun," I say, my eyes never leaving the IV. "What happened?"

"I had another seizure," she says casually, turning to shuffle around some pillows. "The pain after was terrible. One of the home-care nurses came by to put in this IV."

"What is it for?"

"It's a morphine drip," she says. "And fluids. But tell me about the prom. I want to hear details."

I sigh, knowing she won't rest until I've described the evening in painstaking detail. I give her as much as I can, detailing everything from the decorations to the food to the music. Finally, she looks satisfied.

"Wonderful," she says, looking happy. "I'm so glad. You look so beautiful, like a princess." A shadow passes across her face, and I can tell she's in pain. Her breathing becomes more labored, and her eyes close briefly.

"Mom?" I reach for her hand. "Mom, are you okay?"

"Cat." She pats the bed, inviting me to join her, and I crawl in next to her like I used to as a little girl. I wrap my arms around her, tucking my knees beneath hers as if we are a pair of spoons.

"Cat," she says again. "I can't take this anymore."

"What do you mean?" I ask. My heart pounds with fear; I don't want to hear the answer. Instead, I bury my face into her back, inhaling her scent, the soft silk of her dress against my nose and forehead.

"The pain." She reaches for one of my hands and squeezes it. "The pain is so bad."

"We should call the nurse," I say, bolting upwards. "She can call those palliative-care people the doctor told us about. They can come in and make you more comfortable—"

"No." Mom cuts me off, shaking her head. "I don't want to linger like this in bed, weaving in and out of consciousness from the drugs."

"So what are you saying?" I ask in a small voice.

"I'm going to end it." Her tone is calm. She gestures

toward her nightstand, which is cluttered with bottles of pills. Big ones, little ones, yellow ones, blue ones. "See those blue ones? They'll make this stop."

"Stop?" My tone is high-pitched. "Stop what, exactly?"

"This. Suffering. The end." She puts her hand gently on mine. "I googled it. I'll just fall asleep. It will be painless."

I stare at her, brimming with horror. "You can't be serious."

"Please, Cat," she says, anguished. "I want it to be tonight. I want you to remember me like this, with my hair and makeup done. It was such a nice evening. I can't bear to just keep deteriorating. I can't stand the loss of control."

She's crying now, her breathing ragged. "I don't want to die an ugly vegetable," she says quietly, in between sobs. "Please. I want your blessing."

My heart is pounding. *How can she ask me to do this? How can I possibly agree?* I bury my head in my hands as I look at her desperate face. *How can I not?*

"Dad doesn't know anything about this?" I pose it as a question, but I already know the answer.

Mom shakes her head, looking sad. "Dad is still holding out for a miracle," she says.

"So this is it," I whisper. A bead of sweat trickles down my neck. I feel it land inside my dress. "Aren't you…aren't you scared?" I think back to English class, to Hamlet and his famous navel-gazing about taking his life. Ultimately, he was too afraid of death—that undiscovered country—to go through with it.

"A little," she admits. She shifts, against her pillow, looking uncomfortable. "But I'm more afraid of losing what little dignity I have left. I don't want to end up comatose, or on a feeding tube."

It's all too much. I sit at the edge of the bed and stare at the portrait on the wall opposite me. It's of my mother and me when I was a newborn. She's cradling me and staring down at me as if I'd hung the moon. Her hair is long in the picture, and her eyes are luminous. The expression on her face is one of pure joy.

She sees where I'm looking and speaks up. "It was the best day of my life, when you were born." She sounds wistful. "We didn't know you'd be a girl, and I didn't care either way, but when you came out, you were so beautiful, and I was just so grateful to have a daughter." She takes a deep breath. "You're my daughter, but you've always been more than that. You're my best friend."

Silent tears pour down my face. I turn back to her and wipe my cheek, noting my black hands.

"You have eye makeup everywhere," Mom confirms with a small smile. "We should have used waterproof. That was foolish, under the circumstances."

I laugh, in spite of myself. Same old Mom, talking about suicide and mascara in the same breath.

I stifle a sob and bend over to her. I've made my decision. "If this is what you want, I won't tell you not to do it," I say. My tone is full of both conviction and fear. "I want you to die feeling at peace."

"Oh, Cat." She reaches for me again. "I knew I could count on you. My wonderful girl. My special little girl."

I can't believe it. I can't believe what I've agreed to do, but more than that I can't believe this is the last time I'll ever see my mother, the last time I will ever hear her voice and feel her skin and smell her hair.

"Better like this, where I can say good-bye." Her voice is steady, but her eyes are full of tears. "I'm so sorry to do this to you. To make you do this. To leave you as a teenager." She shakes her head, her voice breaking. "I would have loved to see the amazing woman I know you'll become. As a mother, with children of your own." Her voice trails off, and I can't answer. My voice feels stuck in my throat, my vocal cords paralyzed with sorrow.

She reaches into the drawer of her bedside table and pulls out an envelope with my name across the front in her familiar script. "This is for you," she says. "Don't read it until after, okay?"

"Oh, God." I groan loudly, slumping on the bed. "Mom, please—please don't do it."

"No, please!" She grabs my arm and her eyes are full of such pain and terror that I know I have no choice. "Give me this. It's all I have left."

I breathe deeply. "I'm not ready yet," I say.

"No," she agrees. "Lie with me here, Cat. Let me hold you." Her eyes travel again to the portrait.

I climb back in to the bed with her and cry into the sheets until they're soaked.

"Shh," Mom whispers in my ear, rocking me gently. "Don't cry. I'm sorry, baby. I'm so sorry. I just want to sleep, Cat. I don't want to suffer anymore."

To die, to sleep—No more; and by a sleep, to say we end the Heart-ache, and the thousand Natural shocks That Flesh is heir to. Again, I recall Hamlet's words. I want peace for my mother, and the thousand natural shocks that pain her. When Mom finally closes her eyes for the last time, there is no end to the heartache. The heartache is all mine.

Chapter 26

After

He knows right away, from the look on my face. I haven't even opened my mouth when his shoulders slump. "You're leaving," he says quietly.

"Not yet," I say, surprising myself with my own words. "I want to stay out my term, help Anna and Valentina. But eventually, yes."

"You don't want to stay with me?" His expression is that of a wounded puppy, a mutt who's been kicked by his owner. "I love you, Cat."

"Rafael." I sigh, and settle down next to him. The cot creaks, sagging precariously. I rest my hand on top of his, and as our skin touches I feel a strange mix of anger, desire, and despair, like a recipe with too many competing ingredients. I try to speak, but the words don't come, and my breathing is erratic with the effort not to cry.

"Catalina," he says softly, brushing his lips against my ear. "Please. Stay. Help me and Calantes."

I shake my head furiously, blinking away my tears. "Don't call me that," I gasp.

"Cat." He tries again, wrapping an arm around me. "Please."

"Rafael," I say again. "I don't belong here, the way you do. And I definitely don't belong with the terrorists who shot Melody."

Rafael bristles. "They are not terrorists," he says, defensive. "They have the same goals as us. They—"

I cut him off gently. "They shot her," I say again. "She's dead, Rafael. She came here to help, too, and she's gone."

Rafael tightens his grip on my shoulder. "Melody, that was an accident, that was—"

"But she's dead because you invited the narcos," I interrupt him softly. "Think, Rafael. Is this the change you want? Is this your big dream?"

He looks uncertain, confused.

"I just want to do some good for my country." He looks away. "Look at history, Cat. When is there ever change, without revolution? Without violence? This is the path I have to take."

I struggle to find the right words. "That may be," I say carefully. "But it's not my path."

"But my parents!" He pulls away from me picks up an empty glass jar from a bedside crate and heaves it across the tent. It strikes the canvas and slithers to the ground, where it breaks into three neat pieces. I wince at the sound and at the sudden display of rage. "You of all people, Cat. You should understand. I did it for them. For my mama, in prison, and papa, who's dead."

"I'm sorry about your parents," I say, reaching for him again. "I truly am. But, Rafael—is this what they would want? Are you doing this for them? Or for you?"

He doesn't turn towards me again. For a long time, we sit there, in silence. I stare at the pieces of broken glass and wonder if they could be glued back together, if it would be possible with the right supplies. I put my arm out for Rafael, but he once again pulls away, and this time I sense a difference in his body language.

"I think you should go," he says. His voice is barely above a whisper, but it is firm.

I nod. "Yes," I say. I rise, pausing to wipe the tears from the corners of my eyes.

"Good-bye, Catalina." His eyes meet mine.

"Good-bye, Rafael."

I'm tempted to turn around again, to rush back into his arms, but I don't. As I leave the village, I hear Anna Catalina crying in the distance, and I feel a rush of hope that makes me feel I have made the right choice.

• • •

I don't see Rafael again. When I return to the village the following day, he is gone. Eduardo breaks the news to me, his expression sad.

"He left," he says. His voice is regretful. "We are not sure where he has gone."

He's lying, trying to spare me. I think about asking more questions, seeing if he knows anything further, but instead I nod and turn away. With a deep breath, I walk toward the infirmary. I haven't been since Melody's death, sticking to Valentina's tent and the base.

"Cat!" says Anna, her face full of surprise. "I did not think you would come back."

"I just needed some time," I say. I reach for my apron, still in its usual spot. It's been laundered, but there are still bloodstains across the front. Some things you can't erase, even with soap and boiling water.

"I am very glad you are here," she says sincerely. She wraps me in a hug, and I press my cheek against hers.

"Me, too," I say honestly. "I want to help."

Epilogue

It took me a moment to spot my father at the Cleveland airport. Hands in his pockets, Gatsby notably absent, he stared at me for a moment and then broke into a run.

This was so unlike Dad that my first thought was, who is this lunatic running in my direction? But I didn't have time to dwell on it as he enveloped me in a tight bear hug.

"Cat," he whispered, cradling my head. "We're going to be okay."

We, not you. The significance of the words was not lost on me. "I love you, Dad." I wound my arms around his neck the way I used to when I was a little girl.

"I'm so sorry, Caitlin." His voice warbled with emotion. "I'm so sorry."

"Don't be," I said firmly, recalling my friends' words about Melody and Calantes and saving the world. "It wasn't your fault. It wasn't anyone's fault."

...

We're living in California now. Dad got a new job at a little liberal-arts college less than a two-hour drive from Stanford. Once I start school, he says, I can visit as little or as often as I want, but at least he'll be close by. It's a comforting thought.

I have a new therapist out here. Strangely, I was sad to say good-bye to Dr. Shapiro, even with all his beard-stroking and drug-pushing. He wasn't all bad, though I never admitted flushing the Abilify. I have confessed it all, however, to Dr. Elizabeth J. Lancaster, or Liz, as she insists I call her. Liz wears thick-framed plastic purple glasses and has long bangs that she's always brushing out of her eyes. She's in her early thirties and swears a lot during sessions. At first I thought this was a ploy to seem young and cool and gain my trust, but the more I get to know her, the more I think she just likes to use the F word a lot. She dismissed the bipolar diagnosis as a load of shit—her words, not mine—and put me on a basic antidepressant and an indefinite course of something called cognitive-behavioral therapy. I can't tell if it's helping with the post-traumatic stress yet, but it's done wonders for my IBS.

I'm in regular touch with Margo and Taylor. We weathered the initial media storm together—everyone wanted to hear the exiting and tragic story of noble and altruistic North American teenagers whose comrade was shot in cold blood. No one, of course, wanted to hear the reality—to discuss Rafael or the villagers, the violence and the poverty, or Melody's own dark past.

It was bitterly frustrating, but I try to tell myself that before Melody, no one had even heard of Calantes, and now, at least, it's had its fifteen minutes: it's on the map in all its glory. We've got a Kickstarter campaign going, and it's doing surprisingly well. We plan to send all the money to Anna, at the infirmary.

Margo and Taylor are doing well. After a breakthrough in family therapy, Margo has her sights on a Master's degree in medical illustration. Her parents aren't entirely thrilled, but she sprung it upon them shortly after her early return from Calantes, and they were too grateful that she was alive to put up a fuss. Taylor was permitted re-entry to his program, and has been working hard to keep his grades up. He's seeing someone seriously named David, who looks an awful lot like Eduardo, a fact Margo and I remain silent about. We're all planning to meet up next summer. Margo said she's never leaving Canada again, but then Taylor suggested San Francisco, and Margo said that was probably safe, being somewhat Canada-like in its politics, so we'll see. I've suggested having a private memorial service for Melody, just the three of us. I tried to track down her family once I was settled here in California, but when I called the number I wheedled out of SWB administration, the man on the other end slammed the phone down without a word. I wonder if he blames me for Melody's death. I also wonder if he is the man who haunted her nightmares. I settled on sending a letter to Melody's sister to SWB, with the instructions that it be forwarded. I don't know if she ever got it. As Liz tells me, not all stories can have a happy ending.

A couple of weeks ago, I got a message from Emerson, my

old mentor from SWB. His term had ended around the time
Melody died, and we'd never really said good-bye. He tracked
me down on Facebook and suggested we meet for coffee—he
lives within an hour's drive of here. I'm starting to think he
might want more than just coffee, and I can't decide how I
feel about that. Still, it was cathartic to spend time with someone who gets it, who understands. We spent hours just talking
about the jungle, dissecting the flora and fauna, the sights and
sounds. It's funny; when I was in Calantes, the macaws, mosquitoes, and monkeys felt so foreign. I always felt like I stuck
out, didn't quite fit. But now that I'm back, there's a part of
me that knows the jungle, that lives and breathes the birdcalls
and insect hums. It's a part that will forever exist in the heart
of the rainforest.

I miss my mom. Liz beams when I say this, because apparently it takes some people years and years of therapy to admit
basic feelings toward their parents, but I don't see what the big
deal is. She was my best friend, and she's gone. I compare it to
losing an arm—eventually, you adapt and learn to live without
it, and over time the pain subsides, but you're never truly whole
again, not really. You're constantly reminded when you try to
lift things or write or type or brush your teeth. That's what it's
like without my mom. Yesterday, I went to the mall for some
new sneakers, and I watched all the moms and daughters: fighting over hem lengths, laughing over ice cream, arguing about
jean prices. The longing was so great, so suffocating, that I had
to step outside, gasping for air. Liz says the pain is still raw, like
a tooth that needs filling. She promises that she's like a dentist,

and things will get better over time. I told her I appreciate the metaphor, but I really hate the dentist, so could we skip the cavity references.

Liz says that I shouldn't feel responsible for what happened with Mom, at the end. That I was brave, and free from blame of any kind. She convinced me to tell Dad, and I did, one night, on our new front porch. We sat on the two-seater swing together, and I told him everything. He cried a lot, but he wasn't angry. I think he was ashamed that Mom had to come to me. Dad is full of guilt over his handling of my mom's illness, as well as at his own romance with the Frito-Lay corporation and the impact it had on me. He has finally agreed to try therapy again, this time with an earnest-but-annoying little man named Brian, who wears the same long-sleeved plaid shirt every time I've seen him (does he have multiple shirts, or is he a laundry freak?). I'm still angry with Dad at times, but I'm working through it, with forgiveness and understanding on the horizon. As Liz reminds me, depression is an illness, and my father wasn't trying to fail me. He was sick, too, and battling his own army of demons.

Liz and I talk a lot about grief, about its intersection with madness, and the many forms it may take. When you try to visualize the concept of grief before you've truly experienced it, you get the movie version. Black-clothed, somber-faced people crowded under black umbrellas at a graveside. In reality, grief is much more complicated. My dad's grief sent him on a Gatsby-clutching downward spiral. Mine sent me to Calantes. Melody's led her to Jesus, and, ultimately, to oblivion. And Rafael's grief propelled him to betray not only the people he cared about but the very principles that made him who he was. Liz says I don't have to forgive Rafael, but I do. When I talked to Tess about all this, she dug out an old book of poetry and introduced me to a beautiful poem by Emily Dickinson. In my darker moments, I turn to its words for comfort:

> *I measure every Grief I meet*
> *With narrow, probing, eyes—*
> *I wonder if It weighs like Mine—*
> *Or has an Easier size.*

Liz also supports my decision not to undergo genetic testing—for now. But we both agree, it's something that I might consider later down the road. She hooked me up with a support group for potential BRCA carriers, and I actually go. It's a relief to speak to people who really get it, and don't just give you the Cancer Face. There's no bullshit: all of us have moms who've gone through it.

"Cat?" My dad pokes his head into my room, and I look up from my laptop, blinking. I'm writing in an e-journal, one of the therapeutic exercises recommended by Liz that I was skeptical about initially, but ultimately find surprisingly cathartic.

I snap the screen shut. "What's up?" I swivel my chair and face him, expectant.

"This came." He waves an envelope, and I see the pink ribbon symbol on it. Involuntarily, I recoil.

"What is it?" I ask warily. He places it on the desk next to me, and I nudge it gingerly, as if it might detonate.

"It's one of those fundraising things. You run to raise money, for breast cancer."

"You're going to run?" I look up him, amused. I rarely ever see my father walk, let alone run. He's the sort who will circle a parking lot for the closest possible spot to the door.

"I thought maybe *we* could run. Together."

I blink, surprised. I don't run, either. But I can see he's making an effort. We've made progress, these past months, but at times things are still strained. As Liz says, forgiveness is a journey.

"It's not for months, so there would be lots of time to train," he says tentatively. I can hear the hope in his voice, and I pick the envelope up, nodding. It is an olive branch, and I am a pacifist.

"Okay," I say. "Yes. We'll do it for Mom."

Dad's eyes are teary. "We'll do it for all of us," he says.

• • •

For months, I couldn't bring myself to open my mother's letter, the one she gave me before she died. I would pick it up, stare at my name in her neat cursive on the front, and place it back, unopened, on my bedside table. Some part of me intended to wait until the anniversary of her death, or her birthday, or else mine, but today, after running a mile with Dad, I just felt ready and I leaned over and tore into it.

There was a lot in there, a lot of love and sorrow and insight. "I know I'm supposed to think, oh, I wish I had traveled to Australia, or that I should have climbed Mount Everest," she wrote. "But I don't, because I'm not that person. Cancer doesn't change who you are. I could only ever be the person I was, and I'm not a mountain climber. I was your Mom, and that was enough for me."

Part of me wishes I'd read the letter before Calantes, Rafael, and Melody, all the rest of it, because maybe I would have thought twice about going. But it's part of who I am, now, and perhaps that's the person I really have always been. Maybe I am a mountain climber.

"Be happy, Caitlin," my mom wrote at the end of the letter. "I don't know what I believe, if anything, about what happens when we die. But I need to know, wherever I am, that you are happy. I need to know you'll at least try."

And so I'm trying. I cannot save the world, maybe, but I can try to save myself, to master my own grief. Each day, it gets a little easier. It's a beautiful evening, here in sunny California, all pink and golden skies and songbirds. I stand at the porch window and close my eyes, humming softly to myself.

Goodnight, Mom.

From Mrs. Marks's Letter to Cat:
Lessons for Life from a Mother to Daughter

Always have dessert. A time may come when you are too sick to eat and enjoy that slice of chocolate mousse cake. Think of all the poor souls on the *Titanic* who declined their *gâteau*, only to drown in the freezing cold.

Don't worry so much what other people are thinking. Most of the time, they're so busy worrying about themselves that they don't even notice you.

Try to do something you love. I know it sounds cliché, but all the money in the world won't make you happy as an investment banker if what you really want to do is breed show cats.

Don't spend too much time making the bed. I spent years fussing over throw pillows, and no one ever really saw them except for me and Dad, and I'm not sure he ever even noticed they were there.

If you get married, wear a really big wedding dress. It's your one chance to wear a huge dress. There is a lifetime to wear those little slip dresses or whatever. Don't blow your one night to be a princess.

Turn off your phone at dinner. I didn't do this enough, and I regret it. Life is about the people you're with at the moment, not about inane text messages or emails from the office.

Don't be afraid to change your hair. I was too scared to ever change mine much, and then it all fell out. Go blonde, red, long, short. It's just hair.

Appreciate how thin and beautiful you are now—don't waste time moaning over five pounds or minor facial flaws. When you look back at pictures of yourself young, you won't believe how lovely you were. Trust me.

Read a lot. It will make you a more interesting person, and it will take you places you may never get to (or want to) go.

Have children. They are the true love of your life.

Acknowledgments

This book wouldn't have been possible without the assistance and support of many people, so I will try to thank them all here: First, to Margie Wolfe, Kathryn Cole, Carolyn Jackson, Melissa Kaita, Emma Rodgers, and the staff of Second Story Press for believing in the story and bringing it to publication; and to Lana Popovic, for indefatigably advocating on the book's behalf.

Thanks also to Dr. Vivian Glenns and the staff at North York General Hospital's Breast Cancer Care program and Sunnybrook Hospital's radiation oncology department for helping my mother through breast cancer, and for working tirelessly in a health care system that often undervalues your work. We all owe you a great debt.

To my mother, Karen Gold, who wasn't allowed to read drafts of this manuscript because I didn't want to make her cry—thank you for inspiring me to write this story, and for the lifetime of steadfast support and belief in me that makes my writing possible. Thank you as well to my father, Howard Gold, for the love and support you can always be relied on to provide, and for bragging about me to friends, colleagues, and strangers you encounter in elevators.

Thanks to Dara Laxer and Cheryl Ellison for your friendship, counsel, and cheerleading, and to Paul and Jess Gold and Michael and Deborah Goodman for always being interested in and supportive of my work. Thanks too to my colleague Adam Farber, who has spent ten years listening to me vent, and who is sure he gave me some ideas for this book.

Finally, thank you to my husband Adam Goodman, and our children Teddy and Violet, for everything from inspiring me to making time for me to write. It's you guys who make me want to keep going, to be the best person I can be. Thank you for being yourselves; you are the loves of my life.

About the Author

Jennifer Gold is a lawyer and mother of two. She is the author of the YA novels *Soldier Doll* and *Undiscovered Country*. A history buff, she also has degrees in psychology, law, and public health. She lives in Toronto with her family. Visit her online at www.jennifergold.ca.